DELIGHT

Mazo
de la
Roche

DELIGHT

INTRODUCTION: *Desmond Pacey*

GENERAL EDITOR: *Malcolm Ross*

NEW CANADIAN LIBRARY NO. 21

Toronto / Montreal

The following dedication
appeared in the original edition:

TO MY DEAR CAROLYN

THE STORY OF DELIGHT

IS LOVINGLY INSCRIBED

Christmas, 1925

PRINTED AND BOUND IN CANADA BY
T. H. BEST PRINTING COMPANY LIMITED

CONTENTS

	The Author	vi
	Introduction	vii
I	The Duke of York	11
II	Albert and May	24
III	The Firemen's Ball	41
IV	Canadian Ada and English May	66
V	Men and Women	86
VI	Mrs Jessop Roused	99
VII	August Berries	109
VIII	September Kisses	128
IX	Beemer's	134
X	The Rising Tide	146
XI	The Lagoon	158
XII	The Trial by Water	159

THE AUTHOR

Born in 1885, Mazo de la Roche is a native of Toronto which has been her home throughout her life. Although she was intended for a career in art, she soon developed a preference for writing, and published her first novel in 1923. But it was with *Jalna*, which won the $10,000 *Atlantic Monthly* prize in 1927, that her fame became assured, and the international popularity which she has enjoyed ever since.

Fourteen titles followed in the Jalna series: *Finch's Fortune* (1931), *The Master of Jalna* (1933), *Young Renny* (1935), *Whiteoak Harvest* (1936), *Whiteoaks* (1939), *Whiteoak Heritage* (1940), *Wakefield's Course* (1941), *The Building of Jalna* (1944), *Return to Jalna* (1949), *Mary Wakefield* (1949), *Renny's Daughter* (1951), *The Whiteoak Brothers* (1953), *Variable Winds at Jalna* (1954), and *Centenary at Jalna* (1958). As well as the Jalna books, Miss de la Roche has published *Explorers of the Dawn* (1922), *Possession* (1923), *Delight* (1926), *Low Life* (1928), *Portrait of a Dog* (1930), *The Very House* (1937), *The Two Saplings* (1942), and her autobiography, *Ringing the Changes* (1957).

INTRODUCTION

In May of 1925 Mazo de la Roche, with her cousin Caroline as companion, settled in a small cottage in the woods near Clarkson, Ontario. Nearby lived the Livesays—the journalist, J. F. B. Livesay; his wife Flora Randal, the poetess; and their two young daughters Dorothy and Sophie. Already Miss de la Roche had written three books: *Explorers of the Dawn* (1922), a collection of stories about children; *Possession* (1923), her first novel; and a second novel with a Nova Scotia setting which had been rejected by Hugh Eayrs of the Macmillan Company as an unworthy successor to *Possession*. This is the way she describes the writing of *Delight*, a task she began almost immediately after moving into Trail Cottage, in her autobiography, *Ringing the Changes* (1957):

> *Left to ourselves Bunty* [her dog] *and I settled to the day's work—she to sit close beside me while I wrote, then to explore the woods, to press her way into distant undergrowth, wild blackberry bush, to snuffle into the burrow of rabbit and mole. It was not long before I began a new novel. Not only did I write in the delicious privacy of this tiny birch-embowered cottage but I sat while writing in a chair which had swayed (for it was a cane-seated rocking-chair) beneath the majestic weight of my father's mother. Never before had I owned a rocking-chair. They had not been popular in our family, and how this one now came into my possession I cannot remember. But there it was, slender and graceful in shape, not one of those rocking-chairs that give a protesting thump each time they are tilted backward, but that swayed, with a smooth noiseless sweep, like the rocking of a bird on a bough. . . .*
>
> *Sitting in that chair I began my third novel. At that time I had not heard how often is a second novel a failure and I was astonished and humiliated that this should have happened to me. But this third novel* Delight *would be different. In it I would write of Ontario, the province I knew so well. . . .*
>
> *My drawing-board on my knee, I sat upright when I was writing, but when I was at a loss for one word, or triumphant in the finding of the right one, violently would rock. And so, something invincibly childlike in me was satisfied. As for books of reference, I had only one source. That was Dr Johnson's* Dictionary *in two bulky volumes, those sent to my father when he was a boy by his father. They lay on the floor beside me and each time I wanted to look up a word I heaved up one of the books and often became so fascinated by other words that I quite forgot the one of which I was in search.*

This passage not only affords us a fascinating glimpse of the making of *Delight*, it also reveals several of Miss de la Roche's major interests: her love of animals, and especially of dogs, her sense of tradition and especially of family tradition, and her delight in the exact word.

Delight was published simultaneously in London, Toronto, and New York in 1926. Its reception abroad was uniformly favourable, but in Canada it got a very mixed press. Even the Canadian reviewers who were generally favourable to the book tended to be patronizing toward it. The *Canadian Bookman* review, for example, concluded:

> *The author has created a captivating heroine in Delight Mainprize. Some of the chapters in the story strike one as unconvincing and the character of Kirke is far from being consistent, but the tale moves with a swing and the reader of fiction will be able to pass away a pleasant hour or so in its reading.*

And the *Canadian Forum* ended on a similar note of complaint:

> *It is this duality that is responsible for a certain dissatisfaction that is experienced by the reader. Treated as an idyll, the story could have been charming; as a tragedy it might have been terrific; but Miss de la Roche has tried to fuse the materials for both in a spirit of high comedy, and it can't be done.*

Thus we see the beginnings of a hiatus between the foreign and domestic appraisals of Miss de la Roche's work that has continued almost without exception to this day. When *Jalna* appeared in 1927 and won the *Atlantic Monthly* prize, Canadians for once did almost unanimously praise her, but both before and since they have either condemned her work as trivial or damned it with faint praise.

Now I am not disposed to argue that some of the flaws pointed out in the Canadian reviews of *Delight* are imaginary, nor that Miss de la Roche is one of the great novelists of the English tradition. What I am prepared to contend is that Miss de la Roche is a much better novelist than most of her Canadian critics have granted, and that in seeking out the flaws of *Delight* they almost totally ignored its strengths.

What are the merits of *Delight*? First of all, as in all Miss de la Roche's novels, it is packed with varied, interesting, and unforgettable characters. From the very first chapter we are intrigued by the undemonstrative, casual Kirke, the vindictive Mrs Jessop, and above all by the vivacious, sensuous, passionate Delight Mainprize. Delight in particular is a character creation worthy of Thomas Hardy, the embodiment of womanhood at its most attractive and disturbing. Notice how Miss de la Roche compares her, as does Hardy his Tess, with several of the great charmers of history and legend—with Jezebel, Delilah, Deborah, Eve, and Diana.

The second strength of the novel is the pace and variety of its episodes. From the unexpected arrival of Delight and May in the first chapter to the aroused fury of the village women in the last we are kept in a constant state of excitement and suspense. Nor are these episodes, as some hostile reviews said, merely strung loosely together. They build up to three major crises around which the novel is constructed: the Fireman's Ball, the great storm, and the Fair. These three crises, occurring roughly each seventy pages, have the same structural function as is performed by the scaffold scenes in Hawthorne's *Scarlet Letter.*

The firm structure of the novel is buttressed by the use of thematic symbols. The chief of these symbols is the wild crow, which appears in conjunction with each of the three crises to which I have referred. The crow's symbolic significance is made clear in this speech of Jimmy's near the end of Chapter III:

> *"Look! Look!" cried Jimmy, with a dramatic flourish of the hand skyward. "That's one of the sights I brought you to see. Nobody gives any heed to them here except to fetch a gun and shoot them, but I love them." He went to the water's edge and raised his face to them, circling and cawing above. "I call them my crows. . . . They're savage wild things and yet I love them because I seem to know what they're up to. . . ."*

The crows, in short, are the symbols of freedom, instinct, passion, and the primitive, and are thus the equivalent of Delight herself. Notice how, when Delight is set upon in the final section of the novel by the embattled forces of convention and respectability, the crows set up a wild clamour, beat their heavy wings, and utter cries of fear and rage.

This in turn suggests that the novel has a significant theme: the infringement of instinctive freedom and sensuousness upon a conventional society. Delight is described, near the beginning of Chapter VIII, as "a creature of instincts, emotions, not much more developed intellectually than the soft-eyed Jersey in the byre, nor the wood pigeon that called among the cedars." The sympathy with which Delight is portrayed, and the way in which she is allowed eventually to triumph, leave no doubt that Miss de la Roche exalts instinct over reason, the primitive over the civilized.

Hence the tremendous admiration evident here, as in all her books, for wild nature and the living creatures that inhabit it. Nature description occurs frequently throughout the novel, and always as an objective correlative of the mood of the story. Look, for example, at the beginning of Chapter VI, where the fierce fertility of nature in the spring is used to set the mood of wild jealousy aroused in the characters of the story. This interest in wild nature comes out also in Miss de la Roche's similes, almost all of which involve nature or animals or birds. "Behind his calm brow fearful thoughts, like slow-moving shellfish, circled about." "Like an owl's her round, unblinking gaze was riveted on the one spot. . . ." "Mrs Jessop cast all those cherished years of respectability from her now, as a snake casts its skin."

This stress on the wild, the primitive, and the instinctive suggests, of course, that Miss de la Roche is a romantic artist. It is her romanticism, I believe, that has made her such an embarrassment to Canadian critics. In the mid-'twenties, two ideas were uppermost in the Canadian literary consciousness: a distaste for romanticism, which had given Canada a surfeit of nature poetry and of novels of northern and/or western adventure, and a determination that realistic portrayals of Canadian life should present a recognizable Canadian image to the world. Miss de la Roche was an embarrassment because her skill and craft were such that it was impossible to dismiss her outright as a purveyor of cheap thrills, and yet she did not apply her skill to the realistic portrayal of the Canadian scene. The critics therefore chose to chide her for her failure to be realistic. and refused to accept her on her own terms as a skilful romantic artist. Now that our nationalism is less blatant and more subtle, it should be possible for us to see her achievement at its real worth. Not a profound thinker nor an acute analyst of the social situation, she had other gifts: a sensuous, passionate response to the pulsating life of the natural world, an instinctive preference for and sympathy with the rebellious and nonconformist individual, a natural gaiety and *joie de vivre*, a sense of structure and a sense of style. *Delight* has not the introspective subtlety of *The Scarlet Letter*, the philosophical profundity of *Tess of the D'Urbervilles*, nor the social accuracy of *Our Daily Bread*, but it does have the great merit of giving delight.

DESMOND PACEY

University of New Brunswick
September, 1960

CHAPTER I

THE DUKE OF YORK

I

KIRKE enjoyed this moment more than any other in the day. The evening meal—supper they called it at The Duke of York—was over; the busy hours between seven and eleven were just commencing. A pleasant stir of preparation was in the air, men sauntered in at the open front door, washed and brushed after their day's work, a look of anticipation and good-fellowship softening their features. Shortly the bus from the evening train would be clattering up to the door, leaving a half-dozen travellers or possibly a theatrical troupe. It was time they had a show. There had been nothing on in the Town Hall for weeks.

Kirke lounged against the newel post, filling his pipe and staring with shrewd, light-blue eyes into the faces that passed him. He was in the way where he stood; his legs were long, and he had crossed them, the toe of one foot resting on the linoleum, one sharp elbow thrust outward behind him. He rather liked being in the way. It gave him a feeling of superiority to have people edging their way around him, and he did not in the least mind the surly looks that were occasionally turned on him. Once Charley Bye, the porter who always lent a hand in the evening, tripped over his foot while carrying a tray to one of the small drinking-rooms, and jarred the foaming "head" over the polished glasses; in short, barely saved himself from arriving headlong with the refreshment. Bill Bastien, the head bartender and manager, came to the door of the bar. His erect, lithe figure was thrown out against a glittering background of glasses and mirrors. He was drying his hands on a clean white towel.

"What the hell—" he said.

"Chairley's been falling over himself in his zeal," replied Kirke.

"Mr Bastien," said Charley, breathing heavily, "I stumbled over Mr Kirke's foot which he sticks out that way a-purpose to mortify me."

"That's a dairty lie," observed Kirke, smiling. "He never looks where he's going, and you know it."

Bastien was too busy for argument. His opaque, dark-blue

eyes glanced sharply, first at the offending foot, then at the glasses on the tray. With a frown he strode to the door of the drinking-room and looked in. The customers gathered about the table there were not of the fastidious order. They wanted their drinks and wanted them soon. They were rapping impatiently on the table.

"All right, boys," he said cheerily. "Here we are. Charley's lost his way in the crowd. Next time he'll be smarter." He laid his hand heavily on Charley's broad shoulder and steered him into the room. Then he returned briskly to the bar where business was now becoming lively.

A rich smell of ale and spirits filled the air. A sustained flow of men's voices came from all sides, sometimes ebbing to a low drone, sometimes swelling to a vigorous burst of laughter. Night had fallen. The March air was cold, and the heavy, green door was closed after each fresh arrival. Four men from the dye works came in together, their hands, in spite of scrubbing, stained by the dyes they worked in. Then, half a dozen tannery hands, bringing with them their own peculiar nauseating scent. Kirke knew them and nodded curtly.

"It's a fine nicht," he said, biting off the vowels like bits of ice.

"Yes, it's not bad," agreed one.

"It's blowing up a mist," said another.

"Perhaps you'd call this fine in Scotland," said a third.

"We'd call you a fine fool in Scotland," bit off Kirke, grinning.

The men passed into the bar. The noise increased, rising to a hubbub, then suddenly falling to a murmur accented by low laughs, the clink of glasses, the drawing of corks. The smell of dyes, the smell of the tannery, mingled with the smell of the bar. A blue cloud of tobacco smoke formed before Kirke's eyes. It floated in long level shreds that moved quiveringly together till they formed one mass that hung like a magic carpet in the hall. He watched it contemplatively, his lips still in the formation of exhaling. He hoped very much that Charley Bye would not pass through it before he reached the dining-room door.

In the most select of the three little drinking-rooms a hand was striking a table bell at sharp, regular intervals: ding, ding, ding-ding, ding. Charley appeared to take the order.

"Chairley, dive under yon cloud, d'ye hear?" said Kirke, indicating the magic carpet with his pipe. "Dive under, mon, or it'll be the worse for ye."

With a bewildered look, like a timid bull that desires only to avoid the tormenting matador, Charley ducked heavily under the smoke cloud and disappeared into the drinking-room. Still perfect, of a lovely azure against the dark walls, the magic carpet floated on. Kirke was in good humour. In another moment the bus would arrive. He would see what passengers there were, and then saunter into the bar with Mr Fowler, the owner of the bus. Fowler probably would treat him. He usually did. And if not, well, he would have one anyway.

II

The horses' hoofs made a tremendous clatter on the pavement. The driver's voice was raised in hoarse "whoas" and "backs." The wheels crashed with a jar against the high curb which always made one wonder how the bus (to say nothing of the passengers) withstood it. The front door was thrown open, and the jangle of harness, as the horses threw their heads about to ease their wrenched mouths, the depositing of luggage, and the clink of coin could be heard. Kirke put his pipe in his pocket and approached the door. Three commercial travellers entered, two of them young and alert, one elderly, with an expression of mild boredom. They turned into the office to register and choose sample rooms. Kirke looked at them keenly. He had seen all three before. The elderly man nodded to him with a friendly air.

"It's a fine nicht," said Kirke.

Arthur Crosby, old Colonel Crosby's youngest son, came in hurriedly. He pushed past Kirke and entered the bar. Kirke threw an indignant look after him. "Young upstairt," he muttered. He took off the black bowler hat which he wore to one side, and passed a bony hand over his sleek blond head as the sound of women's voices came from the porch. Old Country voices they were.

The women were in the hotel now, followed by old Davy, the ostler, carrying a tin box bearing steamship labels. They were young, Kirke saw that at once; little more than a girl, the big one, and the short one, still fresh enough to be interesting. Fowler came heavily after them.

"Where's the housekeeper?" he asked of Kirke. "I've got the new help here for her."

"It's a fine nicht," said Kirke, his eyes, which had become

two points of pale fire, concentrated on the faces of the girls before him.

"Damp enough," replied the bus driver, shaking himself. "Go straight upstairs, girls, and ask for Mrs Jessop. You'll see to their boxes, Davy. See that they get hold of Mrs Jessop. Speak right up to her, girls, don't be afraid. . . . They only arrived in Montreal yesterday," he said to Kirke. "Come along and have one on me." He moved toward the bar.

"Thanks, I will," said Kirke. "I'll take the girls upstairs first, and find Mrs Jessop. It's an easy place to get lost in. You'd better carry their boxes through and take them up the backstairs, Davy. Mrs Jessop'll no like ye mounting the front with them, at this hour, with the commaircial gentlemen about."

As they ascended the stairway, the shorter of the two girls said: "I'm sure we're much obliged to you, sir, for your trouble. We're a bit dazed after the long journey, and with the strange plice and all."

"Ay, it's a long way to come for two young geerls," said Kirke. "I wonder sometimes how you get the pluck. But you will do it. I suppose there are motives to bring ye, eh?" He gave a short laugh like a bark and grinned down at her.

"Well, a girl 'as to live, 'asn't she?" There was an exhilarating spice of impudence in her tone. The electric lamp at the head of the stairs cast its pale, searching light over her short, freshly coloured face, surrounded by frizzed, sandy hair, under a drooping white hat that registered in its dents and smudges every day and night of the long journey. Her red lips parted over teeth that were not her own, but good ones nevertheless: probably much whiter and more even than the original set.

"Ay, and live on the fat of the land she will, though the rest of us stairve. Isn't that so? What does your friend think? Has she no word to say?" He looked from the point he had reached at the top of the stairs down at the figure coming slowly up, weighted by a canvas-covered basket. Her hat shielded her face, but he saw the curve of a splendid young breast under a thin black blouse, and a rounded throat that gleamed like white satin.

"Make 'aste, my dear," said the short one. She turned with a smile to Kirke. "Such a sleepy'ead as she is I never seen. Just like a 'ealthy kiddie. Eat, and sleep, and enjoy 'erself."

"I'm tired, I am," came a low, deep voice from under the hat.

Kirke went down a few steps and took the basket from her. "Weel," he said, "it's weighty enough. What have ye got in here, anyway? Gold sovereigns?"

"It's a tea set," she explained. "It was my grandmother's what brought me up. I've never been parted from it on any journey, and I shan't be, if it was ever so."

She was now in the clear light. Kirke all but let the basket drop in the fulness of his astonishment. He was used to pretty girls. There had been many a pretty face and form among the maids in The Duke of York. The girls in the glove factory and the jam factory were often much more than passable. His bright, questing eyes had not roved unappeased. But now he realized that he had never before seen real beauty. He was like a hunter who had sauntered forth in search of rabbit and suddenly, without a sign, a footprint to warn him, come upon a milk-white doe that gazed at him out of liquid eyes of unconcern. He caught his breath with a sort of snarl of surprise. He bit his lip, and tugged at his small, straw-coloured moustache. For the first time since he was grown to manhood he could find nothing to say.

The three walked in silence through an empty hallway past rows of closed, numbered doors, along a narrow passage that branched off from it, down three deeply worn uncarpeted steps, stopped in a still narrower passage, pervaded by a smell of past meals from the kitchens below, and lighted by an oil lamp in a bracket.

"These are the help's quarters," muttered Kirke, setting down the basket. He knocked on a door, under which a line of light shone. "Mrs Jessop!" he called. At the same instant Davy was seen at the top of the backstairs along the passage carrying the tin box on his shoulder. He set it down with a small crash. "Ha!" he exclaimed, "you young maids have to bring your finery with you!"

The door on which Kirke had knocked opened and Mrs Jessop appeared against a background of wooden boxes, tin tea, coffee, and spice containers and sides of smoked meat suspended from the ceiling. She was the housekeeper, a short stout woman with coarse grey hair and a wide mouth which could change a broad smile into lines of grimness or ferocity with amazing quickness. She had private means, in fact, was the widow of a small hotelkeeper, and was always talking about retiring from her present situation and "living private," but for some reason she remained. It was whispered in the scullery that her love for Bill Bastien, nearly twenty years her junior, was the reason.

"So," she said, staring hard at the two young women, "you're the girls sent out by the agency. Ever worked in a hotel before?"

"Yes," answered the short one, "I've been five years a 'ousemaid in a public 'ouse in Camden Town. I can do laundry work too, and know how to clean silver and brasses, and put a cake together in a pinch."

"What is your name?"

"May Phillips."

"They told you what wages I'd give at the agency, did they?"

"Oh, yes."

"And you," she said, turning to the tall girl, beside whom Kirke still stood, not looking at her but feeling the subtle power of her presence in every nerve. "What have you been used to?"

"Waiting at table," came in her low, husky voice, with a slight Somerset accent.

"That's good. What's your name?"

The girl hesitated, and her companion answered for her, "Miss Mainprize, 'er nime is."

"H'm. We don't do any 'Miss-ing' here. I want your first name."

May Phillips giggled and looked at her friend teasingly. "She's a bit shy about 'er first nime."

Mrs Jessop grinned. "Go ahead, girl. Don't be shy of me. I guess I've heard all the funny names that ever got tacked on to anyone."

"Out with it," interposed Kirke. "It'll no raise a laugh out o' me, if it's Hepzibah, or Keziah."

"It's not funny," answered the girl, an angry tremor in her voice. "It's beautiful. It's too beautiful for here. I'd not have coom here if I'd thought you'd make game of me."

Mrs Jessop jingled the keys in her apron pocket and laughed loudly but good-humouredly. "Very well," she said. "I'll show you your room now, and you can whisper your name to me after the lights are out." She flung open a door across the passage and turned the light in a small room, scantily furnished, but clean.

"I'll give a hand with your boxes," she said cheerfully. May Phillips and she began at once to drag the two tin boxes across the linoleum-covered floor into the bedroom. Kirke and the stately girl were left alone in the passage, beneath the oil lamp. She was almost as tall as he. With a sigh she pulled off her drooping hat, disarranging the hair about her ears. It was a shining, pale gold, springing from the roots with strong vitality, waving closely over her head, and clinging in little curls about her temples and nape. But her skin was not blond. Rather the exquisite, golden brown of some rare brunettes, with a warm glow on the cheeks, as when firelight touches the surface of a lovely brazen urn. Her eyes were an intense, dark brown, sleepy now, under thick lashes that seemed to cling together wilfully as though to veil the emotion reflected in their depths. Here was mystery, thought Kirke. And her mouth, he thought, was the very throne of sweetness, as it curved with parted lips, pink as a pigeon's feet. His shrewd eyes observed the lovely line that swept from her round chin to her breast, her perfect shoulders, her strong neck, her hands coarsened by work. He moved closer to her.

"Come, my dear," he said, "tell me your name."

She shook her head. "You'd laugh."

"I'm as likely to greet as to laugh. Out with it," he persisted.

She was too tired to resist him. "I'll whisper it," she said.

He took off his bowler hat and bent his ear toward her mouth, a grin stretching his thin lips.

"It's Delight," she whispered. "Delight. That's all. Delight Mainprize."

"Delight," he whispered back. "It's a bonny name. It suits ye fine. Delight. Ha! I'll no' forget it."

He did not raise his head but screwed his eyes around till they were looking into her face now so close to his. Her eyes were no longer sleepy. Laughing lights played in and out of them. She blinked as though trying to separate her lashes. Her face had broadened, dimples dented her cheeks, her wide mouth curved upward showing two rows of square white teeth. Little ripples of laughter seemed to quiver over her face. Expectancy, curiosity, simple animal joy in life were there. Delight indeed! She was well named.

III

Kirke almost ran downstairs. His stiff, high-shouldered figure in light-grey tweed elbowed a way through the crowd that now thronged the hall and bar. He found Fowler and had a drink with him but he was restless. His eyes were constantly on the doorway. It seemed that Lovering, his friend and roommate, would never come. Then, at last, his burly figure filled the opening. Their eyes met. Kirke beckoned with a jerk of the chin. Fowler muttered good night and Lovering took his place, leaning against the counter and strumming on it with his thick fingers. He was a Yorkshireman with curly dark hair and violet eyes. He ordered a glass of beer in a deep rolling voice.

"Charley Bye's got it in for you," he said. "He says you tripped him oop in the hall and then complained of him to Bill."

"Lovering," said Kirke, "you should see the new geerl. Two came on the bus just now. Man, she's a screaming beauty if ever one screamed. You never saw the like. I've just come down from taking her to Mrs Jessop. Lovering, she'll mak' that cairly hair of yours stand on end when you see her."

Lovering took his face from his glass. "Tha' art always oop in the air about some lass," he said skeptically.

"Ay, but never one like this."

"A fine looker, eh? What is she like?"

"I can't describe her, except that she's tall and nobly built, and she's got a red-hot look in the eyes that mak's your blood tingle."

Lovering gave his slow grin. "Tha' art gone on her already, then."

Kirke stiffened. "Ye know I look higher than that, Lovering, but I can admire the lass."

"Listen to what Fergussen's saying," interrupted Lovering. "What a fellow he is to talk!"

Fergussen, the fishmonger, was standing with his back to the wall, a smile broadening his blunt-featured face. He had been born in Halifax, of Scotch parents, had gone to England as a child, had shipped aboard a West Indian trader at fifteen, had worked on a sheep farm in Australia, a coffee plantation in Ceylon, had fought in the Boer War, was, as he said, one of the strands that held the Empire together.

He took another sip from his glass, smacked his lips, and said: "To continoo our conversation, what gets me is 'ow some people can be so stoopid. They don't know nothing. When I sees 'em, I says to myself—'Fergussen, they're not made of the same stuff as you are. They have no brain power, no sense. Not as much sense as the ground they stands on.' For the ground, mind you, 'as a certain amount of sense. It knows enough to grow things. It knows enough to cover up a dead man when he's laid in it, now isn't that so? But a lot of the people I meet, their ignorance makes me sick." He took another drink, set down his glass, and went on—"Perhaps I make them sick, too. Like I did an old cadger once. I was courtin' his daughter. Not that I was very serious, mind, but I was willin' to pass a silly hour with 'er, now and again, even if it did cost me a dollar. And she liked a silly hour with me, and she liked the look of my dough. . . . This night there was a big storm on and we were sittin' close by the fire and 'er old people was in bed in the next room. Suddenly the old man says to 'is old woman—'Well, my old dearie, you and me is safe under our own roof, and none but a fool of no account, whatsomever, would be out a night like this!' Those were his words out of the darkness of his bed, and you can bet it wasn't long till I was makin' the way shorter 'ome."

"Did you ever go back?" shouted a voice from the hall.

Fergussen puffed out his lips. "Do I look like a man who would go sneakin' back arter a hinsult like that? Do I now?"

"What about the girl?" asked another.

"Ho! You expect me to tell you about the girl, eh? Well, I'll just say this, that we spent a few more silly hours together in spite of the old folk." He gave a jolly wink at Bastien.

Three men off a barge and the stoker of a coaling schooner now came in, for Brancepeth was a lake port, as well as the centre of a fruit-growing district.

The bar was now full. Business was at its height. The air quivered with light, with the mingled odours of the men's bodies and of the trades they worked in, with the grateful smell of wine and spirits. The din of voices crashed against the rows of delicately shining glasses. Flushed, laughing, or argumentative faces were reflected in the long mirrors. Someone on the street outside was playing a Jew's-harp. Fergussen began to do a hornpipe in his crowded corner, now and again uttering a sharp yell. Edwin Silk, a broken-down remittance man, feebly drunk, tried to pull him off his feet. "Don't dance, you damned fishmonger," he ordered, "it makesh me dizhy." Fergussen knocked him down without ceasing to dance. At a nod from Bastien, Charley Bye helped Silk to his feet and mildly led him outside.

Lovering, with his eternal lazy smile, still strummed with his fingers on the bar. "Now, about this lass, Kirke. Tell me more about her. What is her name?"

Two bright spots burned on Kirke's high cheek-bones.

"Delight," he returned slowly, as though he savoured the name on his tongue, and he proceeded to give a minute description of her.

IV

Upstairs, in a small room, lighted by a smoky oil lamp, the two girls were getting ready for bed. May Phillips, in pink stays and a short, wrinkled green silk petticoat, was trying to drag a comb through her frizzed hair. Hairpins flew in all directions.

"Ow, damn my 'air!" she exclaimed. "I 'ave to pull it out by the roots almost, to comb it. I 'ope I don't reely look the speckled beauty this glass shows me. Where's my curling-pins now? Kid! Do you know?"

"In the little pink bag. Why don't you give your hair a rest? It never gets out of one frizz till you put it in another. It 'ud be pretty a little bit straight like."

"It's all very well for you to talk with a crop of natural curls as thick as a seryphim's. If I didn't frizz my 'air there'd be nothing of it."

"Well, frizz away, but do hurry. Oo-er, I'm tired." She had been sitting on the side of the bed pulling off her stockings, and now she flung herself back onto the pillow, opening her mouth in a wide yawn and stretching her arms above her head. Her chemise, drawn upward, disclosed her strong, white thighs, glistening in the lamplight. She rocked her body from side to side in an abandon of relaxation.

"Oo-er, it's nice to get your duds off! What do you think of this place, May?"

"It's 'ard to tell the first night. Old Jessop's on 'er good be'aviour. I make a guess that she's a tartar. The other two girls seem nice, but you can't never tell. Cook's got a pleasant way wiv 'er. I think I'll like cook."

"Oh, May, ain't her tooth funny?"

"If I 'ad it, I'd bite that soft-'eaded 'usband of 'ers, Charley, wiv it. I can't stand a simple man."

Delight rolled over on her face and smothered her laughter. "Oh, you are a rip, May!"

"Stop your laughing or you'll 'ave old Jessop in 'ere arter us. Stow it now, or I'll be over to you wiv the brush. You're pretty 'andy, lying like that. Did your Granny ever take the brush to you, Delight?"

"No. She never gave me more than a little tap with her hand."

"You'd be a better girl if she 'ad."

"Oh, May, I'm not bad."

"Well, perhaps not, but I bet your Granny would be glad you'd got me to look arter you."

"I bet she would." She lay still a moment, then rolled over on her back again and looked up at her friend with dancing eyes. "I say, May, what do you think of the brawny Scot? 'Fine nicht!' he said. I'm going to call him 'Fine Nicht.' Isn't it a good name for him? Isn't he a scream?"

"I think 'e's 'andsome. And look 'ow kind 'e was, carrying your basket and all. You're too uppish, Delight."

"He wasn't just kind, May; he was curious. He made me tell him my name, out there in the passage. I mean to have a little fun with him."

May, now in her nightdress, her head covered with curling-pins, said solemnly: "You better be careful of men out 'ere. You're in a strange country, and you 'aven't no one to look arter you but me."

"You hop into bed, old Lady Croak. You hate men yourself, don't you?"

May turned out the light and got into the narrow, lumpy bed beside her. She had not opened the window, and the air was filled with the smell of the charred wick. A steady hum of voices rose from the bar. She turned toward the young girl and laid her arms across her supple hips.

"Is my tea set safe?" whispered Delight.

"In a corner of the clothes cupboard. I laid a petticoat over it in case anyone comes nosing around in the morning."

"I think I'll put it under the bed tomorrow. It'd be safer there."

"Oh, you silly, under the bed's the first place any burglar 'ud look."

"Under the bed! Oo—May, s'pose there was someone under the bed now! S'pose he'd been there waitin' for us!" She wriggled frantically against May. "S'pose it was Fine Nicht! Oo—May." They laughed hysterically, clutching each other.

"Well, I'm not going to get out and look," said May. "If he wants to sleep under the bed he can."

"Oh, May, do strike a light and see."

"You settle down. You're worse than a kid." She administered a slight smack.

They lay still save for an occasional giggle that quivered through their muscles. At last the elder spoke, seriously: "Delight, I'm going to tell you a secret. I never intended to, but now, just at the last minute, I must. I can't go asleep till I do. Ain't it funny?"

"How can I tell till I hear it?"

"Oh, the secret ain't a bit funny. You wait till you 'ear it."

"Get it out, old girl."

May buried her face in Delight's curls and, with her mouth against her ear, whispered: "I'm married."

"Married! Oh, May, and you never told me!"

"Ssh! Don't talk out loud. I couldn't make up my mind to before. I wanted to see wot the plice was like first. But now I've got to. I'm so worried."

"Is he *here*? Are you coming out to him?"

"Yes. 'E works in the tannery. 'E boards in this very hotel. Ain't it thrillin'? But the trouble is I got Annie to tell me the nimes of the boarders tonight, and she never mentioned 'is. I'm frightened. S'pose 'e's gone away! Wouldn't it be awful?"

"Why wasn't he at the station to meet you?"

"'E don't know I'm comin'. 'E was to send for me when 'e 'ad saved up enough, but 'e kept putting me off and I'd worked 'ard myself and saved every penny I could till I'd enough for my passage and to furnish a couple of rooms, then I didn't write or nothink but just come straight out to surprise 'im."

"Lord, May, I can't think of you as married. What's his name?"

"Albert. Albert Masters."

"You're May Masters, then, reely, not May Phillips."

"Yes."

"What's he like? Handsome as Fine Nicht?"

"'E's not 'andsome at all. 'E's a little thickset fellow wiv bulgy blue eyes and a space between 'is two front teeth wot makes 'is smile sort of infantile, too. Oh, 'e ain't wot you'd ever call 'andsome, Delight, but 'e's charmin', 'e reely is."

"H'm," said Delight, pondering deeply.

"And 'e's got a masterful way wiv 'im, too, that a girl likes. 'E quite scares me sometimes, 'specially when 'e 'as a bit o' drink inside 'im. But then, again, 'e'll cry if I look cross at 'im."

"Oh, May, it must be funny to be married."

"Sometimes. Sometimes it's awful. When you don't know where 'e is, or wot 'e's up to. Just s'pose 'e's gone off wiv another woman."

"He'd never leave you for a Canadian girl."

"You can't tell wot they'll do when they gets out to Canader. Oh, I feel it in my bones there's something wrong. W'y ain't 'e 'ere?" She began to sob hysterically.

Delight pressed her to her breast. "Don't you take on, May," she whispered. Tomorrow night it'll be Albert 'stead of me."

"Oh, if I only were sure," sobbed May. But she was too tired to cry for long. The heaving of her shoulders ceased. She lay supine in Delight's arms. The girl still rhythmically patted her back. She drew her head back on the pillow, for one of May's curling-pins pressed cruelly into her cheek. "Poor old girl," she thought. "It must be awful to be married."

Faces of men floated before her half-closed eyes. The pimply face of the son of the publican for whom she had last worked. He had squatted beside her on the floor she was wiping up, and had put his heavy arm around her and tried to kiss her. How funny his face had looked when she had slopped the soapy water over his shiny shoes. Then there came the face of Artie Blythe who had come to see her off at Southampton. Poor little Artie with his pasty clerk's face all woebegone and a funny bunch of flowers held out toward her. Then the waiter on the steamship who used to glide to her in the dark with dainties stolen from the first-cabin pantries. Then the trainman who leant over her seat to point out mountains and valleys, and teach her to say the names of the French villages. How he laughed at the way she said them! Funny creatures, men! Now, here was Kirke. She saw his piercing eyes, the pink spots on his cheek-bones, his red tie, tied just so. She couldn't help it if men liked her, wanted to stare at her and get close to her. She couldn't help it any more than her mother could. Her mother could not have been very much ashamed of having her or she would not have called her Delight. It sounded as though she'd been glad to have her. Well, anyway, God had made her the same as other folk. She began to laugh softly, opening her mouth wide in the darkness, making little clucking noises. What fun God must have had making her! Her hair for one thing. Well, even God would laugh to think of all those tight yellow curls. And her eyes—God must have laughed into them, for there was always a laugh behind them.

Oh, it was wicked to think of God in that way! Just as though He would laugh like other folk! Or even smile! No wonder Gran had worried about her. As soon as she could find time she would unpack Gran's tea set and see if it had got a crack or chip coming over.

Down in the bar someone was playing a fiddle. She had often heard that queer, jiggy tune at home. Perhaps it wouldn't be so different here, after all. . . . Like waves the men's voices rose and fell and, at last, submerged her in sleep.

CHAPTER II

ALBERT AND MAY

I

THE red glow of the sunrise flamed into the room at the same moment that Charley Bye knocked on the bedroom door.

"Up, lasses," he said, in his rich, ponderous tones. "Be you going to lie all day?"

He passed on to the door behind which Annie and Pearl slumbered, and repeated his call.

It was impossible to believe that a whole night had passed. Impossible to believe that they had been sleeping, resting sweetly on that lumpy bed, for hours and hours. A sort of stupor held them in its grip. Dimly they heard stove lids clanging below. Coals rattling out of the scuttle. The creaking of a pump in the stable yard beneath their window, the heavy feet of horses on the paving-stones.

All they longed for was to be allowed to sleep for ever. But presently another knock, light but sharp, sounded on the door.

"Say, you girls," came Annie's voice, "you'd better get a move on. Mrs Jessop won't like it if she's down before you are. There's a troupe come on the midnight train, too, so hurry up. Are you all right?"

"Right as rain, my dear," answered May, springing up with sudden energy. "Down directly." Annie clattered downstairs.

May bent over Delight. "Do you want a wet wash-rag

in the eye, duckie? I'll just give you till I count ten. One—two—three—four—five—"

Delight was out on the floor, pulling her nightdress over her head. "Oo—May," she wailed, "I'm so—sleepy. Couldn't you tell them I'm having a spell of some kind?"

"You aren't 'ired to 'ave spells, my girl. 'Ere, 'op into yer duds." She threw an armful of underclothes at her.

As one in a dream, Delight caught them and stood blinking sleepily out of the window. The red sunlight stained the warm whiteness of her body to the blush of an apple blossom. Her breasts, gently rising and falling, lay like sleeping flowers between her rounded arms. A tangle of yellow curls hung over her drowsy dark eyes. May suddenly beheld her.

"Get back from before that window!" she screamed in a whisper. "Do you want to make a show for the whole town?" She added, solemnly—"Delight, I'm afraid this ain't no place for you. But then I don't know what would be a place for you, I really don't."

"Silly," said Delight, pulling on her stockings. "I fit in anywhere."

II

Breakfast was ready. Already half the boarders were in their places. These were tannery hands, men from the dye works and jam factory, who had to be at their work early. They sat at a long table by themselves, distinct from the commercial table, the table for other transients, and the table for boarders of a higher class. They were boarded at a low rate, had, in consequence, no table napkins or bill-of-fare, wiping their mouths on their handkerchiefs when through eating, and being told what choice there was for them by the waitress. It was this table that Delight was to serve.

She and May were in the pantry between the dining-room and kitchen. She was all a-tremble with excitement.

"Do I look tidy, May?" she whispered, glancing over her neat black dress with its sleeves to the wrists and modestly rounded neck, for it was a time when clothes were still made to conceal, and one might even cross the street to see a motorcar in Brancepeth.

"Your apron's a bit at one side," answered May, straightening it, "but you look as fresh as a daisy. Oh, Delight, do be on the watch for 'im. You'll know 'im the minute you set eyes on 'im. A kind of bullet 'ead, and those blue eyes like a biby, and 'is teeth just a space apart."

"Lord, d'you expect me to turn his face up and look into his mouth?"

"Don't be 'ateful," replied May, her eyes filling with tears. "If you only knew the ache in me 'ere," she pressed her hand to her heart.

"Now, don't you worry, May! I'm just skittish 'cause I'm nervy. Tell me again what I'm to say to him."

"Lean over 'im and whisper—'Remember your May. Be on the watch tonight.' That'll fetch 'im."

Annie threw open the swing door from the kitchen and fastened it. "Mrs Jessop's looking for you," she said to May. "She wants you to get busy on the bedrooms. Come on, Delight."

Annie led the way to the dining-room with an air of deserved superiority. She met an early traveller at the door, led him to the commercial table, seated him, and handed him the bill-of-fare. He took out a pair of eyeglasses, adjusted them to his nose, and was about to read when his eyes fell on Delight. For a moment he stared through his glasses; next he bent his head and looked over them; then he took them off and stared. Then he looked up at Annie. "I've never seen that girl here before, have I?" he asked.

"No, sir. She's a new one, just out from the Old Country. She don't know much yet. I've got to take her in hand."

"Well, well." He turned with a sigh, and picked up the bill-of-fare.

Delight, in her close, black dress that strained darkly to cover her exuberant charms, swayed above the boarders. She was happy. These hungry men, with the odours of their occupations hanging about them, seemed like her little children whom she was about to feed. She had been told by Mrs Bye, the cook, to ask them whether they would have oatmeal porridge or Force. Force was a breakfast food of the day. As she bent over each she asked gently:

"Oatmeal porridge or Forces?"

For some reason she did not like the sound of the singular Force. It was a harsh, disagreeable word. It made her think of wife-beating. But Forces—that was different—she had heard of forces at work. Well, these men must work, so why not work on Forces! From her the word seemed a caress, as she softly rolled the r.

The boarders preferred the good porridge, but it was impossible to resist the seduction of that tone.

"F-or-rces," softly rolled each deep voice after hers.

In the kitchen cook was aghast, outraged. "Whatever has come over the men?" she exclaimed. "Here's my whole pot of porridge going to waste, and package after package of that breakfast food opened. Mrs Jessop'll be in a fine taking."

"It's that new girl," replied her husband. "You may depend upon it. Women are kittle-cattle, every one on 'em, but she's the worst I seen yet. I knowed we'd have trouble with her the minute I set eyes on her."

"But why?" cried Mrs Bye. "Why don't she want them to eat their porridge same as usual?"

Charley wagged his head. "Just spite, missus. She seen you had a big pot o' porridge made, and she undertook that you'd have it left on you."

"Well, I'll teach her! I'll get Mrs Jessop after her. . . ."

But there was one boarder who did not weakly ask for Forces. This was Kirke. Eye to eye, he and Delight faced each other, then he bit off the one word:

"Parritch."

Delight's lids fell. She swayed to the kitchen and said to Mrs Bye:

"Forces."

When the dish was set before Kirke, a heavy scowl darkened his white forehead. "I asked for parritch," he snarled.

Delight leaned over him almost tenderly, his angry eyes caught the pearly curve beneath her chin. "There aren't any porridge," she breathed. "There's just Forces."

Forces indeed. Terrible forces at work to make Kirke and all the others eat just what she chose that they should have!

So busy was Delight that she forgot for a while to look for Albert Masters. But when the men were eating their finnan haddie and fried potatoes, she suddenly thought with remorse that she had forgotten her mission for May. Her eyes flew along the bent heads. They dwelt a moment on Kirke's narrow sleek one at the end of the table and then moved on. Ah! That must be he. That round, fair head, those round rosy cheeks, those childlike blue eyes that were looking at her with shy pleasure. She smiled. He smiled in return and showed square teeth set a little apart. She went quickly to him, putting the sugar basin within his reach.

"Remember your May," she whispered.

The colour deepened in his cheeks. He looked sheepishly from side to side to see if the others had heard. Then he nodded.

When the others straggled out he remained apparently engrossed in a slice of bread and jam. Kirke and Lovering went out together, using toothpicks and joking with the air of swagger fellows. They felt considerably above the other third-floor boarders by virtue of Lovering's position as under-foreman in the dye works, and Kirke's as a shipper in the tannery. But they preferred the cheap accommodation to a more ambitious status.

The dining-room was now empty save for Delight and the young man. He laid down his bread and got nervously to his feet. Delight came and stood beside him, a roguish smile curving toward a dimple in her cheek.

"You heard what I said, eh?" she asked in a low tone.

"Y-yes," he stammered. "You've made me awful proud. When can we get together?"

"I don't quite know. She's upstairs with Mrs Jessop now, makin' beds. Couldn't you go back to your room as though you'd forgotten something?"

"*She?* What do you mean *she?*"

"Why, May, silly. She's terrible keen to see you. You're Albert all right, aren't you?"

"Albert! I say, what are you giving me?"

"Why, May's Albert. Albert Masters. I s'pose you'd like me to tell you where you first met May!" Her smile was sarcastic now. The dimple had gone into retreat.

"Look here," exclaimed the young man, "look here. There's a mistake. I'm not Albert. I'm Jimmy Sykes. Albert don't board here now. He's away up near the station." His face was blank with disappointment. "I guess you didn't mean anything by your whispering, then."

"Lor', what did you think I meant?"

"Well, you said—'Remember, you may'!"

"Oh, listen to the boy! I said—'Remember *your* May'! What did you think I *meant*—'Remember, you may'?"

"I thought you meant I might make love to you." He stared into her eyes imploringly. "Just a little. I'd be awfully disappointed if I thought it was all off between us."

"Oh, well," she moved a little closer to him, her head drooping toward her breast. "I'd be pretty lonely here if there was no one to like me or take me out evenings."

He caught her hand and held it in both of his. "Oh, let me

take you out, let me keep company with you just a little. Why, look here, if you only knew what I felt like when you asked me this morning if I would have oatmeal porridge or Forces, you'd be surprised, I bet."

Her deep, mirthful eyes met his. "Tell me," she whispered, "what did you feel like?"

"Oh, I can't hardly explain. All tickly up the backbone, and weak, and in a kind of haze, and I wanted to eat whatever you'd bring me if it was poison."

She smiled, showing her small white teeth; her eyelashes seemed to get irrevocably tangled. With a frantic look toward the door Jimmy Sykes caught her in his arms and planted a kiss on her cheek, then fled, late for his work.

Delight tiptoed to the commercial table and took a lump of loaf sugar from the silver bowl. She laid it on her tapering tongue, then closed her lips and sucked like a happy child. Annie opened the door and said—"You'd have time for a bite of breakfast now before the troupe comes down. You can look after them. You've done real well."

III

"Just chuck those sausages into the stockpot," said the cook to Delight. "Every bit helps. Then come and get your breakfast while you've time."

"Yes, cook," replied Delight meekly, sliding the two left-over sausages into the simmering beaded liquid.

Mrs Bye was a tall, thin, unbelievably active woman of forty. She had a hatchet face, prominent bright blue eyes, a large nose, and a chin that receded slightly. She had long ago lost a front tooth, and its fellow, moving gradually forward to fill the space, now occupied the centre of her jaw, projecting slightly and giving her face the expression of a very eager squirrel. Her natural pallor was changed for the flush that always came to her cheeks at mealtime, for she was excitable, anxious and fearful of Mrs Jessop who she fancied was not friendly toward her.

The kitchen was terribly hot, the stove lids pinkish from the coals that Charley had heaped beneath them. The girls were all talking at once, old Davy and Charley were dragging their chairs noisily across the bare floor, and Queenie, the Byes' only child, was marching up and down the length of the kitchen singing her newest kindergarten song at the top of her lungs.

She was nearly six years old and had inherited Charley's classic regularity of feature, his fair, almost transparent skin, and his clumsy body. But nature had withheld from her the proper palate with which Charley was endowed, so that Queenie's marching song, while spirited, for she never sang and marched so well as in the high tide of excitement in the kitchen, came haltingly as to words. She sang:

We aw mar'h toge'her,
We aw mar'h toge'her,
We aw mar'h toge'her,
Nih'ly in a waow.

With uplifted face, starry eyes, and flaxen hair flying, she swept past the minions that slaved about her, under trays, under kettles of boiling water, under scuttles of coal, she passed unscathed. If only she could have taken this splendid hauteur with her to school where, because of her affliction, she was the butt of the class, returning home in tears, day after day, chased to the very door by children who took her slate pencils, pulled her hair, and mimicked her unintelligible speech!

"Will you have some haddie?" asked Mrs Bye, treating Delight as a guest. "And potatoes?"

"Yes, please."

"I don't s'pose you'd like any porridge?" This was said with a certain aggressiveness.

"Oh, Mrs Bye, it wasn't my fault about the porridge, truly. The men just fancied Forces this morning. They'll be back to their porridge right enough tomorrow."

"Well, for goodness sake try to get them back or we'll have housekeeper after us."

They sat down with dishes of hot food before them, Annie, her sleek dark head bent in a listening posture, kept one ear open for a step in the dining-room. Pearl, a fat girl with sleepy hazel eyes, slowly consumed a large bowl of porridge and milk. Mrs Bye rarely ate anything but bread and tea. She called coaxingly to Queenie:

"Come along, my poppet, and have a nice boiled egg."

"Naow," replied Queenie, shaking her head, "ah wanha mar'h."

"She's contankerous like all females," observed Charley, withdrawing a long fishbone from his mouth. "They're all alike. As I was a-remarking to my woife a bit ago, women is all kittle-cattle, and you can't get away from it. I'm the man as knows, for I had a first woife and foive daughters, a second woife and a daughter, her as you see paradin' herself this minute, and I live in this kitchen surrounded by women, like a oasis in a desert, and I say they're kittle-cattle, and the less a man has to do with any one on 'em the better for his natur', human and otherwise."

"Aw, Mr Bye, you don't really mean that," said Pearl.

"I allers stick up for the women," said Old Davey. "What is a home without a wife? I say it's a hotel without a bar."

"Good, good!" said Pearl. "Davy's got you there, Mr Bye."

"I grant that's true," said Charley, "but the bar's where all the trouble begins, isn't it? All the contankerousness and noise. I don't ask for anything but peace. I'd like to be back in the Old Land in my truck garden, I would, and breedin' rabbits. I had one old buck rabbit there, that had a natur' so like my own that we was more like brothers than man and rabbit. He felt just the same as I did about the female of the species. And when I think of my lettuces and cabbages settin' there, day arter day, in the same place, just where I'd put them, it brings the tears to my eyes."

A redheaded boy looked in at the door. "Bill Bastien wants you, Charley," he said. "And he says be sharp about it."

Charley filled his mouth with the last of his fried potatoes, emptied his coffeecup, and got heavily to his feet. He tripped over his own toes as he went out, leaving a smile on the faces of those behind him.

"One would think he was simple to hear him talk about his cabbages and all," said Mrs Bye apologetically, "but he's got a grand head for business, I can tell you that."

"He has," agreed old Davy admiringly. "When him and me carry anything together, I always get the heavy end, and I never know how he manages it."

The sound of footsteps came from the dining-room. Annie quickly wiped her lips and fingers and went in. Mrs Bye stirred the porridge and put fresh tea to steep. Old Davy returned to his stable. Pearl continued placidly to eat greasy, hashed potatoes. Delight snatched up Queenie and carried her to the window.

"You're a rum little kiddie," she said, looking into her upturned face.

"Ah hi poo."

"Do you? I like you too, if that's what you're saying. Can you count? Let's hear you count."

"Wa—poo—pee—paw—pi—pih—pebbin—"

"My word, you're fond of p's, ain't you?"

"Ay. Ah hi poo." And she clutched her neck and kissed her.

Annie rushed in with her tray. "Come along, Delight, you're needed. The whole troupe's there, and three of the second-floor boarders. Put the kid down and get a move on. Three ham and eggs, and two fish, cook. My goodness, you ought to see the troupe. Dr De Silva and his College Girls. Funny-lookin' college girls. You ought to see the fat one with a yellow wig and a dirty pink kimono. That coffee hot?"

IV

The tables had been cleared, the floor swept, the crumbs taken up, and the two canaries brought out to have their cages cleaned, before Delight had a chance to speak to May. Suddenly she saw her in the dark cavern of the backstairs. She had set down her mop and pail, and was looking down at Delight with an expression of anxious appeal.

"I'll be back and finish these cages in a minute," said the girl to Mrs Bye. "I must run up to my room for something."

She could hear May's breath coming in little gasps, as she stood beside her in the dark stairway.

"Oh," she panted, "I didn't get no chance to come down before. That awful old Jessop stuck to me like a leech. Did you find 'im?"

"No."

"Ow, my Gawd, 'e's gone! I may never find 'im in this unnatural country!"

"Don't you take on, May. I know where he is. Boarding in a house up near the station." She put her strong arm around her friend and supported her. "Don't take on! We'll find him."

May rested her head on Delight's shoulder, still grasping her mop. " 'Ow did you find out where 'e's gone?"

"Why, there was a nice chubby boy in there that I made sure was Albert. He had baby-blue eyes, and I smiled at him, and when he smiled back, there was his teeth a bit apart like you said, and I whispered—'Remember your May,' and if he didn't think I was trying to say he might be sweet on me. He stopped after the others had gone, then I found out he wasn't Albert, and I got out of him where Albert lives."

"You didn't tell 'im about me, did you?"

"He never asked. He was pretty well amazed. He's a simple lad. I'll look after him, May."

"Oh, Delight, 'ow can I ever get a'old of Albert tonight?"

"Look here. There's a closet between the dining-room and the bar! It's a dark, narrow one and it isn't often used now. It has a little frosted glass window in the wall where drinks used to be handed through for the dining-room. And, look here, May, some Nosey Parker of a girl has scraped a bit of the frosting off the pane, just enough to fit the eye, and what's to prevent you hiding in there tonight and watching for your boy? You say he likes his glass."

"Oh, 'e does, and 'e's a little terror all right w'en 'e's got a bit more than 'e can carry."

"Well, get him before he takes that much. Scratch on the pane like a little mouse." In the dusk of the stairway her long eyes were glistening with mischief. "Oo—May, it'd be fun! I wish you'd let me do it for you."

V

May passed the day in a waking dream. Before her, as she dusted banisters, polished looking-glasses, and slid her mop over linoleums, floated the round face of Albert. The cast in his left eye gave the face an elusive, almost sinister appearance. He seemed to be looking two ways at once, accusingly at her with one eye, shiftily away from her with the other. She saw this face in shining doorknobs, in mirrors, in the puddles on the linoleum. She felt that if she did not see the real face soon she would go mad. Yet she worked on doggedly. Mrs Jessop was pleased with her. She liked her better than Delight, whom she suspected of being "worth watching."

It was eight o'clock before she was able to go to her bedroom. Mrs Bye was in her room next door putting Queenie to bed. May could hear the child's little voice piping—

Ow I ay ee 'ow' oo peep
Paya Lor' my ho oo heep.

She heard Mrs Bye say: "Now, Lovey, hop straight in and go bye-bye."

She could picture Queenie hopping on to her mattress on the floor in the corner of the room next the stovepipe. For a moment the vision of Albert was gone, she breathed more easily. Then it danced before her again in the lamplight and her heart began to pound in her throat. Hastily she pulled off her working-dress and put on a blue one of cheap silk, with a velvet girdle and a lace collar fastened by a gilt bar pin on which two little gilt birds perched, one of Albert's presents. She put on high-heeled shoes that hurt her, and back-combed the hair about her ears till it framed her frightened face like a fabulous halo.

She turned out the light and crept down the backstairs. The kitchen was empty save for old Davy who was poring over the pages of *The Family Herald*, moving his grey unshaven lips as he read some tale of high life. The other girls were in the scullery. Annie and Pearl were wrestling like two boys while Delight sat perched on a table clapping her hands and singing an old Somerset Fair song she had from her Granny.

May stole into the dining-room, and passed from there into the narrow cupboard behind the bar. It was pitch-dark there except for the golden square of the frosted window. The business of the evening was in full swing on the other side of the glass. May soon found the little transparent spot scratched by the nail of some other curious girl. She must have been a tall girl, for it was necessary for May to stand on her toes to see through it. It flashed through her mind that perhaps Delight had been up to her tricks already. . . .

May put her eye to the spot. She could not see very much at first, for a man had moved almost directly in front and his hand, curving about a glass, rose before her anxious eyes like some symbol of a quest. It was a dark supple hand, and on it gleamed a diamond ring. Whoever he was he imbibed his drink slowly. The hand would rise, remaining but long enough for a sip. May watched the fall of the amber liquid in the glass, as a skipper watches the barometer in stressful weather. A steady jargon of voices came to her stabbed by sudden gusts of laughter. . .

Suddenly the man moved. Now he was gone and the length of the bar stretched before her. It was almost full of men. Her eyes flew from one face to another in search of Albert. If only they had stood quite still, but they moved to make way for newcomers. Charley tottered in and out carrying trays to the private rooms, twice Bastien passed before her vision in his white apron, his head forward, his teeth gleaming, a corkscrew in his hand. With the constant dissolving and resetting of the picture before her, and her strained position, her head began to ache and her eyes to burn, but she never ceased watching. At last he came. . . .

Short, thickset, with a bullet head under a tweed cap, he entered alone. He went to the counter and bought a glass of beer from young Steve, the assistant bartender.

All May's anxiety and suspicion flamed into joyous love at the sight of him. She felt as though her body had become a burning torch inside the dark cupboard, that the blaze of her must shine through into the bar.

Albert absorbed his beer solemnly while he listened to something Steve was saying to Kirke and Lovering who were leaning against the counter together. May riveted her eye on him and tried to force him to come toward her. But he did not move. Then right beside her window a man's voice called—"Masters"—and Albert came and stood almost against the glass. May's eye looked directly on to his ear. "Albert, oh, Albert," she moaned under her breath. "Oh, my dearie, look round at me. 'Ere I am."

Cautiously she tried the window to see if it would rise. She slid it up an inch. Her mouth to the crack, she sighed. She sighed again more loudly. She breathed his name. He put his hand behind his shoulder and twiddled his fingers. Oh, what devils men were! But perhaps he guessed it was she.

"Come 'ere," she said softly.

In a second he had left the window. A moment more and she heard his hand fumbling softly for the handle of the cupboard door. It closed behind him. She had him in her arms, clutched to her breast, kissing him violently, savagely, her own Albert. He struggled feebly, then succumbed.

"My word," he gasped, "you're a 'ot 'un."

"Oh, Albert, my 'usband," she said chokily, "my own dearie."

The words went through his body like an electric shock. He tore himself from her grasp. In the pallid light of the frosted window his face showed as a staring disk with distorted features. He looked like the man in the moon.

"Albert, don't you know me?"

"My Gawd!" He grasped his head between his hands and rocked himself in bewilderment. "You, M'y—you!"

"Yes, me. W'y not? Oh, Albert, don't be frightened. Did you think I was a ghos'? My goodness, it's only your own little May come to you! Your nerves are shockin' bad, ain't they, dearie?" She wrapped her arms about him again.

" 'Ow the 'ell did you come 'ere?" he demanded, trying

again to extricate himself. She held him to her firmly, her hands clasped between his shoulder blades.

"I couldn't wait no longer. I reely couldn't. And I saved—pinched and saved. And there was a guessing contest and I won the prize—five pounds; and I found a stone out of a ring on the street and got a reward—three pounds more—oh, Albert, everything's been comin' my w'y! And now I've come yours—to st'y, for ever and ever. Say you're glad."

"Glad—" he moaned— " 'ow the 'ell can I be glad. You *'ave* made a bloody mess o' things! Well, you may just as well 'ave it now as any time, M'y! I'm *married. Yus. To a gal out 'ere. In this town.* 'Ave you got that in yer noddle? *I'm married.* Now don't go screamin' or you'll 'ave the 'ole bloomin' bar in 'ere. 'Ang on to yerself. It weren't my fault. She reg'larly chivied me into it. Now you know."

Her arms had dropped from him like the antennæ of a devilfish when the body had been wounded. He breathed more freely and peered through the dimness to see her face. If his had looked like the full moon, hers was now its shrunken, wan, last quarter.

"Married," she repeated. "You went and got *married.* And me in England, believin' you was savin' for me to come out to you! Me *comin'* out, filled with a fool's pride 'cause I'd saved enough to get me passage and buy a few sticks of furniture for us to begin with! *Married!* You call *that* married! I call it *adulatory*. She ain't your wife. *I'm* your wife. You brute. You dirty, low, little brute."

"Keep yer voice down, for Gawd's sake! Do you want me arrested? 'Ow! M'y, you don't understand."

"Understand! Understand! I understand that you've committed bigermy, and I'll 'ave the law of yer! You miserable, connivin' little brute."

" 'Ow, I know it's orful for you," he moaned, "but I didn't go fer to do it—she chivied me inter it. I wish I'd never seen 'er ugly red 'ead, I do."

"Red 'ead," repeated May dully. "I can't 'ardly believe it. Red 'ead on the piller beside yours. . . . Wot's her nime?"

"Ader."

"Ader. Ader wot?"

"Ader Masters."

"Liar—" screamed May. "It ain't Masters! She ain't yer wife. I'm yer wife. I'll 'ave 'er in the gaol tomorrer!"

Luckily a sudden roar of voices from the bar deadened her scream. Suddenly Albert dropped on his knees before her, clutching her legs and hiding his face in her skirt.

"She's a regular baggage, she are," he moaned. "She leads me a life. If you're crool to me, I'll just go 'n' make w'y wiv myself." His shoulders began to heave. The smell of the tannery rose to her from his kneeling body. There was no air in the dark little room. She was stifling. Sweat trickled from her forehead and mingled with the tears on her cheeks. The feel of him kneeling there sobbing wrung her heart. Mechanically she began to stroke his head.

"And me eatin' my 'eart out in old London for you," she said in a strange, thick voice.

"That's orl very well *in* old London." He wagged his head resentfully. "But it's another story 'ere. Wot wiv the bloomin' climate, and the stink of the vats allus in a feller's nose, 'e ain't responsible for wot 'e does. As for me, I'm that derbilitated that I'm scared o' me own shadder."

"You weren't scared to tike a second wife."

"That was just it. I was scared. I took 'er fer peace sike. She wouldn't let me be. She worked in the jam factory and 'er 'ome was in one o' them cottages be'ind the hotel and she'd 'ang around no matter wot the weather was and walk to and fro wiv me and twinkle 'er eyes at me in a w'y—ow, you've no idear—w'y she *arsked* me to marry 'er, now I come to think of it!"

" 'Ad she a *reason?*"

"Nao. None but 'er own cussedness. She was out to get married and I was the man 'er fawncy lit on."

" 'Ow long ago was this?"

"Six months."

"Six months out of my life she's taken! And I don't s'pose she sets half the store on you I did." She slid to the floor beside him, her back against the wall, trembling from weakness.

His arm slid about her. "She don't set no store by me at all. 'Er one idear is to get all she can out o' me. She's a hard 'un, she is. Talk about bigermy—if she knowed about you she'd 'ave me clapped in gaol before you could say scat—and you'd be disgriced in this bloomin' country!"

They sat in silence now, two little cockney animals that had crept into this dark burrow out of the storm. His lips sought hers. He stroked her cheek. Like a solemn threnody the voices in the bar surged over them. They might have been at the bottom of the sea.

VI

Delight was sitting before the chest of drawers, with her Granny's apple-green tea set spread out before her, when May entered. She turned toward her, a happy smile curving her lips.

"What do you s'pose, May?" she said. "Not a blessed cup or saucer's been chipped. Even the teapot spout never got a nick. . . . Oh, for goodness sake! What's up?"

May stood before her, glassy-eyed, with a terrible twist to her mouth. "I've seen 'im," she answered, in a queer coughing way.

"Oh, Albert, eh? Wasn't he nice to you, May?"

"Nice to me! Listen to the girl! Ow, yes, 'e was nice to me! Very nice to me, 'e was! Loverly to me, I'd s'y, if the queen came around in 'er carriage and ast me."

"May, are you crazy?"

"Small wonder if I was. Wot do you s'pose that 'e's done but get married! To a Canadian girl out 'ere. Married and livin' with 'er this six months. Ader, 'er nime is. Red-'aired."

Delight flew to her and would have folded her in her arms but May backed from her till she stood against the bedroom door. She stretched her arms upon it and broke into hysterical laughter. "Ow, 'e's made a proper wreck of me, 'e 'as!" she laughed, "ain't it a joke?"

"Hang on to yourself," said Delight, "or you'll have the others in. Shall I throw cold water on you now?"

Quick steps were coming from the next room. Mrs Bye pushed the door open, and looked round it at May. At the sight of her May laughed louder than ever. "Married, ain't yer?" she cried. "Are you sure you're married?"

Mrs Bye shut the door and took her by the arm. "May, May," she said. "You'll have Mrs Jessop in. Do quieten yourself."

"I tell her the others 'll all be getting oop," said Delight. "I was just going to empty a mug of water on her."

May was calmed by the sight of Mrs Bye. She sat down on the side of the bed and pressed back the damp hair from her forehead. "It's just a touch of hystrikes," she said. "I've 'ad them before, 'aven't I, Delight?"

Mrs Bye brought her a mug of water and patted her

back as she drank it. The motherly touch had a softening effect. May laid her head against Mrs Bye and sobbed like a little child.

"If it's anything to do with a man, don't waste your tears now," said the cook. "Save them till you're married. You'll need them worse, then." She nodded her head wisely, looking almost like a girl with her ugly kitchen dress exchanged for a long blue wrapper over her nightgown and a little pigtail down her back.

Charley had come up to bed and, hearing his wife's voice in the girls' bedroom, he gave the door a thump and said:

"Come along to bed, missus. D'ye want me to be losing my rest when you well know how early I must rise?"

"In a moment," answered Mrs Bye.

"Is it some fellow that had promised her in the Old Land?" she asked of Delight. "Don't tell me if May had rather not. I don't want to pry, dear knows."

"Well, they were all but promised," answered Delight cautiously. "But now she's coom over, he is trying to back out."

May sobbed. "He's my cousin."

"Well, then, be glad you're shut of him," said Mrs Bye. "I don't approve of cousins marryin'. Nature never intended that we should overdo relations that way, and if we do, likely as not, the children 'll come underdone."

"You'd think marriage was a pie to hear you talk," said Delight.

"It's a pie you'd better keep your finger out of, till you're a bit more sensible."

"Me?" cried Delight. "I'm as sensible as can be. It'd take more than a jilting to upset me."

Charley thumped on the wall. "Missus! Missus!" he called. "Be you going to gadabout all night?"

"Please don't tell the other girls anything of this," implored May. "I couldn't bear it."

"Never a breath," said Mrs Bye. "And you put your cousin out of your mind. There's other nice young fellers here that 'ud like nothing better than to walk out with a smart-looking girl like you." She whisked out with her long stride to her own room, exactly as though it were an oven and Charley a cake burning.

"I wonder what relation *they* were," mused Delight.

"Who?"

"Why, cook and Charley. Look at Queenie. She's a bit queer. No roof to her mouth, I mean, and all."

"Oh, you silly! I've got a brother whose toes are all webbed jus' like a duck's and my parents was no more relation than 'Enery the Eighth and the Queen of Sheba."

Delight persisted. "Well, anyway, May, since Albert *is* your cousin—"

"E's not my cousin, but I've promised 'im to s'y 'e is for the time being."

"Where's the use?"

"Oh, well, we'll be able to meet and talk things over. Folk won't be suspicious if they think we're cousins."

Delight was scornful. "You promised him to keep quiet, eh? After what he's done to you!"

May threw herself back on her pillow, her face swollen from crying, her eyes bloodshot. "You just wait, my beauty, till you're in a fix like this with a man some d'y. You don't know what you'd do. You don't know anythink."

Delight hung over the foot of the bed looking down at her. "I know I'd never, never promise—"

"Oh, shut up! I'd ha' promised 'im anything down in that dark cubby 'ole."

"Well, o' course, if you're going to let him get *around* you."

"You'd have done the sime, Delight. 'E reely is charmin'. 'E just 'ung on to me and cried like a little child. 'E says 'e's that debilertated wiv the climate and all that 'e's scared of 'is own shadder, pore lad."

Between pity for him and pity for her own plight May's tears fell like rain on the pillow. Delight helped her to undress and put her into bed, then thoughtfully set away her Granny's tea set. The house was quiet, save for Charley's sonorous snore in the next room, and the occasional stamp of a horse in the stable. She sat with her chin on her hand, staring at her reflection in the spotted looking-glass. She smiled sleepily at herself, glad that she was still her very own, that no man had the power to make her promise unnatural things in a stuffy little cubby hole, and then cry herself to sleep.

CHAPTER III

THE FIREMEN'S BALL

I

MAY did not wear her damaged heart upon her sleeve. What tears she shed were shed in the shelter of Delight's strong young arms when they were safe in bed. It was a comfort to her to be in their embrace and pour into sympathetic ears all her recollections of her short married life with Albert in England. She told her, too, of her meetings with him in the little dark street behind The Duke of York, for he dared not refuse to meet her. She had him in her power. Among the other servants her glib cockney tongue, her quick wit, and her brisk ways made her a favourite. She mended old Davy's socks for him, and watered the sickly geraniums he kept on the window sill in his bedroom. She went with Mrs Bye to buy clothes for Queenie, and taught the child to do a clog dance, and stamp and snap her fingers. She persuaded Annie and Pearl to cut their hair in fringes and curl them. She soon knew all the gossip about Bill Bastien and the housekeeper, and even learned the ins and outs of things in the rival house next door.

Delight was not such a favourite. Her tongue was slow, she took little interest in the things which did not directly concern herself, and she was always ready to neglect her work to lean over a window sill in the spring sunshine or squat before the pack of a pedlar, or listen to Charley's sagas of his rabbits and cauliflowers in the Old Land.

Also her great beauty separated her definitely from the other girls. When she stood by the serving-table waiting for an order she was remote as a sculptured goddess. When she laughed and talked with them, they forgot what she was saying, for gazing in fascinated envy into her deep, mirthful eyes.

On a morning a fortnight after the arrival of the two girls in Brancepeth, a gypsy pedlar had pushed her way into the scullery and opened out her wares on the floor. The women clustered about her; Queenie, home from school with a cold, peeping from behind her mother's skirts.

"Nicey, nicey—" said the gypsy, holding up a pink silk

scarf embroidered in silver. "Ah, dis look nice, young lady, on you." She threw it about Pearl's plump shoulders.

"Aw, it's too swell for me," objected Pearl. "Isn't it, Mrs Bye?"

Mrs Bye eyed her judicially. "Well, I don't know as you'd get much good out of it. It's a flimsy thing. But it 'ud be lovely for you to wear at the Firemen's Ball. It's not a bit too swell for that."

"How much?" asked Pearl of the gypsy.

"Ah, nicey, nicey. Two dollars. Cheap."

"Oh, say, I can't afford two dollars."

The pedlar's swarthy hands lifted the scarf deftly from Pearl's shoulders and threw it about Delight's. "Ah!" she exclaimed. "Dis tall girl buy. Ah, see, how booti-ful!" Her dark face lighted, she clasped her hands passionately to her breast.

"Here, don't be so swift," said Pearl. "I didn't say I wouldn't buy it. What do you think, Annie? Would it become me?"

"Beat her down to one-fifty," whispered Annie. "They always expect you to haggle."

"I'll give you one-fifty," repeated Pearl stolidly, "not a cent more." She half turned away.

The gypsy's questioning eyes sought Delight's.

"You, lovely lady, you?" she asked in a cooing tone.

Delight shook her head. "Not my colour."

"Take then, Miss," said the gypsy, thrusting the scarf upon Pearl. "Nicey, nicey, for you."

One by one they succumbed to the pedlar's wiles. Annie bought a scarf like Pearl's, but blue to match her eyes. Mrs Bye took a string of beads for Queenie. May, a bangle bracelet for her own thick little wrist. Even Mrs Jessop, though she called the bright wares trash, could not resist a necklet of imitation jet. It was not fair to herself, she had reflected, never to buy a new ornament. It was not fair to Bastien who admired her. . . . One by one they left the kitchen to get the money for their purchases.

Delight and the pedlar were left alone. They looked into each other's eyes. "What have you got for me?" asked the girl in a low voice.

The two understood each other perfectly. The gypsy took a small velvet box from a corner of her pack and put it in Delight's hand. "Dese for you," she said.

Queenie came marching out from the kitchen in time to hear the whispered words.

"Dee po' woo!" she repeated, marching around them. "Po' woo—po' woo—po' woo." She was transported by the gaiety of the occasion.

Delight opened the box and peeped inside. "Oh," she gasped. "How terrible lovely!"

On the satin lining, a pair of long earrings lay, slender crescent moons. From the tip of each hung suspended a twinkling green star.

"For you," repeated the gypsy. "I not show dose odders. Dey are de earth, you de star, de moon, bootiful. You buy?"

"How much?"

"Seex dollar. I gif *you* for five."

"Oh, but I haven't five. I'm newly come over from England, and I haven't earned my first month's wage yet."

The gypsy laughed and shrugged her shawled shoulders.

"Ah, you get de money. Dat easy. All de men love you in dese, and de women, dey jealous. See—green, de colour of jealous." She touched the winking green stars. The tip of her tongue showed between her teeth.

Delight's heart danced out to the earrings. They made her feel as her Granny's apple-green tea set made her feel—good, pure, almost religious. It was funny but it was so. She couldn't account for it. . . . But the five dollars! She had only a dollar and fifteen cents in her little red purse upstairs. She stood perplexed, filled with longing. "There's no use, I can't," she said, at last, and put them from her toward the gypsy. She only smiled and shook her head.

"You keep dose for tonight," she said. "I stop here in town. I call tomorrow for money. You get it. Easy get—for you."

The others were returning to the scullery with their money. Mrs Jessop was looking annoyed at the waste of time. Like one powerless in a dream, Delight pushed the box into the front of her blouse.

"Ain't you going to buy anything, Delight?" asked Pearl.

Delight shook her head.

"I've no money."

May whispered, good-naturedly: "I'll lend you a dollar if you fancy a bracelet like mine. It seems a pity for you not ter 'ave a bit of new joolery for the ball."

"I don't want anything," said Delight, turning away. "I've got to make haste and dress for dinner."

She ran upstairs. In the bedroom she took the earrings out of their box and laid them on her palm. The two crescent moons shone palely, the green stones—emeralds she guessed they were—winked up at her like seductive green eyes. She smiled at them, then impulsively pressed them to her lips. Again she felt that delicious sense of goodness, of being good to the very inmost inside of her. And then, a deep delight in being good.

Oh, for five dollars! She could not ask May for it. May would think she was crazy. She might force her to return the earrings to the pedlar, she was that strong-minded. No, she could not ask May who had offered to lend her a dollar. She thought of Bill Bastien, but her instinct warned her not to ask him to lend her money. No, there was something fierce and cruel about him. What about Kirke—Fine Nicht? The thought made her laugh. That canny Scot would never part with five dollars to a stranger, without proper security. No, she must think of someone else.

II

That feeling of deep and enfolding goodness remained with her all day. Every time she thought of the earrings, and especially of the little trembling, green stars, the feeling grew stronger, till she seemed shut off from the others in a cloistral retreat, sweet and safe from the clatter of dishes and tongues. She ceased to worry about the money. Something, she felt sure, would happen before the next day. The gypsy might even die in the night. She had heard of people going off like that in a hurry from some secret sickness.

When she was dressing to wait at the supper table she went to her Granny's apple-green teapot where she had hidden the earrings and took them out. She held one beneath each ear and went to the looking-glass to enjoy the effect. For a second her eyes danced with delight; then a terrible discovery made her suddenly feel quite faint. Her ears had never been pierced!

She sat down on the side of the bed. Her hands dropped to her lap, and the earrings rolled from her relaxed fingers. When she had bought them and all the long day she had never once thought of that. Now the discovery chilled her like a plunge into cold water. And the Firemen's Ball was in less than a week! Something must be done. She must have her ears pierced. She would do it herself. . . . She sprang to the chest of drawers and took a pin from the pin tray. She pressed it determinedly against the lobe of her ear. A little scream of pain escaped her. She dropped the pin and pressed her hand to her ear. In the glass she saw a ruddy drop hanging there. She turned pale realizing that, though she could bear pain, she could not inflict it upon herself.

What should she do? Perhaps there was an easier way—less stabbing and cruel. She suddenly remembered that Queenie's little ears were pierced. She would ask Mrs Bye. When supper was over she followed the cook into the pantry.

"Cook," she said, "how was it you came to have Queenie's ears pierced?"

"I wonder if I dare try this raisin pie on them tomorrow," mused Mrs Bye. "The boarders'll have to eat it anyway, it must not be wasted."

"Oh, it looks purfickly good," replied Delight. "I'll see that they take it." She picked out a plump raisin from the pie and thoughtfully sucked it.

"How was it you came to pierce young Queenie's ears?" she repeated, when she had swallowed the raisin.

Mrs Bye replied—"To cure her eyes. She had sore eyes."

"Poh eye," repeated Queenie, and she began to march up and down, singing—

I 'ad a poh eye,
I 'ad a poh eye.

"However did you do it?"

"Oh, I didn't do it. A neighbour—a Mrs Bliss—did it. Her 'usband was the butcher"—Delight shuddered—"and she did it beautiful. You just pinches the lobe up a bit to stop the circulation, and then you holds a cork behind for to steady the ear against, then you sticks the needle threaded with a silk thread right through and ties the thread firmly. You have to turn the thread around in the wound every day to keep it from healing. Poor little Queenie did a bit of yelling then, but her eyes have been better ever since."

"Did it hurt very much, Queenie?" Delight asked of the child, as she drew up beside her mother's skirt.

"Ay," whined Queenie, "ih hurh."

Again Delight shuddered, but she was desperate. Her ears must be pierced that day so that they might have time to heal before the ball. She searched through the little plaid silk "housewife" in the shape of a bellows that her Granny had made for her on her twelfth birthday and chose a long sharp needle. She threaded it with silk from a reel belonging to May. She had already procured a cork from the kitchen. The hour was eight. Supper was over and the other girls had agreed to do her share of the clearing up, for she had said she was suffering from a very queer stomach. Her stomach did indeed feel queer and her cheeks were pale.

She locked herself in the bedroom and took the implements of torture from the top drawer. Mechanically she began to pinch the lobe of her left ear. Even pinching hurt. Then suddenly she snatched up the cork, pressed it behind the lobe, and jabbed the needle against the tender flesh. In spite of herself a cry escaped her. She clapped her hands to her mouth and bent double in pain for a moment. Then she straightened herself with a feeling of triumph. She had pierced one, at any rate. It was not so bad, after all. Now she must draw the thread through and tie it. She bent toward the looking-glass expecting to see the needle sticking through the plump punctured lobe, but the needle was not there, and only a tiny drop of blood showed where she had pricked it.

She was almost in despair. She picked up the needle and the cork from the floor where they had fallen, her lips thrust forward like an angry, hurt child's. She sat down on the side of the bed, trying to think of someone who might help her.

Suddenly the ruddy, square face of Jimmy Sykes rose before her, smiling, eager to help. She had walked out with him on two different evenings and he had bought her oranges and a bag of sweets. Why had she not thought of him before? She was to have met him this evening, so he would probably be in his room now waiting till she had finished her work. She wasted no more time, but went to seek young Sykes. The passages were deserted, the doors shut. It was a cold night and a fire burned in the Quebec heater on the third-floor hallway.

She knocked softly on Sykes' door. There was the rustle of a newspaper inside, a step, then the door opened. Jimmy Sykes' cheeks flamed. He came out to her shyly.

"Why, Delight, is it you?"

She pushed past him into the room and closed the door behind her. "Yes, it's me. I want you to do something for me."

He timidly touched her hand. "There's nothing I wouldn't do for you."

She went very close to him. Her deep, dark eyes were on a level with his, and he felt her breath, sweet and warm, on his face.

"I'll tell you what it is," she breathed, "you've got to put a hole through my ears. I won't ask any of the other girls to do it. I want them to think I've always had earrings. Oh, don't say you won't do it! It 'ud break my heart if I couldn't wear 'em to the Firemen's Ball. Look here, I've tried myself and that is all I could do, and it hurt me cruel, too." She dragged back her hair and showed the wounded ear lobe.

Jimmy was dazed by this unexpected demand on his skill, his courage, and his manhood. The sudden leap into intimacy with this glorious creature filled him with exultation and yet fear. He was afraid he could not do what she wanted him to do. In fact, he hardly understood what it was she wanted. He took the needle and the cork dumbly from her while she poured forth the tale of the gypsy, the secret purchase, and the directions for piercing her ears.

"Now," she said finally, sitting down in a chair and holding her head very erect while she fixed him with her glowing gaze, "you must press my ear firmly against the cork, then jab the needle right through and no mistake, and then tie the thread in a knot." She tilted her head, presenting the sacrificial ear. An adorable ear, Jimmy thought, pink and curving like a shell.

"I wish you'd not given me the ear with the little drop of blood oozing," he said. "It seems so awful cruel to stick it again."

"Do as I tell you," she ordered, clenching her hands and setting her teeth.

Jimmy took the ear tenderly between his finger and thumb. A tremor of fear shook his sturdy frame.

"Pinch it," she commanded. He pinched it, getting very red about his own ears.

"Now stick the needle through, where the drop o' blood is."

Gingerly he pressed the point of the needle against the wound.

"Ouch!" she cried, throwing him a glance of anguish. "Get it through, quick!"

With a groan he jabbed the needle through the delicate flesh and drew the thread after it. She was white, she looked faint. The dark red drops trickled into his palm.

"Is it done?" she asked shakily.

"Yes," he muttered. He tied the thread and went and sat down on the window sill.

"What ails you?" she asked.

"I'm not feeling well."

"You don't mean to say that wee drop of blood upset you?"

"It was *your* blood, Delight."

A smile trembled on her lips, her eyes filled with tears. "Jimmy!" she said gently. "I do like you, I do." But she took the needle and placed it in his hand. "Now, do the other," she commanded.

He sprang to his feet, his face set and white. "If I do the other, I'll be sick, do you hear? You'll have to get someone else to do the other."

"You do it this minute," she persisted.

"By thunder, I won't!" He folded his arms across his chest.

"Then you don't like me." Her lashes were sticking together with tears. "You've turned against me, Jimmy."

"Like you! Like you! That's the trouble. I like you so well I'd do anything reasonable for you. But this ain't reasonable. It's unnatural, and it's making me sick. P-please don't ask me, Delight." He made a pillow of his bent arm and laid his face against it. He, too, was crying.

III

Kirke and Lovering had come up to their room together after supper. Lovering was writing his weekly letter home to his wife. His broad figure bent over the shaky little table, his fist grasping the pen so firmly that the nib sputtered ink at each period, he threw himself into his task. His lips moved as he wrote as though he were indeed holding converse with his wife, and when he frowned and nodded, it seemed to Kirke that he was arguing with her, or explaining why he was not sending more money.

Kirke was tilted in a chair, his feet resting on another, his pipe in his mouth. He was supposedly reading a daily paper he had taken from the reading-room, but his gaze wandered from Lovering to the window from which he could see the flagged side entrance and pump of the house, the yard and poultry runs and, just up the street, a broadside view of The British American House, the rival hotel. There was not a bedroom in The Duke of York which Kirke would have liked so well, for there was none with quite the same view, the same intimate angle on the affairs of the two hotels. His insatiable curiosity toward life, his satirical pleasure in the rôle of onlooker at the follies of those about him, found endless scope here.

A dray was being unloaded of casks of ale in the entrance below. Bill Bastien was talking with the driver, counting the casks. Kirke counted them too. Charley Bye and Davy were putting them into the cellar. Kirke wondered how much of that ale would be sold by Bastien dishonestly and the money appropriated for himself. He was a thief, and Mrs Jessop no better, lining their pockets with the absent owner's profits.

"How d'you spell voluptuous?" inquired Lovering.

"Man," said Kirke, grinning, "that's an awful word to use in a letter to your wife. You'll have her over here before you can say scat."

"You be damned!" replied Lovering. "Tell me how to spell the word."

"I really think you mak' a mistake," went on his friend, "in using such words to a simple wifely body. You'll instill bad ideas into her head."

"She not a simple body. She's a fier-ry piece—is my wife."

"All the more reason, then," said Kirke, "not to excite her. But—perhaps you were describing Miss Mainprize to her."

"Tha'rt gone on that bitch thyself, Duncan," said Lovering.

"Nonsense," replied Kirke calmly. "Now for veeluptuous —v-o-l-u-p-t-u-o-u-s. It's a fine mouthful of a word to fling at your fiery wife across the sea."

Lovering did not answer. He was busy getting down the word. Kirke turned once more to the window. The lorry had disappeared. Pearl and Edwin Silk, the remittance man, were standing together by the pump. His thin neck was bent as he looked into her face. Was he beginning to pay Pearl attention? Kirke focused his eyes on them with a boring expression, like two gimlets. Pearl evidently said she was thirsty, for Silk pumped a glass of water for her. She would not drink from the common vessel but poured a little into her pink palm and drank daintily from it. When she had finished Silk snatched up her hand and put it to his mouth, drinking the last drops greedily from it. Kirke's thin lips stretched in a grin; he bent closer to the pane.

But now a sound other than the scratching of Lovering's nib shot through his sensitive nerves. It was the sound of a sob.

A woman's sob. The transom above his door was open and, turning his head sideways toward it like a shrewd, aquiline bird, he made out that the second sob came from the room across the passage. Silently he rose and went to the door, frowning down at Lovering as he stood with his hand on the knob. No, he would not tell Lovering. Let him go on with his stupid letter. He would only spoil things. He stole out into the passage and closed the door behind him.

"Wait for me, Duncan," called Lovering. "I'll be done in a minute."

Kirke's finger twitched. Gladly would he have throttled his friend. He looked back into the room, smiling. "All richt," he said. "I'll just go down as far as the reading-room and leave this paper in."

He closed the door again and fixed his attention on the door opposite. It was Jimmy Sykes' door. The transom was closed but the sound of another sob came appealingly. He tiptoed to the door and put his eye to the keyhole. Against the red glow of the western window opposite he saw the form of Delight Mainprize, seated droopingly in a chair. Beside her stood the stocky figure of Sykes, his head pillowed on his arm. They were both crying.

IV

"Weel," said Kirke, stepping inside, "it's a fine nicht."

Delight gave a stifled scream, and Jimmy uncovered his miserable face and looked at Kirke, quite unabashed. "It's her ear," he said. "She wants me to pierce it and I can't."

"Say that again," said Kirke. "I'm not taking it in. What about her ear?"

"She's bought new earrings. They're to wear at the Firemen's Ball. She wants her ears pierced. I've done one b-but I can't do the other. I'll be sick."

"Weel, you are a flaming coward," said Kirke. "Let's see the job you've done." He bent over the gently sobbing girl and examined her ear.

"Give me the needle," he ordered Sykes.

Delight said in a smothered voice, not uncovering her face: "See that it's threaded."

Kirke threaded the needle skilfully, he was used to doing his own mending. "Now," he bit off, "tairn your head over."

With a little moan, and keeping her eyes tightly shut,

Delight rolled her head over, presenting the other ear. Kirke grasped it firmly between his finger and thumb.

"Here's the cork," gulped Jimmy. "You do something with the cork."

"Cork be damned!" said Kirke.

With pitiless precision he pierced the ear, tied the thread in a neat knot, and patted Delight's shoulder. "Good geerl," he said. "If you had as many ears as a field of corn I'd pierce them for you."

"Oh, thank you," Delight said, looking up at him with wet eyes. "I can wear my earrings now, and you won't tell a soul, will you?"

"Now, do I look like a man that would go about telling secrets? Sykes is the one to watch, though considering the booby's pairt he played, I expect he'll hold his tongue."

"It was just that he was so tender."

"Well, a tender man's no good to you. How are you going to hide those ears, now?"

"My hair's so thick I can just pull it a bit farther over them."

"I hear Lovering going down. I must get after him. You're not going to stop here all nicht, are you?"

"Don't you be insultin' to me, Mr Kirke."

"No, you'd better not," said Jimmy. "I may be chicken-hearted where a girl's concerned, but I've yet to see the man I'm afraid of."

Kirke broke into hoots of metallic laughter and hurried down the passage after Lovering.

"Isn't he a beast?" said Delight. "Never mind, I like you far the best of anyone here. I like you even more because you didn't want to hurt me."

Jimmy put his arm tenderly about her. "I'd do anything for you, Delight. Only give me a chance. Can't you think of *anything* I could do for you? Isn't there anything?"

Delight hung her head. "There's one thing," she whispered, "that's troubling me sorely, and that's the money for the earrings. They're not paid for yet, and I've been wondering all day who I can find to borrow the money from."

"Oh, let me!" cried Jimmy. "I'd rather do it than anything. How much is it?"

"I'm afraid to tell you."

"Delight!"

"Well, it's five dollars. I know I'm terrible extravagant."

Jimmy tore a little canvas bag from his pocket. It was untidily crammed with bills of small denominations. Delight watched him like a greedy child as he drew out a two and three ones.

"There you are," he said, beaming, "and if ever you speak of returning it to me I'll turn cruel, too, and stick a needle into you." He went on to talk of Kirke to cover her embarrassment, which was not so great as he thought. "If you'd only seen his face when he was piercing your ears. It was as cruel as the mischief. I bet he just liked doing it. He looked as though he'd like to be able to hurt you every day."

Delight shivered and smiled at Jimmy. "I want to kiss you," she said, "for being so good."

V

A soft thunder rumbled through the house, mingling, at first, almost inaudibly with the men's loud voices in the hall and bar, but gradually increasing to a metallic clamour that beat insistently above all else.

Delight stood in the open door of the dining-room. In her left hand the copper Japanese gong hung by a red silk cord; in her right she grasped a short stick with a padded ball at the end, with which she beat it. Her lips were parted in earnestness showing the even rim of her teeth, her bright hair covered all but the tips of her ears which were now healed.

It was the night of the Firemen's Ball.

Kirke was standing in his favourite position by the newel post, ready, at the last stroke of the gong, to enter the dining-room. He was invariably the first at meals, yet he always came in with his angular, nonchalant swagger, as though he felt nothing but contempt for the food and the girls that served it. Delight now lowered the gong and, as its vibrations ceased, the surge of men's voices once more possessed the hall. As Kirke came abreast of her, he peered closely at the ear nearest him.

"How's the ear?" he asked, and gave the lobe a little pinch.

Delight drew back her head. "Don't be so free with your hands." Her eyes flashed.

"You didn't object to me handling your ear when you wanted it pierced," he observed, following her in and taking his seat.

"That was different."

"You mean you wanted to mak' use of me then?"

Once he was in his chair he became to Delight, as did all the other boarders, her little child, to be cajoled and fed. "Beefsteak?" she asked, leaning over him and admiring the parting in his hair.

"Is that all?" he asked sharply. "Last nicht it was like leather."

"There's sausages," she said softly.

"Bring me some. You were trying to hold me off them," he added bitterly.

"Well, be nice then," she whispered and floated from the room.

Kirke sat scowling at his knife and fork till his plate was set before him. On it lay a piece of underdone steak, such as he liked, and two sausages.

"Delight," he bit off, "you're a terrible woman. I believe you're going to be the curse of this hotel. The whole town has its eye on you already."

"Why, what have I done, Mr Kirke, but just be myself?"

"Ay, that's the trouble," answered Kirke, "you're just yourself. And so was Jezebel, and so was Jael, and so was Delilah and Deborah."

"My goodness," said Delight, open-eyed, "you *do* know your Bible, don't you?"

VI

The four girls were dressing for the ball. As ill fortune would have it, there was a fruit-growers' convention in Brancepeth next day, the dining-room had been crowded, and the girls were later than usual in leaving the kitchen. Their faces were burning, their breath came in gasps. May's and Pearl's hands were red and swollen from hot dish-water. Mrs Bye, with Queenie at her heels, rushed from room to room helping them to dress. Before each looking-glass blazed two coal-oil lamps, the basins on the washing-stands swam with soapy water; there was a smell of burning hair and cheap toilet powder. It was stifling hot. The freshly laundered petticoats of the four girls rustled as they flew here and there.

"My word," cried Mrs Bye. "I can't lay my hands on a single hairpin! May, you've got your hair frizzed so that I'll never get this ribbon bound in it."

"The frizz'll come out soon enough when I've done a few dances. Oh, Lord, there's my garter broke!"

"Somebody pull my corset lace," implored Pearl. "I must have gained ten pounds since the last dance."

"Oh, oh," moaned Annie, "I've been on my feet so much today that they're all swelled up. I can hardly get these slippers on."

Queenie burst into hymn:

Puh po a hoh, buhher,
Puh po a hoh—

Delight alone was silent. The windowpane against the night gave her back a dark but clear reflection of herself. Standing there no one could accuse her of monopolizing a looking-glass. She was already dressed, having curling hair that needed no coaxing, and taking little care with the details of her costume. Now she gazed in a rapt, impersonal delight at the sombre beauty of the reflection. She was wearing a dress that had been her mother's, a deep, old-gold satin, with black lace about the low-cut neck and short sleeves. The satin was cotton-backed, the lace cheap, but the effect with the girl's bewitching dark eyes and golden hair was barbarously beautiful. Annie and Pearl were sorry for her in that old-fashioned dress. They felt superior in their white dresses with the pink and blue scarves they had bought from the gypsy about their shoulders. Yet those earrings —where had she got those earrings? She was a deep one, not a bit like May who hid nothing. Still, they liked Delight. Her admiration of their dresses and beads and scarves was so childlike and open that they couldn't help liking her.

"I declare it makes me wish I was a girl again," said Mrs Bye when they were ready. "Many's the gay dance I've been to, and not with Charley neither!"

On a sudden impulse they all kissed her good-bye as though they were going away for a long time, pressing their fresh lips to her thin cheek in turn. The unusual ceremony touched some deep well-spring of pity in Queenie. She lifted her voice and wailed loudly in great compassion for them and for herself.

VII

Tonight they did not go out by the back door as usual but with conscious dignity through the front entrance. Jimmy Sykes and Edwin Silk were waiting in the hall for them. Jimmy wore a navy-blue serge suit and white tie. Silk appeared in wrinkled evening clothes, a flat opera hat shadowing his haggard face. Pearl broke into embarrassed giggles as he moved to her side through the crowd. Men stopped talking and drinking to look at the girls and to offer bantering advice to them and their escorts. Bill Bastien came out of the bar and said in a low tone to Annie—

"I'll be over after closing time, so don't fill your card."

Annie beamed up at him, her whole face breaking into ripples of pleasure like a little lake over which hot, bright sunlight has suddenly burst.

Outside, on the porch, Kirke and Lovering were standing. "Are tha coomin' aht to the ball, Duncan?" asked Lovering.

"I micht."

"Well, luk 'ere, we'd better just walk along with the girls. They're in the hall." He could see through the narrow windows on either side of the front door.

"I've never taken servant geerls out yet," rejoined Kirke, lighting his pipe. The tiny blaze illumined his bright light eyes and pink cheek-bones.

"My wife was a servant lass," said Lovering simply.

"Ah, but she was a veeluptuous one," sneered Kirke.

"Blast thy eyes!" growled Lovering. "I daresay you've got a servant girl wife of your own in the Old Land."

"I was never churched with any woman," said the Scot, with composure. "A mon's but a mon."

"Well, I'm going with them, anyhow." He stepped up to May and Annie and asked with little trace of his Yorkshire accent, which he reserved for his friend Kirke, whether he might accompany them to the hall.

The group of seven hurried through the clear, frosty evening of late March, a great full moon sailing above them, and a handful of twinkling stars clustered about the chimneys of the Town Hall. Every window was alight; the vigorous music of a brass band made the girls forget the weariness of their legs, and set their blood to dancing in anticipation.

It was nearly eleven when they had hung their wraps in the cloak room and appeared on the dancing-floor. Jimmy and Delight took their places among the other dancers, also Pearl with Edwin Silk, Annie with Lovering, and May with a boarder named Slee. May, in the midst of the whirling crowd, was continually on the watch for Albert. He had promised he would be there. He dared not refuse her. And he was to bring Ada, too, that May might look on the face of her rival. . . . Like hopping marionettes, they suddenly appeared before her. Albert red-faced, with wilted collar; Ada, taller than he by half a head, her red hair in elaborate puffs, her thick curling lips and beady eyes expressing an abandon of physical exuberance. Before this moment, May's hatred of her had been hatred for an unknown barrier between herself and Albert; now, when she saw her solidly in the flesh, the fierceness of her jealousy, her abhorrence for this coarse interloper, numbed her legs and took away her breath.

"I can't"—she gasped—"can't dance."

Slee halted and looked down into her face.

"Swoony?" he asked. "Have a glass of something?"

Her eyes had pierced into Albert's consciousness. His jaws dropped. Then, somewhat recovering himself, he steered Ada toward May. "Hullo, cousin," he got out.

"She's a bit swoony," explained Slee, ostentatiously supporting her.

Angry looks were thrown at them by the other dancers. They were jostled. The two men led the girls to a corner. They sat down on four chairs, under draperies of red and white bunting. Slee tilted his chair against the wall, leaning back and gazing at the ceiling to show that there would be no intrusion from him on a family party.

"So this is Albert's cousin, at last," exclaimed Ada, grasping May's small icy hand in her large hot one. "I've been coming to see you I don't know how many evenings but I couldn't get Albert out. He's getting to be a reg'lar old stogie and, of course, I knowed you'd be busy all day. Say, do y' know Albert never let on to me he had a cousin till you landed here. I tell him it's a shame, the way he's cut himself off from his relations, and it's mean to me, too, because I like to be friendly. My! You don't look a bit like Albert, do you?"

"Shut up, can't you, and give someone else a chance," interrupted Albert. "Feelin' any better now, M'y?"

"Yes. It were just the crowd." Ada leaned across Albert to look into May's face. "You look awful," she said. "Get her a lemonade, Albert? I guess you're not used to much society. I was in the jam factory and we was always gettin' up impromtoo dances."

"I'm better now," said May stiffly. "That's another dance strikin' up. I'd like to dance it with Albert for old time's sake. Let me interduce you to my friend, Mr Slee."

Mr Slee brought the front legs of his chair to the floor, bowed to Ada, and asked her if he might have the honour of a dance.

"Thanks," said Ada. "I'd like to. It isn't good style to dance with your own husband all evening." She slapped Albert playfully on the shoulder. "Be good to your cousin, now, Albert! You let me know if he ain't good to you, Cousin May."

The two couples were whirled apart. The devil himself seemed to put new life into May. "I'll 'cousin' her! I'll 'cousin' her!" she muttered, grinding her teeth, and dancing like one possessed.

Ada had towered above Albert. Her big solid frame had been difficult to guide among the swaying throng, but May was tiny, agile, like a bit of dancing quicksilver. He clutched her to him, and a grin overspread his moist, flushed face.

May's face was upturned. Her eyes were shining into his. Every now and again she gave little stamps as though she were dancing on Ada's prostrate body.

A change had come over the room. Under the glaring lights, under the red and white bunting, a strange blight seemed to have fallen on the dancers. May suddenly perceived that, except for one other couple, she and Albert were the only ones dancing. The rest stood about the walls, silent; their faces, under the white lights, had become round, meaningless disks like the faces of daisies in a flower border. The other dancers were Jimmy Sykes and Delight.

"They don't seem used to girls wot can dance, 'ere," said May. "They're all standin' up to watch Delight and me." She turned her head, laughing, kicking up her heels, so that more and more of her petticoat and twisted pink cotton stockings were visible. At last a man in a red fireman's coat growled at them, as they passed:

"Get off the earth, can't you? Nobody wants to look at you."

Albert and May were struck motionless. Hurriedly they escaped into the crowd of onlookers, and their faces, too, became round, watching daisy faces.

Jimmy and Delight danced on. He was a well-proportioned, agile young fellow, and he danced with grace and vigour, inspired by the knowledge that he held the loveliest girl in Brancepeth (in the world, he believed) in his arms. Delight's long eyes were half-closed in the ecstasy of the dance, in the somnolent, heavy throbbing of the band, in the admiring light of all these rows and rows of eyes that watched her every motion. She was conscious of every part of herself, as one might think a star would be conscious of its every glittering point. She was conscious of her curls dancing on her head, of her long lashes, as they swept toward her cheek, of her firm breasts that seemed to hold the rhythm of the dance, of her strong thighs that never tired, of her gay, tripping feet. She was conscious, too, of Jimmy's body beside her, guiding her caressingly. But she was only dimly conscious of that.

"Who is she? Who is she?" gasped Ada in Albert's ear. Everyone was asking the same question.

"My goodness, what a show she's making of herself!" went on Ada angrily. "This Firemen's Ball is gettin' a little *too* common for me. For two cents I'd go home."

"You'd go alone, then," returned Albert, "for I'm goin' to daunce as long as there's a ruddy 'op in me."

The music had stopped. The crowd surged into a kaleidoscopic pattern. Bastien and Kirke had strolled in together, just before the dance had ceased. The effect of the spectacle on the two men was strikingly different. Bastien's dark-blue eyes bulged in astonishment; he showed every tooth in a delighted grin, but a sombre satisfaction gleamed from the Scot's shrewd face.

"Well, me next, I guess," said Bastien lightly. "I bought tickets for the four girls, and it's up to me to dance with each of 'em in turn."

He went briskly to Delight's side. "Look here," he said, "you'll need a bodyguard to take you home. The other women'll mob you as sure as your name is Delight."

He put his arm around her as the band struck up. He had not expected that the dance was to be a duet, and he flashed a look, half-pleading, half-bold, about the room when he found they were to have the floor to themselves. He was known to them all, admired, feared; he did what he liked, and Brancepeth might be damned.

Bastien was straight as a rod. His clothes were made by a city tailor. His was a very different figure from that of poor Jimmy in his Old Country workingman's clothes. Jimmy's flush of triumph paled into mordant despair as he saw Delight floating in bold submission against Bastien's breast.

The bandsmen leant forward over their music to see the dancers. The eyes of the horn-blowers bulged almost out of their sockets. Job Watson, the drummer, accented the waltz with a ferocity that was almost obscene. In the white glare the two waltzers seemed the only animated two on earth, with rows of staring ghosts to watch them. . . .

The band ceased. Bastien and Delight were surrounded. Bill introduced his protégée, Miss Mainprize. There was time for only one more dance before supper. For not much longer could the onsweeping tide of women be withheld. But Kirke was fiercely determined to be Delight's partner in another triumph. He went to her and took her hand.

"If you're ready, I'm ready," he bit off.

She said nothing. She seemed not capable of speech but only of glorious movement. The simple, lovely creature stood facing the throng about her with the majesty of a Greek goddess. She scarcely saw them, though her inner consciousness absorbed the admiring looks of the men as the sun absorbs dew; somewhere, too, there was a tingling sense of the jealousy of the women. The little green stars, the colour of jealousy, seemed to burn against her ears. Her fingers returned the pressure of Kirke's hard hand. She was ready.

He had already spoken to old Donald McKay, the piper. He knew he could not hope to vie with Bastien in waltzing to the accompaniment of the band. He felt that he was a very special sort of man, not at all like the other chaps. He had good blood in him, good Highland blood, and he needed Scottish music to stir it. Delight was a special sort of girl, too. Not an ordinary servant. One could tell that by her graceful movements, her pretty feet and ankles.

"Can ye dance a Scotch reel?" he asked, a sudden doubt making him hesitate as he led her to the centre of the floor.

"Oh, I can dance anything," she said. "I've got the dance in me, you see. I'll just follow you."

Old Donald, a little thin man in kilts who looked scarcely large enough to cope with the great lusty pipes he carried but who could draw from them a piercing volume of sound, began to stride the length of the hall, playing as he strode. The crowd pressed back, leaving Kirke and Delight isolated in an expanse of polished floor. He stood facing her, an expression of ferocious energy lighting his eyes that stared compellingly into hers.

Suddenly he was galvanized into motion, flinging himself with a kind of angular grace into the reel, his red tie working up over his collar at the back, under his chin at the front, a stiff crest of blond hair standing upright on his crown. As a pool reflects the image of an eagle, so Delight reflected the darting vigour of Kirke's dance; now one hand on her hip, the other above her head; now twirling interlaced with him. A noisy clapping of hands came from the men in the rear.

To have every eye focused on him, to have this girl imitating his every movement, to know that he was preventing others who had paid their money to dance from dancing was bliss to Kirke. It was better than standing draped against the newel post in the hall at night in everyone's way. He was gloriously happy.

Not till Delight's steps flagged and her breath came in open-mouthed gasps would he signal old Donald to lower his pipes. The bandsmen had left their seats, using the opportunity to get something to drink. Supper was ready in the basement. The smell of coffee and hot meat pasties rose to them up the flag-draped stairway. With a loud burst of talk and laughter the crowd now moved toward the supper-room. Kirke and Delight were engulfed, swept along down the stairs. Girls below threw back envious and inquisitive glances at her.

"Are ye tired?" inquired Kirke.

"A little," she breathed, clinging to him. "Not really tired; just out o' breath."

"You'd soon do it fine. I must give you some lessons. It's ten years since I had a dance like that mysel'."

At the foot of the stairs Jimmy Sykes was standing, anxious and boyish.

"Here's your partner!" said Kirke, abruptly handing her over to him. "You'll find she's a grand appetite for supper. You can wait on her for a change. If he gets a timid spell, Delight, and is afraid to sairve you, just let me know and I'll come to your rescue." With his hard, staccato laugh he moved away. He was eager to mingle with the other men and hear what they had to say about the dance. Besides, he did not want to take her in to supper. It was one thing to dance with a servant—a lord of the manor might do that—but to take her in to supper was quite another thing. Instead, he took in the daughter of Mr Wickham, the jeweller, and they sat with a select few at one of the small tables in a corner.

VIII

It was after five on a windy March morning when Jimmy and Delight left the hall. Spring had come in the night. While they had been dancing in the hot, crowded hall, spring had danced across the shining floor of the inland sea, borne in the arms of a southwest wind, to the music of booming, singing, sighing waves. When they had passed through the streets last night they had shivered in the dark, cold air, now their hot, flushed faces were swept by a wind pregnant with the sweet fire of life and growth. Above, the sky was a tremulous melting grey-blue; the drowsy moon shone faintly; a silver band confined the east.

Jimmy grasped Delight's arm and began to hurry her down a side street.

"Why, Jimmy," she said, "this isn't the way we came. See, the others have gone along the main street."

"I know," he said mysteriously, "but I want to get away from the others. I want to show you something. You've hardly seen anything of this old town yet. I want to show you something pretty."

"But what?"

"You wait and see. I bet you'll think it's pretty when you see it. Don't say you won't. It's only a little bit of a way. I've got things I want to say to you. I can't tell you how I feel with all those fools about us shouting to each other."

Still urging her he turned his face toward hers and looked into her eyes as into darkly dangerous pools. "Don't refuse me this," he pleaded. "If I thought you doted on me, I couldn't refuse you anything. Not that I would anyway, even if you hated me but, you know—when a fellow—oh, Delight, come along, it's only a little way."

"O-o, I'm so sleepy," she yawned, opening her mouth widely like a child and, like a child, suffering herself to be led along. "I'm so sleepy that I'd like to go straight to bed. . . . Jimmy, did you see young Mr Crosby dancing with me?"

"Yes, I did, curse him!" Jimmy growled.

"Oh, no. He's nice. He admired my earrings."

"Just your earrings, eh? Not you!"

Delight's head drooped.

Jimmy was suddenly angry. "Oh, I know what girls are like! Just because his father's a colonel, you'd let him say anything."

"But he didn't, Jimmy. He didn't say half the things you do."

"Well, he'd better not," returned Jimmy stoutly. "I know his kind. And how I hated to see you dancing with Bastien! Gosh, he's a bad 'un. And that beast Kirke and his old reel—"

" 'Fine Nicht' I call him. You know the funny way he talks. Scotch. Are we nearly there, Jimmy? I think you're awful, truly I do."

Jimmy passionately pressed her arm against his ribs. "One minute more and you'll see. I bet you don't know where we are, do you?"

Confidingly she shook her head.

"Well, I'll tell you. We're not far from the old Duke that you're so anxious to get to, but we're behind it, west of it, near the race course and the lagoon. It's that I want you to see. It'll be pretty in the sunrise. I bet you'll get the surprise of your life."

"I must go back soon and change into my day clothes. O-o, Jimmy, wasn't the dance lovely? Wouldn't you like to dance on and on like that forever?"

"If I was dancing with you but not to see you swinging round in other chaps' arms."

"I meant with you, of course."

"Oh, you dear girl, Delight!" He slipped his arm about her waist and gave it a little squeeze. His manhood seemed to melt within him at her nearness and dearness.

"Here we are," he said, in a choky voice.

They had come, at the end of a narrow, dim street, to a high, closely boarded fence. A large gateway was barred against the road, but at the end of the wooden sidewalk, a narrow gate hung ajar, showing a glimpse of a smooth open space beyond. They went through the gate and Jimmy latched it after them.

Before them stretched a level expanse of turf, moist and palely green, on it lying, like a vast ring, the half-mile race track. At one end of the enclosure rose the covered grandstand. On the far side. low stables and sheds and, beyond, the wet roofs of houses, showing here and there, a window, gleaming red in the first beams of the sun.

Toward the sunrise the end of the enclosure merged into a dense growth of shrubs, willows, and underbrush, now leafless and discovering the glint of water beyond. The wind struck their faces, fresh and moist from the lagoon. Among the bushes a little bird broke into a song, fragile as crystal, unpremeditated as the song of the wind.

For an instant Delight's heart stood still while every nerve responded to the sudden rush of open space and freedom. Then a shiver of sensuous pleasure rippled over her relaxed body. She closed her eyes and snuffed the air like a young animal.

"Ain't you glad you came?" whispered Jimmy. "Isn't it as pretty as I said?"

She did not answer but began to run from him, not in a straight line, not as the crow flies, but in sudden darts, here and there, looking back at him once over her shoulder in a terrified way. He was half-frightened for a moment. Whatever was the girl up to? Why, she looked as though she had gone fey! Perhaps —Jimmy's face went crimson as this thought came—perhaps she was afraid of him, thought he had brought her here—

"Delight! Delight!" he shouted, filled with anger and shame. "Come back here, darn you!"

Still she ran on, but now, as if she were tracing some strange linear design, she ran back toward him, her hat fallen off, her yellow hair flying, her satin skirt plastered between her legs. He could see her face now. She wasn't frightened. She was laughing. She was playing, full of play as a young lamb gambolling on the first morning of spring, or a butterfly darting its zigzag course. Jimmy, like another butterfly, felt the warm fire on his wings. His eyes glowed. He began to chase her.

Here and there they ran, at first in the open, till she realized that she would soon be captured there, then among the shrubs and willows, where brambles tore at her skirt, and the lush grass wet her ankles. At last on the brink of the lagoon he caught her in his arms and they clung together, panting.

"My, but you're a wild one," he breathed. "You gave me a chase."

He could feel her heart thudding against his side. His arms closed tightly about her. She half turned her face toward his.

"Delight!" he cried, low, "let me kiss you. My darling girl."

He kissed her again and again, clutching her to his breast. Deep sobs shook his shoulders.

She said, surprised: "Jimmy, you're crying."

"I know," he sobbed. "It's because I'm 'fraid I'll lose you —all those others—I want to marry you. I'm just about crazy over you."

The lagoon lay, red as the petal of a rose, before them; the red sun glared like a staring wild bird at them; little rills of water sought their way, whispering, among the reeds and sedges.

"Will you let me buy you a little ring?" he whispered. "Just a pretty little ring to hold you fast by like a pigeon? Eh, Delight, will you?" His lips were against her cheek.

"Oo, Jimmy, I don't want to be tied up! I want to be my very own, I do."

"Why, look here," he blazed, "you'll be your very own,

and you'll have me, too. That'll be the only difference. You'll have two 'stead of one. That's all. Come along, now, say you will. Oh, if I only knew the sort of words swell fellows say! I'd just pour them out of me, and you'd have to say yes."

She shook her head. "I'd like the nice little ring but I don't want to be married."

"Well, you needn't be for a long time. But just to wear it so's I'd know you'd be mine some day."

"There you go! You said *mine*. That shows. Men are all alike. They *say* yours. But they *mean* mine."

"This man don't," he said fiercely. "Anyway, it's from other men I want to protect you. You're too beautiful—"

"Jimmy, you can give me something that folk won't know what it means like a ring. Something pretty, and different like."

"You do love me, don't you?" he asked, stroking her hair.

She gave a comforting little grunt, something like a cat purring in acquiescent gratification of the senses. "M-m," she purred.

"A watch and chain!" cried Jimmy, inspired. "Will you have a watch and chain?"

She considered. "Yes, I'd like a watch and chain, 'cause then I'd know the time to get up, without old Charley Bye calling me."

He wanted to say—"Some morning the watch will tell you it's time to get married," but he was afraid of making her withdraw from him. He must not urge her, this spirited creature; he must give her time to realize the tenderness of his devotion to her, time to get used to the idea of marriage.

Now he could only hope to hold her by being a pleasant-like companion to her so that she wouldn't be chafing against a fancied curb. He would tell her about the crows that lived in the wood beyond the lagoon. Many a morning he had risen an hour earlier that he might spend the time watching them, so wild, so free, slaves to no factory whistle.

Across the lagoon stood the dark pine wood, remnant of the ancient forest not yet destroyed. The tapering treetops rose like delicate minarets against the morning sky. From among the branches a sudden clamour rose, and a black battalion of crows flew upward from its fastness. Densely the cloud ascended, then broke into flying fragments. In all directions the dark birds sped, cleaving the air with vigorous strokes. The sweet morning air was rent by the tumult of their cries.

"Look! Look!" cried Jimmy, with a dramatic flourish of the

hand skyward. "That's one of the sights I brought you to see. Nobody gives any heed to them here except to fetch a gun and shoot them, but I love them." He went to the water's edge and raised his face to them, circling and cawing above. "I call them my crows. . . . They're savage wild things and yet I love them because I seem to know what they're up to. They've got a plan of action, mind you, like an army. They've captains, and sentries, and they're all told off in the direction they're to go. Listen, now, and hear them."

She came and leant against his shoulder, her face raised, too; her lips parted in a wide, wondering smile. Jimmy went on—

"Listen to them! They're like sailors setting off for new lands! 'Bill—Bill—Bill—where's Bill? Hurry up, Bill! Jake—Jake—where's Jake? Up, lads—up, lads—heave ho! ho! ho! Call the gals! Where are the gals? Down below—below. Get 'em up! Rouse 'em up! Maggie! Kate! Kate! Kate!' "

In a cloud the birds sped overhead, leaning on the breeze, shouting, dipping, stretching their wings, sailing, sweeping, screaming. The shadow of their mass swept with pomp across the red lagoon.

Jimmy was enraptured. He had to shout to make himself heard above the din. "Hear that chap calling—'Kate—Kate—Kate'?"

She nodded and he gripped her waist.

"They're married, you know. They've got their women. But they're rough with 'em. They don't know how to treat 'em, 'cause they're rough fellows—just roughs. They don't know any better. But they love them, you bet, and you should see them teaching the young ones to fly in the summer. And the hubbub they make if one of 'em gets lost in the fall. Lord, you'd think they'd crack the sky with their calling to him."

Delight touched his hot cheek with her fingers. "My word, you're a rum one, Jimmy."

He sputtered into sudden, embarrassed laughter. "Oh, I know I am. . . . Any other girl'd think I was crazy, but you understand, don't you, Delight?"

"I think you've comical ways. That's all. But I love you for them! I reely do."

CHAPTER IV

CANADIAN ADA AND ENGLISH MAY

I

THE bedroom was in a state of disorder. The floor was strewn with hairpins, the chest of drawers vomited forth its contents, the basin was full to the brim with ice-cold soapy water. May's party clothes were thrown across a chair; her slippers, toeing in, lay in the middle of the floor, her pink cotton stockings, like fabulous pink snakes, beside them. Only the bed was decent, undisturbed. Delight longed to cast herself upon it, just as she was, half-undressed, and sleep, snatch a little rest, if only an hour, before the day's work began. But she must put on the neat black dress and white apron, and hurry down to the dining-room. Already she was late. She heard the factory whistle blowing for a quarter to seven. Annie would be waiting on the boarders, out of temper, too, and no wonder, having Delight's work put on to her.

She dipped a corner of the towel into the ewer and scrubbed her face and neck, and gave a hurried wipe with the other end.

"That's what Granny used to call a lick and a promise," she said, aloud, trying to be company for herself. She felt very lonely now it was morning, she hardly knew why, and she added—"Didn't you, Gran?" to bring her grandmother into the conversation.

She took out the earrings, very cautiously, for her ear lobes were inflamed and sore, and hid them as usual in the apple-green teapot. A sudden impulse made her cuddle the teapot to her breast, then passionately imprint a kiss on its shining round belly.

"Well, you're a silly, if ever there be's one," she said, in her grandmother's voice, and a tear splashed into the sugar basin.

At last she was ready, going down the stairs on swollen feet that had had to be forcibly compressed into unyielding, cheap shoes. In the kitchen, Mrs Bye was glaring into a pot, from which issued a smell of burning. Queenie was sitting on the bottom step of the backstairs, a handkerchief bound about her head.

"I goh a poh 'ead," she explained, raising her face, as Delight stepped over her.

"Got a sore head, have you? Pore little kid. One 'ud think you'd been to the ball. Well, I've got sore feet. How does your feet feel, Annie?"

"All right," replied Annie curtly.

Then she added, turning away with her tray in her hands:

"I've waited on your table. There's no need for you to come into the dining-room."

"But, Annie—"

"I say there's no need." She passed out of sight through the serving pantry.

Delight went and stood by the cook. "What's ailing Annie?" she whispered, so that Pearl would not hear, and putting her arm about Mrs Bye's waist.

"Oh, I don't know, except that her heels are blistered."

"But she said her feet felt all right. And she won't let me go in the dining-room, and me hastening to dress oop and all."

Mrs Bye spoke cryptically from the cloud of steam in which her head was enveloped. "She's in a state that's best left alone. You might go and wipe the dishes for Pearl. She's in a kind of maze this morning. Drat these parties anyway, I say. Everything's at sixes and sevens after them."

Delight picked up a large, soapy platter from the heap of dishes beside Pearl, and began, mechanically, to dry it on a moist tea towel. Out of the corner of her eye she timidly regarded the plump, pigeon-like girl. It was apparent, even to her, that, though Pearl's hands were stewing in the dishwater, her spirit dwelt on some remote plane. Her clear, hazel eyes were wide but they saw nothing; her tender, affectionate mouth hung loosely open as though she slept.

"Good gracious," thought Delight, "of all the unnatural places this is this morning! I hope May hasn't been taken queer, too."

She asked, on a note of assumed lightness:

"Where's May this morning?"

A slight smile curved Pearl's mouth; she made a somnolent slushing in the dishpan but uttered no word.

"Where's May?" repeated Delight, loudly and desperately.

"Clea'ing pih," replied Queenie, pressing one tiny hand to her brow. "I goh a poh 'ead."

"She says May's cleaning fish," said Mrs Bye. "Come now, my poppet, you must get ready for school, head or no, if you're going to get an edication." She took the child on her lap and began to lace the heavy boots that dangled below the thin little legs. Queenie turned her face, as though she would shut out all the world, against her mother's floury breast.

"I shouldn't send her to school this morning," said Delight pityingly.

"Bless you, her daddy 'ud never tolerate her wastin' her time. He's all for edication, Charley is. He's got a good edication, himself. To be sure, I say to him sometimes—'Well, your learning hasn't made much of you.' But then he says—'Think what I might have been without it.' Nobody can dispute that; and, as teacher says, the only way we can overcome this impederment in Queenie's speech is by edication. Come, come, dearie, raise your head and let mammy put on your pretty hair ribbon."

"De poy puh my 'air," whined Queenie.

"Well, well, tell them you've a sore head this morning and they'll leave you be."

Queenie looked unconvinced but, with folded hands, resigned herself to her toilet.

When Annie came to the kitchen, Delight did not raise her eyes. Annie's coldness perturbed her. She preferred a quick-tempered girl like May who said what she thought and had it over. She was ravenously hungry. The cold meats and cake and coffee of the ball seemed distant memories. She took a piece of buttered toast from the plate that stood in the open oven, snatching bites as she wiped the dishes. The melted butter oozed through to the table, making a little oily square. "How delicious!" thought the girl. "I never had such good food in my life, and so much of it. I'll be getting fat. Now I smell bacon. How I wish I were a commercial, sitting in there at the best table, and Annie waiting on me! I'd keep her moving—'make it nippy,' I'd say. Blistered heel and all. I'd blister her."

The door softly opened and Edwin Silk entered. His cheeks were hollowed by weariness. He might have been in his bed sleeping soundly, but he could not rest because of his love for Pearl which made his lips red and his heavy eyes glisten. He came and stood by the table, resting his hands on it and staring into Pearl's face. His evening clothes hung loosely on his thin frame and, in the daylight, showed green and shiny. To Pearl he was an exquisite. She noted his long pointed chin, the little drab of dark whisker before each ear, and his slender tapering fingers.

Two respectable unmarried sisters denied themselves things that they needed in order to send him the remittance that kept him out of England. He was always months behind with his board money. Mrs Jessop would have turned him out but Bastien had a tender spot in his heart for Silk. He was proud of him, too. He was an institution, and travellers would ask after him when once they had made his acquaintance. Not every hotel could afford to keep an elegant derelict, such as he, drifting about its corridors and bar. At The British American House, for instance, everyone had to pay at the tick, but The Duke of York could afford to be open-handed.

So Silk stayed on, mysterious, out of a mysterious past, sickly, cringing, arrogant in turn. Leaning toward Pearl, he looked like a drooping fungus growth beside a blowsy pink peony.

"My dear, beautiful girl," he said thickly, "I can't bear to see your hands in that dreadful dishwater—that—er—obscene dishwater."

"Oh, that's all right." She smiled into his eyes.

"No, it's all wrong," he mourned. "That little rosy palm from which I drank pure cold water should not be polluted by filthy washings from unspeakable plates, licked by factory hands."

"Oh, Mr Silk, they don't lick them. They'd be insulted if they heard you say such things."

"I want to insult them. I want to insult everyone in the world but you."

Pearl's head drooped toward him. "You'll make me break the dishes if you go on. I feel as weak as a kitten."

He put his arm about her and laid his cheek against her hair. "So do I," he sighed. "Weak as kittens, both of us." Taking her wrist in his sallow fingers, he lifted her hand from the dishpan and held it tenderly aloft, while greasy drops hung from every finger tip.

"Pearl, Pearl," he repeated. "What a beautiful name. Delight. Lovely name. Lovely names. Lovely girls."

"I think I'll go," said Delight. They made no reply.

She passed into the scullery where Mrs Bye was blacking Queenie's boots, grasping her frock between the shoulders with one hand to prevent her being overthrown by the onslaught of the brush wielded by the other.

"I had to come away," exclaimed Delight. "That Silk's too comical for me. He's making love to Pearl over the dishwater just like an orator or something. They were getting so moony I couldn't put up with it."

Cook sucked in the air under her projecting tooth. "I'd never trust that man. I wish Pearlie'd keep clear of him. Is Annie needing me?"

"No. The top-floor boarders are gone. I think there's just the Hair professor in there now. Annie took up the bacon for him herself. She never seemed to notice *them*."

"If Mrs Jessop should notice them, I pity them. She never did like Mr Silk, and she won't have spooning in the kitchen."

Delight snatched up Queenie and kissed her. Her heart was filled with tenderness this morning. "If any boys pull your hair just tell me and I'll attend to them," she enjoined.

"I luh oo," cried Queenie, hugging her. "I 'onh wan a go a poo. Poy puh my 'air."

II

May was scraping the scales from a large salmon trout on a bench outside the scullery door. Grasping the shiny wet tail in one hand, with energetic strokes she wielded the short black knife in the other, sending a shower of silver scales in all directions. They clung to her frizzy fringe and to the short hairs on her arms, one even glittering against the down on her cheek.

"Hullo, May," said Delight, in a conciliatory tone. She felt that, for some reason, she was not a favourite this morning.

"Good morning, Mrs Moth and the Flame," replied May, not looking up.

Delight thoughtfully considered this greeting.

"What do you mean moth and the flame?" she asked. "Which am I, then?"

May turned the fish over and skilfully slit its belly open, disclosing the curious tangle of inwards. "Both," she returned. "You're like the flame 'cause all the men go dancin' abaht yer, like crazy bluebottles, and you're like the moth 'cause you're goin' to singe your silly wings, see?"

"Oh, May," cried Delight. "Don't you go and turn on me! They're all after me this morning."

"Who d'ye mean, all?"

"Why, Pearl won't hardly speak, and when I went to go into the dining-room Annie gave one perishing look and said she'd done all there was to do, and to keep out."

"And no wonder, the w'y you went on wiv Bill."

"I didn't go on with him. I just danced with him. It wasn't my fault if everybody stood staring. Oh, I think you're cruel, May, and me always treating you the very best I know how." Her voice broke and tears filled her eyes. She moved close to May.

May, having gutted the salmon now espied some scales remaining near the tail. She made some vicious passes with the knife, sending a shower of them over Delight's face and head. Flaming with anger, Delight caught her wrist and stayed the knife.

"You're doing that a-purpose," she said bitterly. "You ugly little devil."

"You'd devil me, would you?" cried May. "You're a nice one, you are! You're a nice one to devil anyone, you are! I tell you the 'ole town's a 'otbed of gossip abaht you. Didn't Fergussen, the fishmonger, jus' tell me this minute. 'E says 'e never seen the like o' you and Kirke stampin' abaht each other like a mare an' a bloomin' stallion! Gemme my knife or, by Gawd, I'll stick you wiv it!"

She twisted and writhed, bending her body double over their hands welded on the knife. Two primitive women, filled with fury, fighting, they hardly knew why. Delight was larger, stronger, but May's little body was like wire.

"Leave go that knife," she hissed. "Leave go, I tell you, or I'll put my teeth into you!" Her head was down, her shoulders humped. Delight, looking down on her, was afraid of her ferocity and, deep within her, was a feeling that, after all, May was her dear friend, her only friend in the world, that, somehow, little May was fighting her because there was no one else on whom she could vent the fury of her jealousy of Ada. If you couldn't do things to one person, well, the next best thing was to do them to another.

The back of May's neck was crimson, the fish scales sparkled like pretty spangles in her hair. . . . Suddenly came a sharp sound of some small china-like object striking the ground, a tiny snap, a relaxing of May's body. Delight released her, and they both stood staring at something of red rubber, edged with little white porcelain squares. Whatever it was it was broken....

"Me teeth," said May bleakly. "You've busted me teeth." Her face twitched. Her upper lip was sunken, pitiful. "That Ader's comin' to call on me this afternoon and you've busted me teeth."

Delight, heavy with the catastrophe, picked up the two

fragments and fitted them together. A shiver ran through her. It was like holding one of her friend's organs in her hands, exposed to the ruthless light of day. What if May were dead! Oh, she had no one else but May! And here were her poor teeth. Tears rained down Delight's cheeks.

She handed the teeth back to May who took them in her little red paw that smelled so of fish. The head of the salmon lay on the bench beside them, staring up with a look of shocked surprise. It was all very well for it to be surprised, thought Delight; it had never had any teeth. It didn't know what it was suddenly to be bereft of them.

"Quit yer blubbin'!" said May, but not unkindly. "What we've got to do is to think of a w'y out o' this."

We! Delicious word. It melted all the volcano of anger between them into a flowing lava of sympathy and comradeship. Once more they were May and Delight, two English girls, with this Canadian Ada to deal with.

"Now I'll tell you, May—I'll tell you—" began Delight. She was so anxious to be helpful, to think of a plan before May could.

May looked searchingly at her. "Well, tell aw'y, then. There's no need to linger over it. Wot's your plan?"

"Why, look here, May, say you're sick."

May shook her head. "That won't do. We'd 'ave 'er up, nosin' abaht me bedroom. Besides, the laundry's just come back and I've got to go over the sheets and pillercases wiv Mrs Jessop. She'll need me up to four o'clock when Ader comes."

"Perhaps you might just act a bit haughty and keep your face turned away."

May snorted. "Look 'ere, Delight. If you can't think o' something besides baby talk, don't try to 'elp. The very idear, as though I could be 'aughty wiv me lip all caved in. Keep a stiff upper lip! 'Aven't you ever 'eard o' that saying? Well, 'ow d'you s'pose I'm goin' to keep a stiff upper lip when me teeth's busted?" She dropped her teeth into her apron pocket, picked up the fish and the knife, and faced her friend belligerently.

A man crossed the stable yard driving a team of heavy draught horses. He had left his wagon in the shed and was taking the horses to water. Their sleek sides shone like chestnuts, they lifted their large, hairy legs jauntily. In a moment they plunged their thirsty lips into the trough. The man leaned against the flank of the nearest and stared at the girls.

"I know," cried Delight, inspiration coming when she had

ceased to seek for it. "You must say you've a face ache. Wrap your face up with a great bandage and say you've a gathering tooth."

It was lucky that Mrs Jessop sent Delight to get some camphor for her that morning. The dentist's office was over the chemist's shop, so it did not take her long to fly up the narrow stairway and timidly present the broken plate to the dentist. He was a fatherly man, staring over his spectacles at the bright vision obtruding into his dingy domain. She explained that the teeth had been broken when she and her friend were having a little tussle, nothing much, only play, but the teeth couldn't stand it. He promised that he would try to have them mended by the next day.

May had rushed through the kitchen, her hand to her face, groaning as she ran to her room. Mrs Bye had prescribed a poultice of hot salt to be bound on the cheek, and Delight had run after her carrying it, her brow dented with concern.

"That's what comes of these overheated halls and draughts," observed Mrs Jessop, when she encountered her with the lower half of her face swathed in a bandage, the poultice giving a lifelike imitation of a swelling. "I suppose it's one of your unders, seeing your uppers are not your own. Well, take it a little easy this afternoon. Delight can do some of your work. You don't look very good."

In truth, May's eyes had an anxious expression. She looked forward with some dread to the call from Ada. Yet, entrenched behind the bandage, her thin lips had a malicious twist of pleasure. This was play-acting, she thought, and it was fun to fool Ada, fun to fool everybody, and she wasn't going to display her face with her mouth all sunk in. She did not sit at the table with the others at dinner but carried a bowl of soup and bread to the scullery, and lounged in a rocking-chair to eat. She had a devil-may-care, picnic feeling as she flung fragments to the fowls that collected outside the door. Suddenly she wasn't afraid of Ada any more. Lack of sleep, the fight with Delight, the accident had combined to stimulate her brain. She was a hotbed of desires and plans, as she swung to and fro in the rocker which gave forth a loud crack with each backward plunge, mingling a spice of danger to its soothing.

At four Ada was announced at the kitchen door by Charley in a pompous voice:

"Mrs Masters to call on Miss Phillips."

Charley liked announcing this strapping young woman

in her dashing clothes. He had the sensation of being a butler in a great house. He swelled his chest grandly and his voice deepened to an organ-like sonorousness, as he repeated:

"Mrs Masters' compliments to Miss Phillips. Mrs Bye, send a maid to find Miss Phillips."

The cook was making scones for tea. She felt flustered at this formidable arrival, and stood with the pan of sweet-smelling hot cakes in her hands, while her lashless blue eyes blinked excitedly.

"May's out. At least, she's not well. She's in the scullery. Queenie, run and tell May there's a lady to call."

"May goh a poh too'h," whined Queenie.

Cook ran to the scullery herself (Annie, Pearl, and Delight were snatching a nap), and said:

"Goodness me, it's your cousin's wife, May, and you so out of sorts. That's always the way. Don't do your hair of an afternoon, and a *partic'lar* caller comes." She still held the hot pan of scones, and Queenie, standing on tiptoe, was able to snatch one, with an inarticulate exclamation of glee. She danced about the women, tossing the hot cake from one hand to the other, blowing on her burned fingers.

"My word," said her mother, "if I slapped your hands till they tingled like that we'd hear some whimpering."

May said casually: "Send 'er out 'ere."

"All right," returned Mrs Bye, and loped back to the kitchen. "May'll be pleased to see you," she told Ada who was uneasily shifting from one foot to the other. "She's resting a bit easier. She's in the back sitting-room. Queenie, lead Mrs Masters in."

Queenie pranced ahead, holding her scone aloft. "Miha Maha," she announced shrilly.

May turned her head on the back of the rocking-chair, her eyes staring inscrutably over the bandage. " 'Ow d'ye do," she said, in a muffled tone. "Sit down and make yourself comfortable." She gave a weary gesture toward a yellow kitchen chair.

Ada seated herself, setting her feet well out before her. They were dressed in patent leather high-heeled shoes, the thick ankles glistened in imitation silk. On her red pompadour perched a black velvet hat with a drooping white plume. She wore a green and white plaid ulster and white kid gloves.

She did not know what to make of this queer little cousin of Albert's. There was some mystery about her, something not quite straight. One could never be sure of a husband who had come from a great city like London. There was something shady about May and, whatever it was, Albert knew it. She had tackled him about it one night, a terrible quarrel followed, and he had closed one of her beady eyes for her. "Nah, you cursed Canuck," he had said wrathfully, "I'll teach yer to cast narsty insinooa-tions on my family." It was all very well for Albert to get an-noyed, fussed up about his family and all, but Ada believed May was not all that she should be.

She felt immensely superior, sitting opposite May in her fine clothes. She placed her feet a little farther forward, glanc-ing at May's blue cotton stockings and red felt slippers with a pitying smile.

May began to rock. Instead of drawing her hideous foot-gear under the chair from Ada's sight, she thrust her feet out before her, striking the floor with her toes, and rocking violently so that the insistent explosive sound in the chair's anatomy cracked like defensive guns.

"It must be awful to be swelled up like that," commented Ada. "I thought your teeth looked real good when I met you at the ball."

"It's a wisdom tooth," said May. "I'm just cuttin' it. Onct I get it through I'll 'ave done wiv worryin'."

"Goodness, I used to have toothache and earache, too, but since I'm married I never have so much as an ache. Happiness is a great beautifier, they say." She hunched her shoulders, giv-ing a mischievous smile to Albert's image that rose between them.

May's eyes above the bandage were not to be fathomed. "Yes," she agreed. "That's wot's swelled me fyce. It's just puffed out wiv 'appiness."

"Lord," said Ada brutally. "What have you got to be happy about? Albert always speaks as though you was a mopey little thing."

May rolled her head on the back of the chair. "I am," she said. "I like to be mopey. That's the w'y I'm made."

Ada regarded her doubtfully. She thought she would change the subject. "How is it you and Albert are related? I've never reely understood."

"Our fathers were brothers. Twin brothers."

Ada pounced. "Why isn't your name Masters, then, same as Albert's?"

May rocked, " 'Cause I was adopted by a rich gentleman, nime of Phillips, when I was a little nipper."

Ada mocked. "Rich gentleman! I like that. Where's he gone to? Leavin' you to work in a hotel?"

"Well, yer see, he died," said May softly, "and me hated guardian wanted to marry me, when I was seventeen, so, one dark night, at midnight, I crept down the stairs of the mansion in Mayfair, an' out into the world to seek distraction. The fancy took me lately that I'd like to see Cousin Albert. Dear me, I'd 'ardly 'ave knowed 'im in those workingman's clothes. 'E used to look such a little toff. As true as I sit 'ere I'd 'ave passed 'im by if 'e 'adn't rose 'is 'at to me."

A shock ran through Ada's solid form as she sat on the kitchen chair. The scullery reeled with her. Her bosom was a battle place for jealousy, disbelief, credulity, yet her tone was only surly, as she said:

"You don't seem to go in much for good clothes yourself." Her eyes travelled scornfully over May's felt slippers, her crumpled serge dress, and soiled apron.

May rocked harder than ever. "Ow, clothes don't matter to me in this 'ole. Besides I'm stony broke, 'aven't the price of a 'airnet. But just you wait till I come inter my fortune when I'm of age! Oh, you'll see some dressin' then, if yer 'appen to be in Mayfair!"

"Of age!" cried Ada. "I thought you was thirty if you was a day."

"Just tike ten years off that, Ader. I 'ope to be back in London for my comin' of age party in November. I must not forget ter send you and Cousin Albert an invite."

Ada could not guess the fine sweep of May's designs, but she became almost humble before this magnificence.

"You must come and call on me," she said. "Not tomorrow, because I'm goin' to my aunt's funeral in Milford. I'll be staying the night. But come the next day, and I'll show you my china cabinet and we can run the phonograph. It's likely my aunt'll be leavin' me something pretty nice. I'm her favourite niece."

Mrs Bye came out carrying a tray, set with a pot of tea, four cups and a plate of hot buttered scones.

"I thought you and your friend would be ready for a cup of tea, May. Will you mind if my husband has a cup with us? He always seems to get a little faint about this hour and the sup and bite revive him."

Charley shortly entered the scullery with the impressive air of a churchwarden.

III

A gentle April rain was falling on Brancepeth, dimming the lighted windows, seeming to draw the houses more closely together in a delicate net of intimacy. The lights on the wharves and on the boats anchored in the little bay were blurred like drowsy eyes, and over where the lagoon slept, was blackness indeed, and in the wood where the crows crowded on moist pine branches, was blackness still more profound.

The two girls might have been in bed, sleeping, as Annie and Pearl were. They must have needed rest for, though they were young, they had danced all the night before and worked all day. But May could not settle down; she wanted the air, and to feel the sweet rain on her face after being swathed in a poultice for, it seemed, a lifetime. And she wanted Delight with her. She could not make enough of the girl. Delight was glad in her heart that they had had the fight, for since then they had been more happily intimate than ever before. Why, when they were in their room, changing to their outdoor things, May had simply grabbed her in her arms and kissed her for nothing at all. Delight thought that if Granny could look down and see her little girl out walking so happy with a friend like May, instead of a man, she would have been very pleased with her. Granny seemed very near tonight. Delight could almost feel her hand pressing her arm as she walked rather heavily beside her. Not that Granny was weak, but just a little stiff with the rheumatics and, oh, the rosy cheeks and lovely blue eyes of her! Delight gave a little gulp.

May peered up at her. "What's the matter, lovey? Did yer sigh or something?"

"No, May, I just swallowed a little lump that was in my throat."

"A lump! Not a homesick lump, was it, Delight?"

"N-no. It just comes there when I feel good and suddenly think of Gran."

"You're a rum little toad. Just you rivet your intentions on me, for you may not always 'ave me with you, see? Now, I'm goin' to tell you one thing. Jimmy is a good boy; you stick to 'im. 'E'll never 'arm you. It isn't in 'im. But steer clear of Bastien, and Lovering, and Kirke. . . . I do wish you'd have let Jimmy give you the ring 'e wanted to, 'stead of a watch and chain. Still the watch and chain 'll cost 'im more, unless 'e gave you a diamond, and even some of them's not to be depended on to keep their shine against the wear and tear of life, and then there's no reason the ring shouldn't come later. . . . My advice is, get all the *lasting* things out o' men you can. Small, costly things like joolery that is easy to carry 'round, and can always be pawned, if necessary."

"Goodness, May, you're wise."

"I'd need ter be. I never 'ad anyone to advise me. I've allus 'ad to be my own traffic perliceman, and my own correspondence school, et cetera, and depend on no one. But you're different. You're a beauty. You can't nip around without bein' noticed sime as me. You needs guardin'."

They were swinging lightly along the pavement, arm locked in arm, in a secluded street, where houses stood closely together near the pavement, with only a bit of lawn between. Sometimes the blinds of a window were up, revealing the interior of a cozy room, with people sitting intimately together in the lamplight, and once a young man playing the flute to an old, old deaf lady who leaned forward with one hand to her ear to listen. They lingered as long as they dared at that window.

"Isn't it lovely out, tonight, May?" whispered Delight, as though she feared the houses would hear her. "Shouldn't you like to run and run through the rain like a little old fox till you'd come to your burrow, an' then run down into it with your mate and your cubs, and all snuggle up together, nice an' dry and warm? May, you'd ought to hear the funny things Jimmy was telling me about the crows that live in the woods beyond the lagoon. He took me there to see them—was it last night—or this morning? I'm getting all mixed up with the time. Well, d'ye know, Jimmy can tell every dodge they're up to. They've got girls, and they call 'em by name—Kate, Maggie, an' all the rest. And they're terrible fond of 'em, too. . . I say, May, I believe I'm getting comical like Jimmy, listening to his talk and all. But, honestly, shouldn't you like to be a fox—a real she fox, I mean, not an old boy fox—running through this warm rain?"

"You *are* ratty," said May. "No, I don't want to be a fox. I'd rather be who we are, and meet a couple o' nice boys and 'ave a bit of a lark wiv them. We could do it, too, if it wasn't for me teeth. A girl can't be 'arf jolly when she knows 'er smile's a mockery."

Delight squeezed her arm. "What's in this window?" she

breathed. "Let's look in here. It's where the schoolmaster lives. Jimmy told me one night, I remember, because he said he wished he had his learning. There he sits at his table, studying."

There was a green shade on the lamp in the room. There were small, black-framed pictures on the wall and, on the table before him, a little statue with wings and no head.

"I'll bet 'e's busted the 'ead off that orniment one time in his rage," whispered May. "Schoolmasters is all evil dispositioned."

"Oo, May, I think he's lovely. Look at his white hands, and his long pointed thumb—"

"Ho!" snorted May. "Admirin' of a man's thumb! I never heard the like."

They both shook with smothered laughter.

"I don't care," persisted Delight. "I think he's lovely. That black lock like the letter J on his forehead. I wish he'd come out in to the rain with us. It'd do him good."

"Ask him, then. Run in and tap on the pane and say—'Come along out, schoolmaster!' I dare you."

In the mild darkness of the night, in the intimate rain, anything might be dared. The blood in their veins was filled with unnamed desire. May pushed Delight toward the window. The schoolmaster threw his arms above his head, stretching himself, tired to death of the pile of Easter examination papers before him. He opened his mouth wide in a great yawn.

Delight darted across the strip of drenched grass to the window. She struck her palm sharply on the pane.

"Coom along out, schoolmaster!" she shouted.

The man sprang to his feet. Some young devil of a boy trying to torment him. Wouldn't he cuff him! He did not go to the window but darted through the hall and out the front door. May ran squealing down the dark street, but Delight stood motionless, her long dark eyes peering out of the night at him.

"Why did you do that, girl?" he asked sternly. She imagined a cane behind his back.

Her head drooped. "Ah, just for fun. You looked so lonesome like."

"Are you the girl that danced at the Firemen's Ball?"

Her chin went up and down.

"Well, you're a very forward girl. Let me tell you, you're not the sort of girl we need in Brancepeth. There is enough looseness here already. Everyone is talking of you—even the schoolboys—"

Delight had moved closer to him into the pale shaft of lamplight from the hall. He could only see her indistinctly, as the figure of a girl under water, her features pale, her eyes imploring. She seemed like a drowning girl. He suddenly imagined white limbs struggling in the water. He longed to save her. The rain dripped from the eaves like tears of pity for her. . . . He stepped out into the rain beside her.

"You called me," he said accusingly, yet something in his eyes caressed her.

"I felt sorry for ye," she breathed, and a delicious trembling seized her.

"I am to be pitied," he muttered, and drew her into his arms and kissed her. . . .

May was waiting at the corner, full of amused curiosity. "Whatever did he say? Was he very cross?"

"Yes, he was cross. But he got over it. He says he's to be pitied, poor man. I'm real sorry for him, May. He's stern, and yet, just like a little child. Ain't men the comical things? One minute they make you shake in your shoes and the next minute you could laugh in their face. Just the same a girl needs to be careful with them, May."

"Keep that idear planted in your 'ead, Delight, and I'll rest easier about yer."

"Lord, May, don't talk like that. One 'ud think you was going to die like Gran."

Squeezing her arm, May thought: "Oh, if the pore child only knew what's in me mind to do!"

The rain began to pour down on them, hurrying them back to The Duke of York.

IV

It was almost factory closing time the next day. May stood at the back door of Albert's rough-cast cottage, one arm full of small packages, a huge bundle under the other. Her breath came in short gasps, her parted lips showed rows of little white teeth like sails of errant boats anchored safely once more in their harbour.

The door yielded, creaking on its hinges. A cat appeared out of the dusk of some gooseberry bushes and, pressing past her with little coaxing noises, led the way into the kitchen. A good omen, May thought, and black, too. Black cats were lucky. "Puss, puss," she said, " 'ere I am. . . . My word, wot a dismal 'ouse!"

It was all but dark. She shuffled cautiously across the floor, and laid her packages on the table. She closed the door and stood alone in Albert's house, every nerve alert; desperate resolve smouldering in her sharp eyes. She lifted the stove lid and stirred the grey coals with a poker. A tongue of flame shot up. She opened the draughts and, with a wisp of paper, lighted the oil lamp that sat on a bracket above the stove.

She must fly about and no mistake. There was a good deal to be done before the temple would be prepared and the feast laid for the hungry god of love. How she flew! The cat flew before her and after her, tail straight up in the air, green eyes glowing. He seemed to say: "I understand what you're about. After all, there is nothing like love."

May scrubbed the table; she put a pot of potatoes on to boil. A pan of sausages, smeared with drippings, was soon sputtering in the oven. She found another lamp in the bedroom, trimmed the wick, and polished the glass with the corner of a red shawl that hung on the kitchen door. She set the lamp on the table and flung the shawl in a corner. With a purr of delight the cat pounced on it and, with arched back and ardent claws, began to prepare a bed for himself. He thought: "At last the bed that suits me. Colour and softness. All along of this new female."

As she drew the blinds and laid the table she was rehearsing what she would say to Albert—how she would get him going—first on a full stomach—and then the two of them in the rocking-chair. Everything was ready, she wished he would hurry. Her eyes swept over the table spread for two: mounds of buttered toast, slabs of cheese, a pot of strawberry jam. Ah, the delicious smell of stewing tea!

A step crunched on the gravelled path. A hand fumbled at the latch. Albert entered.

He stood blinking in the unaccustomed brightness of the lights. May had stuck her head in the cupboard.

Albert spoke then, in a sarcastic drawl: "Well, an' wot's the matter wiv *you*, Mrs Ostrich?"

No answer.

"Might I arsk wot brung you 'ome so bright an' hearly, I dunno?"

Silence. But she wondered that he did not hear her heart pounding.

"So you've turned narsty, again, 'ave yer?" And he added, in a complaining tone: "If you 'ad *some* men to deal wiv, you'd get a good smack on the jor."

A titter came from the head in the cupboard but the body did not move. Albert threw his cap on a peg and came toward her, snarling: "Come out o' that and I'll learn yer manners, yer blarsted red'ead!"

Slowly, with a fixed grin, May turned her face over her shoulder to him.

Albert's jaw dropped. He began to shake. "Wot's the matter, any'ow? I've gone balmy. Ader's body—an' M'y's 'ead! I've gone balmy orl right. Two in one—one in two—oh, s'y, can't you speak?"

May's hands shot out and clasped him to her. Her fuzzy hair was against his mouth.

"Don't yer be scared, Awbert"—she used his old pet name—"it's only M'y, come to get your supper. I knew Ader was orf to a funeral and I thought you'd be lonely like. I thought: 'Wot's the 'arm in my doin' for 'im just once like in the old d'ys?' An' I've bought a bit of a treat for us. An' I've scrubbed 'er tyble an 'polished 'er lamp as weren't wot you'd call sparkling. Where's the 'arm in one little evening together?"

He rocked her blissfully in his arms, fear giving way to relief, to warm well-being, to sweet recollections of other nights together.

" 'Arm! There's no 'arm at all. Oh, lovey, I needed yer tonight. I was that depressed—comin' 'ome to a empty 'ouse! Not but wot I'd about as soon come to an empty 'ouse as to *'er!* Oh, M'y, wotever got me tangled up in this 'ere ruddy mess? Lovey, lovey—" he stroked her cheeks with his, pressing her to him.

"The saursages!" she cried. "I smell them burning! Quick, Awbert, let me go!"

She sprang to the oven and drew out the pan.

"Saursages for supper!" He loudly smacked his lips. "This *is* a bit of orl right! Wot does she give me for supper, can you guess? 'Otted-hup pertaters and applesaurce. Applesaurce and *'er* saurce—that's wot *I* get!"

"Never you mind, ducky! You'll 'ave one good supper anyw'y. Draw up yer chair. Don't let's wyste a minute of this precious evening."

She set the plates before him where four and twenty sausages bubbled as though they would fain burst into song like four and twenty blackbirds.

She drew her chair close to his. As he helped her to sausages and mashed potatoes he plied her with questions, his eyes raised every moment to feast on the sight of her there beside him, on her frizzy hair, her blazing cheeks, and her blue eyes bright with resolve. When his mouth became too full for speech he leant toward her and slapped her playfully on the wrist, or stamped rhythmically under the table with his feet.

At last the meal was over. The cat was given the platter to lick. Albert pulled May out of her chair onto his knees. She had to light his fag. He filled her mouth with smoke in a long close kiss and chuckled when she coughed and the smoke puffed out through her nostrils.

She grew suddenly limp and sad in his arms. Her head lay heavy on his shoulder.

"Wot's up, lovey? Too many saursages? Sleepy? Wot about stoppin' the night? Oh, I'm goin' to tyke care of you. In spite of 'er."

"Do you mind the old 'op-pickin' d'ys in Kent, when we first met, Awbert? Those were the times! Do you mind the warm soft evenin's and the nights when the pickers danced and sang 'arf the night through? And we?—aoh, let's forget it!"

"No, no! Tell some more, M'y! Lor', those were the d'ys!"

"Will yer ever forget the nights in old London at the music 'all, and goin' 'ome in the starlight singin' the songs we'd 'eard? They don't do much singin' and dancin' in this country, do they?"

"Noa. The song is froze in their 'earts wiv the cold, and the dance dried up their bones wiv the 'eat. Wot's the use?"

"Awbert, d'you mind the Bank 'Olerd'ys at 'Amstead 'Eath? The donkeys, and the coconut shies, and the swings?"

"And wasn't I waxy, when I caught you dancin' the Mazurker wiv a Jacky?"

"Jackies allers dance better than Tommies somew'y."

"That's because they've the 'ole deck to practise on."

May snuggled closer, pressing her shoulder under his armpit. She breathed: "Awbert, d'you mind the time you knocked me about so? I lay in a swound and—there was blood—"

He hid his face against hers. "Aoh, M'y, don't! You know I was sorry."

"I bet you was! W'y you bought me a hyercinth and it—*bloomed*."

"M'y, are you goin' to stop the night?"

"No. I've come to s'y good-bye, ducky. I'm leavin' for 'ome on the midnight train. I've got all I'm goin' to tyke in that bundle. I'm goin' 'ome."

He threw her from him and sprang to his feet facing her.

"Goin' 'ome! Ter leave me! M'y! 'Ave yer gone balmy? Leavin' me 'ere in this bloomin' 'ole! Wot's got inter you, anyw'y?"

"I'm finished. That's wot." Her eyes were flaming. Her voice cut like a knife. "Wot d'you think I'm myde of? Wot d'you tyke me for? Do you fancy I'll drudge my life out in that hotel wiv *'er* flauntin' 'er plumes in me fice? Do you think I'll be pitied by the other servants for my starved looks wiv *'er* gettin' fat on you! Do you think—oh, 'ave you no 'eart?—that I'll soak my pillow wiv my tears every night, and *'er* red 'ead a-snugglin' where mine should be?"

She panted like a caged thing struggling to be free.

"You think I'll sneak around 'ere bein' yer mistress while *she* pl'ys the wife! Well, you're wrong. I'm finished. I'm goin'. I'll be on the ocean in two d'ys. I've the money. I earned it, and earned it *honest*. I didn't tike up wiv' anyone. I *could* 'ave earned money wrongfully. But I'm honest and—I'm goin' —damn you!"

He was groping toward her, his eyes swimming in tears, his mouth contorted. His voice came in a strangled sob.

"Me too. Me too, M'y. I want to go 'ome. S'elp me, I'll desert 'er, if you've passage money fer *two!*"

May had not yet drained the cup of triumph, though Albert's bag was packed and they were almost ready to steal into the night. She cleared the table of dishes and, with a charred stick, wrote clearly on its clean surface:

Ada, Canadian Ada,
I have come and took my own.
English May.

The cat watched the feverish preparations for departure. He saw the lights put out. With brilliant green eyes, he beheld the two dark figures become one with the outer darkness. The door was closed, and he was alone in the hot little room. He rubbed his furry cheek against a table leg, then the length of his supple body. With tail erect he caressed himself, and thought: "After all, there's nothing like love."

V

Delight was disconsolate without May. How could May have had the heart to leave her so? She did not blame her for taking Albert from Ada, though some did, for Ada had come to the hotel and talked and cried before the men in the hall and the women in the kitchen. The whole town was by the ears. The two had disappeared as if by sorcery. The sleepy old station-master remembered selling two tickets for York to a young female. The midnight train it was, too, but he didn't know her and didn't see the man with her. Delight had found a note under her pillow from May. It was a loving note, and May left Delight the clothes she could not get into her bag. Her new necklace, too, but even that could not make up for the loss of May. She had a bereft feeling, and even Jimmy's arms about her, and his new gold watch tucked under her belt with the long chain about her neck, only made her gently happy. The new gravity of her expression added a fresh charm to the beauty of her face. The boarders, the transients could not eat in peace because of this disturbingly lovely presence. Once a tear dropped from her cheek into the soup of a young dye-works hand and, not knowing which spoonful contained the tear, he sat trembling and choking over the whole plateful, until Kirke leant over him and snarled:

"Swallow it, you cursed fool, or I'll duck your soft heid in it."

By degrees a friendship sprang up between Delight and Pearl. She could not lean on Pearl as she had leant on May, but still the plump, pretty girl was a comfort to her.

Pearl was passing through deep waters, too, those early spring days. Silk's elderly sisters had died within a few days of each other and he had found himself possessed of the tiny fortune which they had by pinching and privation kept intact for him. Where he had been formerly dependent on charity for much of his good cheer, he now found himself the centre of a flattering group, always ready to listen to his endless stories and laugh at his confused jokes. Where he had hung over the most wretched little tannery hand while he drank his beer, in the hope of being treated, he now ordered sherry with his dinner, and thought nothing of treating a dozen at a time in the bar. A new eloquence fired his love scenes with Pearl. Night after night these took place, in the dim streets, in the park, where other shadows haunted the willow-fringed lagoon, or sitting on the decrepit sofa in the hallway on the third floor. He held her plump, red hands in his slender, pallid ones; his puffy eyes burned into the hazel depths of hers. She must be kind to him! What was the good of anything if lovely girls were not kind to poor lonely devils of Englishmen in a strange land? He would take her to England—by God, he would!—and make a lady of her one day. But he did not ask her to marry him. His ardour fanned her own love into a flame that made her toss about the bed all night, and ache with longing in the pale dawn when she dressed. A lady! A lady in England! Oh, if he would only ask her to be his wife. Otherwise she couldn't be a lady. . . . She asked Delight, and Delight said that in her opinion Silk was a proper villain and that Pearl had need to be careful of herself.

Pearl was angry. She would confide no more in Delight. She wondered if any other girl had been so tempted. That night sitting on the sofa, the seat of which sank in two deep holes where the occupants had to fit their own seats, she looked down at Silk's head lying against her shoulder and wondered if life were as strange and difficult for other women as for her. She decided that it could not be, for there was only one Edwin and he loved her.

CHAPTER V

MEN AND WOMEN

I

KIRKE was waiting in the hall for Bastien at closing time. The last straggler had gone. The place was quiet save for the sound of coins being emptied out of the cash register. Kirke wondered very much what had been taken in that day. His mind dwelt for a moment with scorn on the absent owner of The Duke of York who trusted his affairs to Bastien.

The manager came out with his cool, alert air and locked the bar behind him.

"Weel," observed Kirke, "it's a fine nicht."

"Yes," agreed Bastien, putting the key in his pocket. "It begins to feel like spring."

Kirke came close to him, his shrewd light eyes concentrated on Bastien's face. He said in a low tone:

"That's a fine geerl. The one they call Delight, eh?"

A roguish grin slid over Bastien's face and left it impassive as ever.

"You, too? You'll need to step lively."

"I'm not thinking of myself. I'm thinking of the hotel. There's not a man in town but has his eye on her. They're discussing her points. In the little room behind the chemist's, in the tailor shop, the newspaper office, ay, the mayor's office. They can't keep their minds off her. She's come on the town like a blight.

"Ha, ha, a blight! That's good."

"It's guid business if ye'll make it so. Take it from me, man, you could fill the two transients' tables every day of the week, if you'd have her wait on them."

Bastien frowned. "That's Annie's job. She'd kick like the devil. There'd be trouble."

"Weel," sneered Kirke, "if ye prefair Annie's prestige"—he bit off the French word with relish—"to the prestige of The Duke of York—" he swung up the two bottom steps of the stairs.

Bastien's frown deepened.

"Wait a minute, can't you? You know I don't care a darn about Annie's what-d'you-call-it, but I don't want rows. She's got a lot more experience than Delight—"

"Experience," sneered Kirke, leaning over the banister. "Experience with men counts more than being able to keep three orders in your head at once. D'ye think they'd mind if she muddled their orders a bit? I was over in the bar at The British American tonight and I haird Beemer say he'd like to steal her if he could."

"The dirty dog."

"No. He just has the guid sense to see that there's money in her for the business."

"The dining-room is a loss."

"It needn't be if you'll just put your young beauty in the foreground. Ah, man, don't tell me that you can't make that richt with Annie! She's daft about you." He grinned down at Bastien.

"What about old Jessop?"

"She'd be glad to see Annie come down a peg. They're all jealous for ye. It's an awful thing, Bastien, to be such a chairmer. Old and young—"

"I'll think about it," said the manager.

II

He followed Kirke slowly up the first flight of stairs and turned into his own bedroom near the top. He put on the light, and stood a short while with bent head in the middle of the room. He believed that what Kirke said was true. (Was that queer fish really gone on Delight?) But he hated to hurt Annie's feelings. Still he had had complaining letters from Mr Hodgins, the owner; if anything could be done to bring in more revenue, the feelings of a waitress should not stand in the way.

Suddenly an idea came to him. He left his room and went quietly down the hall to the passage that led to the servants' quarters. He could hear Charley Bye's regular snore, unctuous as the beat of waves on a boggy shore. He stopped before Annie's door and listened. With his nail he scratched gently on the panel.

"You there, Annie?" he breathed.

There was a scuffle of stockinged feet on the floor, the door opened a crack, and Annie whispered:

"Is that you, Bill?"

"Yes, can you step out here a minute? Nobody about."

She came out, fully dressed but with her hair down, sticking out in short dark clumps about her tilted head. She looked so childlike he put his hand in the mass of her hair and gave it a tug.

"Oh, you kid," he said, smiling down at her.

She jerked her head away.

"Don't get fresh, Bill."

"You call *that* fresh?"

"I certainly do."

"Annie."

"What d'you want?"

"Annie." He put his arm around her.

"Oh, for goodness sake, Bill. What if Mrs Jessop came along? She's always snooping along this passage."

"Let her snoop. I'll soon show her who's boss here."

He pressed her to him roughly and kissed away the protest her lips were forming.

"Pearl in there?" he asked, glancing toward the bedroom door.

Annie nodded.

"Well, look here," he said, suddenly business-like, releasing her. "I've just been wondering now May's gone if we couldn't get along without hiring another girl."

Annie glared at him.

"My gosh, how hard do you think we can work? My soles are blistered now with being on my feet."

"I don't believe it."

Annie flushed. "Well, do the other thing, then. But they are."

"Show me, then."

"What do you take me for?"

"Oh, you girls! You make me tired. You don't know what real work is. I'm never *off* my feet."

"Well, you better get to bed, then, and rest."

"Now don't start getting at me, Annie. Listen. I'm wondering if you and Pearl could do May's work between you if I gave you something extra. Suppose I gave her three dollars a month more, and you seven. She needn't know there's any difference in the amount."

The prospect of earning more money was alluring. Annie had a widowed mother and six young brothers and sisters. Still, she did not see how she could.

"It'd be awfully hard—"

"Now wait. Look here. Let that big lump Delight do more work. She doesn't do half what she should. Give her the travellers and town tables, and you can look after some of the boarders. It's easy to wait on them. Just slap the food down before them any old way. Why, on quiet days she ought to be able to do the whole thing."

She drew back. "Oh, Billie, I shouldn't like to give up my best tables." Her voice choked. Her pride was cut.

"Now don't be a little fool. What good is it going to do you to wait at those blasted tables? None. But seven a month extra is going to do you a lot of good. Lord, think what it will buy! Then, it will save me a bit each month on another girl's wages. . . . I'm worried, I tell you, Annie. Things are not going as they should. I'd hate to lose my job."

"Oh, Bill, I didn't know." Her voice was full of compassion now. "How awful it'd be here without you. But there's no real danger, is there?"

He was pensive. "I guess we can worry through, but there's no knowing. Mr Hodgins is certainly coming to look into things, and it'll look well if he sees I'm cutting down expenses."

Annie moved closer to him and beseechingly scanned his face.

"Bill, you aren't getting struck on Delight, are you?"

"Have a heart, Annie. Spare one poor devil in the town to be struck on your own little self."

"Ah, Bill, if I only thought you was!" Her lip trembled. . . .

A step sounded down the passage and Pearl appeared.

"Oh, hullo," she said, "I thought you'd be in bed, Annie."

Bastien's brows lowered.

"Funny, isn't it?" he said. "Annie thought you were in bed. Honest. Early-to-bed ladies you are, aren't you? Well, see that you're early to rise."

He turned away.

"Beast," said Pearl calmly. "Thinks he's lord of the manor here. You ought to hear Edwin's opinion of him. . . . Have a toffee drop, Annie, and let's reely get to bed."

III

Delight and Jimmy were sitting on the sagging seat of the old sofa in the third-floor hallway. It was May but a gale was shaking the windows and a flurry of snow dimmed the panes. The deep roar of the lake made the indoors seem cozier. A good fire burned in the Quebec heater. One of the hands of the dye works had fallen in a vat that day, and his clothes hung by the stove on two chairs, giving off vapour and a strange pungent odour.

The two were happy.

Delight's body ached from a hard Saturday's work, but now it was relaxed in Jimmy's gentle embrace; her hands lay resigned and warm in his; every now and again his lips just touched her hair.

"Darling girl," he murmured, "dearest girl in the world."

"Oo—Jimmy, isn't that a funny smell off them clothes?"

"It is queer. Poor Patterson was an awful colour when

he was fished out. . . . Isn't it nice here, just you and me? So quiet like?"

"H'm. I can hear your heart, Jimmy."

"It doesn't beat for anyone but you, Delight."

"Then, it's saying—Delight—isn't it? De-light. De-light—De-light."

"You're not fretting for May now, are you?"

"Not so much. I'm getting used, and I like my new job waiting on the swells' tables."

Jimmy was hurt. "Ah, but it takes you away from me. I've never the same relish for my food any more. It makes me boil to see all those fool town fellows coming here to meals just for the sake of staring at you. You're too good for this place. . . . There's too much danger here for you." He turned his face to hers and whispered against her cheek: "Darling, we could have a little cottage, you and me, if you only would—I'd be so kind, Delight. You'd not need to work half so hard as you do here. When I was a boy I used to keep pigeons—I'd keep you just as safe and gentle as a pigeon."

"I know, Jimmy, and I will. But not yet. I want to be free for a while. I love you but—"

"But what?"

"I want to be just my own."

He saw that her full, curving lips could be stubborn. Once more he resigned himself to be patient.

IV

Charley Bye had had too much to drink though it was only ten in the morning. It did not take much to make the brain behind his white classical forehead flounder like a captive balloon, now soaring in little spurts, now feebly joggling against the earth. He was seated by the kitchen table with a cup of tea and a plate of bread and cheese before him, looking large and solemn while his wife flew hither and thither from bake board to stove, her thin arms white with flour, her lips puckered with anxiety about her projecting tooth.

"Pearl, are you getting them brains ready for the sauce for the calf's head?" she asked.

"Ye-es," answered Pearl, her nose curled. "I hate the sight of them."

"Speaking of brains," said Charley oracularly, "there's nothing like 'em for getting on in the world."

"Well, they haven't done much for this calf," said Pearl.

"Ah, but he hasn't got 'em, that's the p'int. He's now a brainless calf wherever he is."

"And you're a brainless fool," interrupted his wife. "Drink your tea, for goodness sake, and give us your room. We need it more than your company."

Charley took a swig of his tea and then proceeded with dignity:

"Talk of brains I had a buck rabbit that had brains to fit him to be on the town council. Anyone who knew him would co-operate this statement. I vallied him at five guineas. Not a penny less. Him and me was like brothers though I was summat older, being more what you might call Early Victorian in my idears."

Old Davy came into the kitchen and sat down heavily on a bench in a corner.

"What's up, Davy?" inquired Pearl.

"Someone has played me a dirty trick," said the old man. "You know the three geraniums I keep in my room. They set on the window sill and I keep them soaked all winter. They looked kinder sickly but I liked them. Now some dirty skunk has emptied the pots on to the middle of my bed. You never seen such a litter—mud and slop and roots and broken plants. Annie's mad as a hornet because she's got to clean it. If I only knew who it was—"

"Speakin' of litters," observed Charley, "the finest litter my buck rabbit ever got—"

"Darn your rabbits!" shouted Davy. "What do I care for your rabbits? I'm tellin' about my geraniums!"

With a sudden weak and yet fierce gesture Mrs Bye threw her floury apron over her head, and began loudly to weep.

"Oh, oh, I can't bear it!" she wailed, and she sat down on the bottom step of the backstairs.

Pearl ran to her and tried to draw the apron from her head.

"Oh, cook, whatever is the matter?" she cried.

Mrs Bye's head could be seen rolling from side to side under the apron. Her two hands, with little worms of dough clinging to them, were wrung together.

"I can't bear it—" she repeated.

"Don't you go worryin' yourself," consoled Davy. "I'd ha' never told you if I'd thought you'd take on so."

Charley, too, spoke soothingly: "There's other rabbits

where he come from, woife. Not but what I grant ye that there's none equal to him in edication."

"I can't bear it," came from under the apron, and a scream followed.

"For pity's sake get the doctor," said Pearl.

The two men merely stared stupidly, but Bastien who had been passing the door threw it open and strode over to Mrs Bye.

"What's the matter?" he demanded.

"She's been took badly," explained Pearl, white and trembling. "Davy told her of a mean trick someone did and she flew right off the handle."

Bastien resolutely uncovered Mrs Bye's head and looked down into her face. It was dusted with flour from the apron, and little runnels of tears through the flour made a strange, patchwork effect. She seemed to have no pride left, but sat with her poor face exposed to the gaze of all, her mouth sagging, her eyes staring disconsolately before her. She was quiet now.

"I think it's hysterics," said Bastien, and he asked—"Are you in pain?"

"Not now," she answered wearily, "but it'll come back again. . . . If I could only get upstairs."

"Make an effort," advised Charley pompously. "Make an effort same as I do. Say to yourself—'I will conquer this here weakness.' "

"Shut up!" ordered Bastien.

He bent over Mrs Bye. "Put your arms around my neck," he said, and heaved her up against his shoulder. He was of athletic build, and strong. In a moment he had carried Mrs Bye up the stairs and laid her on her own bed. Charley regarded the feat with mild interest.

V

It was certain that Mrs Bye was a very sick woman. When she and Pearl were left alone in the bedroom she raised herself on her elbow and, pointing with a shaking finger at a small box on the dresser, said:

"Hand me those powders, Pearl. I don't want the doctor to see them."

Pearl obeyed, and Mrs Bye, sitting up now, took two folded papers from the box, emptied them into the basin beside the bed, tore the papers and box into small fragments, and ordered the girl to throw them out of the window.

She dropped back on the pillow then and passed before Pearl's eyes into terrible convulsions. Mrs Jessop came, her large mouth set in a grim line.

"Go back to your work, Pearl," she said. "This is no place for you."

The doctor came and stayed for hours. The girls cried in the kitchen. Charley had been sobered by the excitement and, feeling himself the centre of interest as an afflicted husband, passed from bar to kitchen, and kitchen to bar, recounting details of other "spells," staged by both this and the first Mrs Bye. It was a serious business being a husband, and a man had need for a steady head and a sound edication. In fact, it was an edication in itself.

The next day Mrs Bye was said to be out of danger, but she looked so ill that the girls were frightened when they crept in to see her. Her eyes were so large and blue, her face so ivory yellow, and her air so gentle and remote that she seemed to belong to another world.

Mrs Jessop turned to and did the cooking, bringing an atmosphere of solid efficiency into the kitchen, very different from Mrs Bye's nervous haste. There was no loitering when she was at the helm, though she took time to be coy when Bastien came into the kitchen. Once he stole behind her and untied her apron strings and she, grinning widely, dabbed flour at his face.

In a week Mrs Bye was able to sit up, propped by pillows, but Charley began to be anxious about the slowness of her recovery. Mr Hodgins, the owner of The Duke of York, was expected almost any time and Charley was deeply perturbed lest Mrs Jessop should intimate to him that a delicate cook was a doubtful asset. Suppose they should lose their situations! Behind his calm brow fearful thoughts, like slow-moving shellfish, circled about. As his wife had said, behind his seeming foolishness he had a deal of sound sense. Deep misgivings now hung over him like a cloud. He was offended that Mrs Bye did not seem to share them. For the first time since their marriage her mind seemed to be turned inward on her own selfish comforts. While he discoursed at length upon the dangers of a too-prolonged convalescence, she would greedily eat the toast and custard one of the girls had brought her, or play with Queenie's flaxen hair, or even curl up in a ball and shut her eyes. He felt fettered in the struggle to maintain his position.

At last definite word was received that Mr Hodgins was to be expected on Monday at noon.

All through the quiet of Sunday Charley was in a state of portentous calm. As he was undressing that night he addressed almost the first words he had spoken that day to Mrs Bye.

"Mr Hodgins will be here to dinner tomorrow. Are you goin' to get up or are you goin' to lie there forever?"

"Oh," moaned Mrs Bye, "I'm so weak. Do let me be."

"Do you want to lose us our job?"

Mrs Bye rolled up in a ball and shut her eyes.

Charley, in his undershirt and trousers, stood looking down at her. He looked from her to Queenie, sprawled over her little mattress on the floor, her pink face in a halo of silvery hair. A deep resolve to be master in his own house was born in him. He was an Englishman. This shabby, tumbled room, littered with the belongings of three people, was his castle. These two recumbent, obstinate females were his clinging vines, and he the sturdy oak. They'd cling so hard they'd stifle him if they could. But he'd show them oak wasn't to be stifled. Oak had his rights, by gum!

He dropped his boots, truculently, one by his wife's bed, one by his daughter's. Neither flinched nor stirred. He finished his undressing, put out the light, and sank heavily into bed.

His weight caused the mattress to sink so that Mrs Bye rolled from her eminence next the wall, down against him, all her weight on his chest, her hair tickling his nose and mouth.

Queenie spoke in her sleep:

"Dahy! Dahy!"

"Daddy, eh?" Clinging vines! He'd show them!

VI

Toward noon of the next day Mrs Bye was lying flat on her back, listening to the hum and rattle of the kitchen below, her hands, like two ivory claws, palms upward on the dingy counterpane. Queenie was cutting out paper dolls on a stool by the head of the bed. She had difficulty in keeping them quiet once they were cut out, for a playful spring breeze blew in at the window and invested them with a malicious liveliness, waving their arms and legs about and prompting them to scurry to the farthermost corner under the bed.

Mrs Bye was dreaming of her girlhood on a Surrey farm and of a certain young Thomas Clark who used to be sweet on her. She hadn't thought of him for years, but now he stood before her, real as life, smiling shyly as he helped her over a stile. She was smiling, too, when Charley opened the door and looked in at her. . . . Nothing to do but lie there and smile. It made him almost ill himself to think of such selfishness. He came in and slammed the door behind him.

Mrs Bye awoke with a start to see him towering with his back against the door.

"Oh," she said weakly, "what time is it?" She did not want to know the time and only asked because she was afraid he was going to say something unpleasant.

"Time to get up," he answered majestically. "Time for you to get up and hold down your job, missus." He came toward her, creaking the boards beneath him.

"But I'm not able!" she cried, apprehensively clutching the quilt. "Nobody has said nothing against me resting a bit longer, have they?"

"Am *I* nobody? Have *I* said nothing?" Suddenly his voice swelled out, bursting from his barrel-like chest and filling the room. "I say now as you've lain long enough. Do you want us to be sacked along o' *your* laziness? Mrs Jessop's given me a nasty look already this morning. . . . Come, now," he turned the bedclothes back off her, "up you gets, and no nonsense."

Queenie tried to cover her mother up again.

" 'Onh hurh her, Dahy!" she pleaded.

Charley swept her aside as though she had been one of her own paper dolls. He put his hands under his wife's arms and set her up, another doll, as white as paper. But something in his masterful touch brought the answer of her heart. She raised her eyes to him and smiled.

"Hold me a bit," she said, "I'm dizzy."

He supported her and, mollified by her submission, said more kindly:

"You don't have to do nothing but sit still. I'll dress you and carry you down. Where's your clothes?"

The underthings were lying handy on the top of the trunk. He bent over her and breathing hard drew the black cotton stockings over the long thin legs. Between them they got her nightdress off; he, breathing still harder, clasped her corsets about her. . . . Encased in her poor armour of the day, Mrs Bye felt more able to cope with the affairs of life.

She had Charley get a clean print dress for her from the bottom drawer. While he laced her shoes Queenie passed the taken on so beautiful a creature. It disturbed him to think of her in a hotel among a lot of rough fellows.

He stood blinking in the kitchen now, near the fiery range, the women and Charley in a deferential semi-circle about him, Bastien at his back.

Bastien said: "This is Mrs Bye, the cook. She's had a little sick spell but she'll be all right in a day or so. Mrs Jessop's been helping her out with the cooking."

Mrs Jessop grinned. Mrs Bye had risen. Some superhuman force seemed to have given power to those shaking legs of hers. Red patches flared in her cheeks. But there was something in her eyes that held Mr Hodgins. He looked into them and thought: "Poor woman. A nice woman."

Queenie, pressing forward, put the wand of pussy willow into his hand.

"Po' woo," she said.

"What's that?" he asked. "What does she say?"

"She says it's for you," Mrs Bye answered, shaking all over.

"Po' woo," shouted Queenie, joggling his watch-chain.

"Good little girl," he replied. "Here's ten cents for you."

He kissed the child, chatted pleasantly to the women for a moment, and then retreated, carrying the willow wand.

A pleasant man, the women agreed. Everything had gone off well. He had praised the dinner, especially the rhubarb pie with custard sauce.

"I really believe I could try a bit of the pie and custard, with a cup of tea," said Mrs Bye faintly.

Delight observed: "I don't think Mr Hodgins likes me very well. He gave me a stern kind of look as he went out."

"I hope you didn't put yourself forward too much in the dining-room," said Mrs Jessop, cutting the pie.

"Men are always giving her queer looks," said Annie sarcastically.

Delight smiled her lazy smile, and shrugged her goddess-like shoulders.

"Well *I* think they're comical and I don't care who hears me say it. Comical to the very marrow."

stubby hairbrush over her hair, peeking round in her fa
ask:

"Be'er 'ow?"

Yes, she was better. She felt quite courageous a
clung to Charley's great barrel of a body, descending the l
stairs. What ages since Bill had run up with her! Charley
cautiously, feeling for every step. Queenie shuffled after, c
ing a pillow.

She created a sensation in the kitchen.

"Here's a sight for sore eyes," said old Davy who
that in some way he was responsible for Mrs Bye's suc
attack.

"Well, you do look like two sheets and a shadow,"
Jessop declared.

Delight came running with the rocking-chair from
scullery; Annie with a bowl of broth; Pearl with a branch
pussy-willow to which downy great catkins were clingi
Queenie was convulsed with joy to see her mother propped
in the kitchen. She snatched the willow wand and holding
erect began to march up and down, singing:

We aw mar'h toge'her,
We aw mar'h toge'her,
We aw mar'h toge'her,
Nih'ly in a waow.

VII

Mr Hodgins was a nervous little man who knew nothing wha
ever about the hotel business. He had taken a mortgage on Th
Duke of York to help a friend in difficulties and the hotel ha
eventually come into his hands. He had already lost money b
it and he was afraid he would lose more. He dreaded his occa
sional visits to Brancepeth to look into things, for Bastien an
Mrs Jessop intimidated him by their complete knowledge o
what he so little understood and by their airs of aggressive
competence.

However today he felt rather more hopeful. Bastien's
accounts were more satisfactory. He was trying to economize.
The dining-room trade was looking up wonderfully. A good
dinner, tables well filled, and what a waitress! She made a man
blink, positively. He doubted whether Mrs Jessop should have

CHAPTER VI

MRS JESSOP ROUSED

I

THAT year spring had no lovely adolescence. From the morning when she had taken her first timid steps across the fields till she had sprung into fierce maturity was little more than a month. It was almost sad to see her cast her playthings of frail flowers and downy leaf buds so soon aside, and desire nothing more in play, but all in passion.

Land and lake and sky leaped into hot activity in her embrace. The blue sky arched, bluer and more blue, to the zenith. Fruit trees spilled their petals and showed the sour young fruit buds which, in a few weeks, took the distinctive curves of apple, peach, or plum. Strawberries glowed like a myriad of little hearts among the scorching vines. Wagons loaded with crates of them journeyed at sunrise from the surrounding fruit farms to the wharf to be loaded on the early boat. Basket factories were working on long hours in all the fruit district. Groups of dusky Indian pickers appeared on the streets of Brancepeth. They carried bundles and babies, lived their own mysterious lives and, when the season was over, disappeared with the fruit.

It was a time of steady immigration from Britain and there was hope in every heart and work for all.

Business was good at The Duke of York. There was no doubt that Kirke's scheme of placing Delight more prominently in the dining-room had been a good one. She was a never-failing attraction. As Kirke had said, her fame had spread like a blight. not only through the town but through the surrounding farmlands. Farmers who had formerly patronized The British American now came, half-sheepishly, to take their dinner at The Duke, that they might have a glimpse of the strange beauty. And, once they had been, the thought of her gave them no peace, and they must make excuses to return to the town for the pleasure of having her deferentially, even caressingly, place their food before them. Sailors and stokers and train hands who had always haunted the little old rough-cast hotel near the wharf began to appear; and, though they were set at the table with the factory boarders for Annie to wait on, they could watch Delight moving to and fro with heavy trays, from which the flowing lines of her arms merged exquisitely into her breast and waist. Her velvet brown eyes might even rest on them for a moment and her lips part as she thought:

"He hasn't got his face half-clean after his stoking." Or: "What a comical stare this one has!"

No one knew whether she were a loose girl or not. Strange stories floated about concerning her, but nothing could be proved. It was certain that she would accept presents from anyone. Many men testified to this, but they had to lie about the return she made them. Legends sprang up about her origin. Subtle, intimate imaginings concerning her moved in and out of the bar, crept through the streets, filtered into the houses and offices of the well-to-do and, at last, sank to the wharves and mingled with the sighing of the lake.

As the feverish heat of the summer grew and business had to be carried on at a temperature of ninety-five degrees, The Duke of York became the heart of an intricate organism separate from the ordinary life of the town yet fatally bound up in it. The situation in the hotel was strange. Almost everyone in it was watching someone else, was spied on by someone else.

Annie concealed her chagrin at the loss of her position as head waitress. She concealed the fact that Bastien was giving her more wages. She watched him, she watched Mrs Jessop and, most of all, she watched Delight. Pearl's mind was given to observing Silk as her heart was given to loving him. He drank more and more, talked less of returning to England, but she greatly feared he would slip away and leave her in the lurch. He had bought a skiff and, when he was sober enough, he would take her out in it to float about the lagoon. Neither his arms nor heart were strong enough to face the vagaries of the lake. But in the calm lagoon he would collapse in the bottom of the boat, the moonlight shining down on his pallid face, and recite poems of Byron and Tennyson to the poor yearning girl who knew deep down in her soul that he was a slippery customer to be in love with.

Twilight and evening bell
And after that the dark—

his melodious voice would repeat, weaving a hypnotic spell about her.

II

A nascent enmity had arisen between Bastien and Kirke. Scarcely acknowledged yet, it did not raise its head, but it was gaining strength and there was rich food for its development.

Bastien wished to forget that it was Kirke who had proposed elevating Delight to the position she now held. He wanted to regard her as his own creation and he resented the gimlet gaze of the Scotsman that seemed forever fixed on him. He felt as the ringmaster in a circus putting a beautiful filly through her paces, snapping the whip at the right moment, bowing for her to the plaudits of the crowd.

But, if Bastien were comparable to the ringmaster of a circus, Kirke was as a high priest at the altar of a goddess, a priest rather contemptuous toward the poor young goddess herself, but demanding the worship of others with fierce austerity.

When Delight beat the Chinese gong before the door of the dining-room with calculated fervour, ascending from a low, muffled tapping to a thunder that filled the house, his angular body would invariably be draped against the newel post while his hungry light eyes devoured her unconscious beauty. When she lowered the gong, her lips parted in a pleased smile, he always gave his short barking laugh, and looked about him with a kind of snarl to see whether homage were forthcoming.

He said nothing except perhaps to mutter to his friend, Lovering: "A fine geerl." His mind was made up that she should come to no harm through Bastien.

Kirke was annoyed by Edwin Silk's sudden affluence. It angered him to see Silk sought after where he had once been jeered at, and though he was willing to let Silk pay for his drinks, he never hung about him. He despised Silk for taking a kitchen girl rowing on the lagoon. With his education he might have picked up a lass worth while, if he could only have kept sober.

However, luck was to come his own way before the summer was over. His mother died in Dundee and left him a comfortable sum, not so much as Silk had got by a good deal, but still enough to put him on a very different footing in Brancepeth. He looked decently subdued for a few days after the news came. He bought himself a black tie and retired early to his room, but he could not mourn inwardly. He had not seen his mother for twelve years and he had never been fond of her. He remembered with a grimace how she had made his back and legs tingle with a switch, when he was a big growing lad. It was a good thing, he reflected, that his half-sister had died two years before, so that the money did not have to be divided.

He had always wanted to be in a business of his own. He made up his mind to start a small dairy. He gave up his position in the tannery, and did nothing for a fortnight but look about him for suitable premises and interview farmers about the purchase of milk. He bought a horse, a fine tall gelding, and a yellow-wheeled trap. As he drove at full speed along the main street or dashed into the stable yard of The Duke, he felt that every eye in Brancepeth was on him. He was ambitious. The mayor of the town had a plain-faced daughter of thirty. Kirke met her in her father's office when he was seeing about a licence for his dairy business. They met several times after that and at last he asked her to have a drive behind the gelding.

Every shopkeeper in Brancepeth seemed to have his nose against his window as Kirke and Miss Earle drove past. Slow was the pace as they drove out, that every eye might see, but they came back like a whirlwind, the gelding stamping his hoofs in graceful fury, Miss Earle's long green scarf streaming far behind.

Kirke could not conceal his elation that night. When he and Lovering went to bed they lay awake talking of his plans, of milch cows, of marketing butter and cream, and lastly of his taking the mayor's daughter for a drive. Lovering became sleepy but Kirke would not let him be. He even flung his arm about his neck and, hugging him, exclaimed:

"Who knows! I may be Mayor of Brancepeth yet, mysel'." His accent broadened with his emotion.

"Get off me, Duncan," growled Lovering, trying to free his burly neck. "Tha'rt choking me. What's all this fuss about? As for Miss Earle, she has no more life in her than a sheep, and no more beauty. And if tha'rt going to be mayor, I'll get out and that's flat."

III

Like a red lily blooming on a dung heap, Delight lived tranquilly in the midst of all the sordid gossip and sluggish passions surrounding her. She worked till she was tired, she ate little because of the great heat, and slept lightly in the stifling little back room.

The sun had ceased to be a beneficent friend to the fruitgrowers on the Peninsula. Instead he had become a sinister tyrant whose rising was watched with dread, who walked with brazen feet over the vines, scorching, shrivelling, drying the life-blood of the fruit.

The bar of The Duke of York was the coolest place in the town. The kitchen was certainly the hottest. Once more Mrs Bye flew about the panting range; the girls flew at her command, and Mrs Jessop retired to her storeroom and linen closet.

It was Sunday evening and Delight and Jimmy were sitting on the sofa in the third-floor hall. The window was open beside them, and a sultry breeze had sprung up, stirring the boy's hair on his flushed forehead and kissing the girl's bare throat as her head tilted back on his shoulder. . . . There was thunder in the air.

Delight's feet were swollen from being constantly on them the day before. She did not feel like taking a walk and he was content to sit with her here. There was no peace of mind for him in walking out with her, because of the peering of the men they passed, and the feeling that someone was always following them. The thought of being followed may have been only Jimmy's imagination, for things had got sadly on his nerves of late. He dreamed at nights as he had never been wont to do—strange dreams of terrible things befalling Delight. He was getting nervous in his work, too. He would think: "What if I fell into one of those vats now and was suffocated! There'd be no one to look after my girl." His square face, with its short nose and stubborn mouth, had taken on a troubled look, and he carried his compact strong body with an air of nervous aggression.

"Oh, marry me, Delight, and let's have done with all this," he implored, patting her shoulder. "Whatever makes you so mulish-like, my darling? You'd not have to work half so hard, just doing for us two, and all these chaps 'ud quit harrying you."

"Mr Mayberry, the tailor, proposed to me today," she said gently.

"Mayberry, the tailor!" he exclaimed loudly and angrily.

"Don't shout, Jimmy." She laid her finger against his lips.

"Yes, but that old dud! He's bow-legged from sitting cross-legged. How did he get near you in the daytime? What's Mrs Bye thinking about to let him into the kitchen? Has she no sense?"

"He didn't see me. He wrote a nice little letter to me, on pink paper—"

"I'll pink paper him," groaned Jimmy. "Oh, I like his cheek, I do."

Delight sighed. "He's got a nice shop. He makes clothes for the best people in Brancepeth."

"And his poor crippled wife just dead three months! He ought to be horse-whipped."

"Three months is quite a long time, Jimmy. Then, too, he's bought her a beautiful tall monument. He says so in the letter."

"On pink paper! Talking about a monument on pink paper! Where's this here letter? Give it over to me. I'll answer it, by thunder!"

Instinctively her hand went to her bosom. Her attitude became defensive. She could not hand over the poor little tailor's tender missive to another man.

"No, Jimmy. I can't do that. 'Twouldn't be fair."

"Is it fair to me to go carrying another man's letter next to your heart?"

"It isn't doing no one any harm."

"Are you engaged to me or aren't you?" She smiled roguishly at him, and a sudden flash of lightning illuminating her face, twisted her smile into a malicious grin, gave her face a sinister, unknown quality like that of some tormenting stranger. He suddenly felt terrified of her.

The breeze that came in the window was hot and dry with fine dust. The coarse lace window-curtain was whipped up and blown against his face. His nostrils were filled with a musty odour.

"Give me that letter," he snarled, tearing the curtain from his head, "or it'll be the worse for you."

Laughing, Delight put her arm around him and pressed her head against his shoulder, but instead of pacifying him, she only enraged him the more. His arm closed around her like a vice, his chin pressed her head against his breast. With his free hand he thrust sharply into the opening of her blouse. They set their teeth. They struggled. The decrepit sofa creaked. Her blouse was torn. Then, with cheeks crimson with anger and shame, he drew out the pink paper. With a blazing look for it and another for her, he tore envelope and letter into fragments and threw them on the floor.

"There—" he said, "there's your beastly proposal. You can have your old tailor."

A long roll of thunder shook the dark sky, rumbling far

down the lake, till it became but a distant mutter. Then, in the menacing silence that followed, he repeated:

"You can have your darned old tailor."

"Oh, Jimmy, how could you use me so rough? And I've always treated you the very best I know how! You've hurt me cruel."

He did not answer.

"Oh, Jimmy, do you mean it's all over between us?"

Still he made no reply, enjoying with a boy's brutality the distress of one weaker than himself.

She put her arm across her eyes and rose, stumbling across the hall in the darkness. The rain now began to pelt on the roof and the sign outside sorrowfully to creak in the rising gale.

"I'm going," she sobbed, finding the banister. "I'm going, Jimmy."

He wanted to call her but something savage in him held him back. He remembered all she made him suffer in jealousy and longing, and he could not call her back, though already his arms ached to hold her and his heart cried out for her. But he sat with stocky body erect and arms folded while she felt her way down the stairs.

IV

Kirke in his bedroom was sitting by a small table, bending over some neatly ruled sheets of paper. He kept an accurate account of all expenditures in his new venture. He did not notice the thunderstorm.

Lovering flung open the door but without noise and stepped inside.

"What's up with you?" demanded Kirke, regarding him coldly.

Lovering came close, his eyes rolling, his mouth pursed.

"Godamoighty, Duncan," he answered, in a hoarse whisper, "there's summat goin' on downstairs. It's that young rip, Delight. She's in Bastien's room, cryin'. I was just mountin' the stair, and stopped stock-still as a flash of lightning lit the hall when I spied her comin' down. She was sobbing with her hand to her bosom, and Bastien opened his door and came out and spoke to her and led her into his room and made the door fast, and I slipped up to let tha know the soort o' thing that's goin' on. Ah, what a lass to cuddle and kiss. And *Bastien*, Duncan, *Bastien!*"

Kirke's nerves were excited by the news. His senses were gratified by the disclosure of an intrigue beneath the roof. He suddenly became aware of the storm. He felt the air electric with inarticulate feeling, vibrant with passion.

"Stop here, Jack," he said to his friend, unwinding his angular legs from the legs of the chair as he rose. A bright spot burned on either cheek-bone.

"What art goin' to do?" sputtered Lovering, always suspicious yet envious of Kirke.

"Wait here and see. There'll be some fun."

He slunk down the stairs like a shadow. Outside Bastien's door he listened for a second, hearing low voices, and a sob with a little laugh behind it. The young trollop, he thought, going from one man's room to another's with her laughing and her crying. She didn't know how to take care of herself. He'd teach her. Give her a lesson she wouldn't forget. Give that cursed Bastien a lesson. Bastien most of all. He'd make him suffer. . . .

He went through the narrow back passage and tapped at Mrs Jessop's door. Her peaceful snores continued without a break. He tapped again sharply and this time she was out of bed in an instant and at the door.

"Who's that?" she whispered.

His eyebrows went up at her sudden alertness. Used to callers, the sly old vixen.

"Step out here, a bit," he said. "Put a wrapper on. I want to show you something. . . . It's Duncan Kirke speaking."

"I hope there's no nonsense going on, Mr Kirke. My gracious, what a storm!"

"Come along, Mrs Jessop. You'll regret it if you don't."

"What time is it?"

"Time all of us were in our own beds. Are you dressing?"

She came out, dressed in a plaid wrapper, her grey hair in crimping pins, her large grey eyes aggressively staring.

"I hope this is worth getting up for," she said sharply.

Kirke gave a low bark.

"Weel, that depends."

"Where's the trouble?"

"Just follow me, Mrs Jessop."

Outside Bastien's door he stopped. With his long index finger he noiselessly tapped the panel.

"Delight Mainprize is in there with Bill," he breathed.

A peal of thunder drowned Mrs Jessop's sharp exclamation but a lightning flash showed her face distorted with rage. Kirke was standing rigidly, his high shoulders hunched.

The housekeeper grasped the doorknob and wrenched open the door. Kirke backed into the shadow.

In the unshaded electric light Bastien and Delight turned and faced Mrs Jessop. The three stared at each other, spellbound. Lightning blinked against the window glass, frustrated by the glare of the bulb beside the dressing-table. One roll of thunder followed steadily upon another.

Bastien's brow was black. He stood sullenly facing the housekeeper. She darted into the room and grasped the girl's wrist, her fingers digging into the flesh like claws.

"I'll have something to say to you, my girl," she said in a thick voice. "Now go to your room."

"Don't get worked up over nothing," said Bastien. "We weren't into any harm here."

"Shut up!" shouted Mrs Jessop; then steadying herself, she added, brokenly—"Oh, Bill, you'd ought to be ashamed. Look—her dress is torn! Oh, you're a nice one, you are, Delight Mainprize! Get to your room and don't let me see your brazen face again."

"He didn't tear it, Mrs Jessop," sobbed Delight, clutching the torn blouse on her shoulder.

"Don't lie to me. And get out of my sight or, by God, I'll tear your clothes for you! I'll tear them clean off your body and throw you into the street!"

A burst of thunder, like an explosion, engulfed them in its volume. Rain descended in a deluge. The electric power of the town ceased to function and the house was in darkness, except for the ceaseless blue glimmer of lightning through the rain.

Bastien stumbled toward Delight. He would have liked in that blackness to disentagle her from the older woman and bear her to safety some place—some place—a desert island—a cave—wild tales from his boyhood surged through his brain. His hands groped toward her. A flash showed him her wild, frightful eyes. Then Mrs Jessop's woolly wrapper came between them. He knew she'd never let him hear the last of this. . . . Interfering, spiteful woman that she was! Why had he ever got thick with her?

V

Delight was safe in her bedroom, trembling but safe from the houskeeper's hands, the door locked, the washstand dragged over against it, the oil lamp lighted, her own dishevelled figure reflected in the glass, for company.

Oh, if May were only here! Darling, plucky, strong little May. She'd protect her from Mrs Jessop. It was a queer situation that May couldn't face.

She was hot as fire but she was afraid to open the window because of the storm. She sat on the side of the bed fanning herself with a bit of newspaper. Beads of perspiration stood on her forehead and across her nose. There were purple marks on her wrist where Mrs Jessop had wrenched it. Cruel old woman. There had been nothing done or said to deserve those purple marks. Bill had only been kind to her, patted her shoulder, and he had just been going to show her some trinkets he had brought from South Africa when the door had been thrown open and all that row began.

Listen! There was someone at the door now. Through the drumming of the rain she could hear the doorknob rattling. She sprang up and threw her weight against the barricading washstand.

"Who's there?" she cried.

"Mrs Jessop," came in muffled tones.

"I won't let you in. Go away."

"You won't, eh? What are you afraid of? If I was a man you'd let me in fast enough."

"No, I shouldn't. You're a wicked woman to say so."

"Very well, then. If you won't let me in, come close to the door. Put your ear to the crack so's you can hear what I say. Can you hear?"

"Y—yes."

"Now listen. You're nothing but a trollop, and I won't have you in this house another day. There's a train goes through here to the city at five in the morning. You'll go on that, d'you hear. You'll get up quietly and dress without letting on to the other girls. I'll give you your breakfast and a month's wages, and you'll go on that train, see? You'll leave us in peace as we were before you came. Get your trunk packed ready to go. I'll have Davy take it to the station on the wheelbarrow. Don't you dare to leave your room before I call you at half-past three. I'm going to watch your door from my room and if you come out of it and I lay my hands on you, God's my witness, I'll spoil your looks for you. I've got a temper when it's roused and I've stood about all I can from you!"

Delight wrung her hands in the dark.

"Oh, please, mayn't I see Jimmy before I go? Him and me have quarrelled and I'd like to make it up."

Mrs Jessop struck the panel a blow with her clenched hand.

"Just you dare to try seeing anyone! If you do, I'll blazon you over the whole house. I'll get the gong and sound it in the hall, and tell everyone in the town how you've gone from one man's room to another. You've shamed the house, and you're lucky to get off as easy as you're doing, d'yer hear?"

The storm which had rolled down the lake now swept back as though for nothing else than to beat down Mrs Jessop's voice. She could not hear it herself so she knew that the girl behind the door at which she glared could not hear. She returned to her own room and dragged her rocking-chair to the doorway. Seated in it she did not take her eyes from Delight's door for the rest of the night. Like an owl's her round, unblinking gaze was riveted on the one spot, and strange, wild thoughts from an almost forgotten youth rose again within her, oddly familiar after all these years, making her feel young and fierce again.

CHAPTER VII

AUGUST BERRIES

I

DELIGHT'S body lay stretched along the bed, her strong arms thrown out in an attitude of profound relaxation. Her mind, too, was quiet, half-drowsing after wearying emotions. She knew that in an hour or two Mrs Jessop would rap on the door, the signal for her to leave this room forever. . . . Well, she was ready to leave, except for her coat and hat. Her tin trunk, with the basket containing Granny's tea set standing on top of it, was waiting by the door.

She had not known that she loved this poor room so but, in truth, it was the one home she had. On the lumpy bed she and

May had slept happily together; there May had poured out the story of her love for Albert. In this room she had felt remote and safe as in a little house of her own. It was intolerably stuffy, stained, and faded, but she saw none of this. Her heart enfolded it as the shrine where Gran's tea set lived, where memories of May abounded. She was like a poor stall animal that clings to its own manger, its halter, its drinking pail, and would rush there gladly after the day's work. It seemed terrible to her, besides, to be thrown out into the street like this, as though she were a bad girl. She never thought of questioning Mrs Jessop's authority. Mrs Jessop had engaged her, now if she pleased she could throw her out.

But, oh, if she had not quarrelled with Jimmy! If only they had not become bitter over the tailor's proposal. . . . She might marry the tailor. She could go to him in the morning and say—"Mr Mayberry, I'll marry you this morning if you like." He would be glad. And he wasn't so ugly, either. His legs might be a little bowed and his chest flat, but Jimmy was too hard on ugly people. He was too proud of his own compact, strong body. She remembered the feel of him in her arms, so round and firm. Well, he wouldn't have her to put her arms around him any more— He'd have to get some other girl. . . .

Slow tears drenched her eyes. The lamp became a blurred sun, far away. The echoing walls of the rain shut her in. She slept.

II

Thud! Thud! Mrs Jessop's palm struck the door. She did not rap for fear of waking Annie and Pearl in the next room. Delight sat up startled, yet only half awake. The lamp had burned itself out and a smell of charred wick hung in the air. She could dimly see the furniture by the grey glimmer at the window. . . . But why was she dressed? What was it all about? Mrs Jessop softly thumped on the door again.

"Hurry up, there," her voice came thickly. "You've no time to spare. Open the door."

Delight sprang to her feet, fully conscious now, terribly afraid of angering Mrs Jessop still further. She dragged the washstand from before the door, and timidly opened it. Her eyes, wild and mournful, stared out at the housekeeper.

"Phew, what a stink!" exclaimed Mrs Jessop, and she

glared around the twilit room, as though she half expected to find Bastien hidden there.

Delight took her coat and hat from the peg and put them on, avoiding Mrs Jessop's eyes.

"What about my box and basket?" she asked.

"You take one end of the trunk. It ain't very heavy, and I'll take the other. You can carry the basket in your other hand. You're big enough, ain't you?"

Together they carried the trunk down the steep black stairway. Delight was in front, the basket bumping against her leg, the trunk weighing on her cruelly. "Oh," she thought, "what a fix I'm in! What if Mrs Jessop should let go of her end of the trunk and I'd go to the bottom with it on me. I'd be smashed. Perhaps she's planned the whole thing, to kill me." She felt like screaming.

But they reached the kitchen safely.

The fire was lighted. A pot of tea was stewing on the back of the stove. They set down the trunk and faced each other, panting. Mrs Jessop looked ghastly in the electric light, black circles beneath her eyes, her lips blue. She said commandingly:

"Sit down at the table. Here's your month's wage." She handed her some bills. "Count it. Now, will you have a fried egg?"

"No, just a cup of tea and a bit of bread."

"It's for you to say. I'll cook you the egg if you want it."

"No. No. I don't want any egg." It was strange to sit alone at the long table, being waited on by Mrs Jessop. The bread and butter stuck in her throat till she washed it down with strong tea. The strange thing was, she seemed to see Queenie marching up and down the kitchen singing her marching song:

We aw mar'h toge'her,
Nih'ly in a waow.

What a comical way she talked, poor young Queenie!

Mrs Jessop went to the back door and called, but in a low voice:

"Henry!"

A half-grown boy who worked about the stables at odd times entered now and threw a look of dull surprise at Delight. He had never seen anyone who looked at all like her, and he did not like the look of her in the least.

"This is the trunk," said Mrs Jessop. "Got your wheelbarrow outside?"

"M-m," grunted Henry, heaving up the trunk. "Can I go on ahead? She can foller all right."

Delight answered:

"Well, don't go too fast. I'd like to keep near you." She thought of the dim, lonely streets. She would like some company, however stupid, on that last walk through Brancepeth.

Henry grunted again and staggered out with the trunk.

"You said last night that Davy would take my trunk," said Delight. "I'd like to ha' seen one of them again."

"I changed my mind."

"Well, good-bye." Delight swallowed the last of her tea and set down the cup.

With a fierce gesture, Mrs Jessop snatched it up and, with rigid arm, held it before the eyes of the girl.

"You see that cup?"

"Yes."

Mrs Jessop hurled it to the floor, smashing it to fragments. A ferocious smile lighted her face.

"Well, I don't run no risk of ever putting my mouth to that cup, see? All us women hate you. Go!"

III

Henry was already trundling the wheelbarrow up the street when Delight crossed the stable yard. She hurried after him, carrying her basket of dishes, feeling pursued by Mrs Jessop's hatred. The splintering crash of the cup was still in her ears. And the bitter words, too, would not leave her.

What a rain had fallen after the long weeks of drought! Little runnels of water ran across the yard, and joined a gurgling stream in the gutter. The drinking-trough was flooded and stood in a pool, both reflecting the silver light in the east. In the west hung a grand purple cloud, driven through again and again by the pale stilettos of distant lightning, and shaken by far-off thunder.

The crows were up. She heard them coming, emerging from the fastness of their woods by the lagoon.

"Caw—caw—caw— Come along, Kate—come along. Up, Sue! Up, Sue! Speed—speed—speed—Feed, boys, feed!"

They circled above her. Jimmy's crows. Would they perhaps know her for his girl?

They dipped, and rose, and swam through the cool drenched air, peering down at her, she thought, with their bright eyes. A black guard for this last walk through Brancepeth.

"Guard her—speed her—speed her—Jimmy's girl—Who's that? Why, Delight! Delight! Delight!"

Once they fastened on that word Delight how they played with it! They screamed it across the sky till they almost frightened her. They tossed it from one to another, they tore it to fragments and, at last, streamed out of sight, throwing only the last syllable back to her:

"Light! Light! Light! Give us Light!"

Delight was frightened. She half ran up the street trying to catch up to the boy. The wet pavements had now taken on a burnished look. The morning star sank behind the blacksmith shop. A wind rose and pressed on her from behind as though trying to hustle her out of the town. She heard horse's hoofs and the rattle of a cart. It would soon overtake her, all alone in the street.

She stepped into the deep doorway of a shop to hide till the cart should pass. It was almost opposite when the wind caught the sign hanging above her and shook it as though it would cast it down on her. She looked up and saw the name—

JOHN MAYBERRY

TAILOR

Mayberry, the tailor, whose proposal had been the cause of all her troubles! He lived over the shop. He might come down any minute to open his shutters. He might be leaning out of the window now to see who was at his door. She fled out into the street.

A train shrieked in the distance and came roaring toward the town. She would miss her train and be left stranded in this hostile town! Wild with fright she began running toward the station, the dishes rattling unnoticed in the basket. At the first corner the driver of the cart turned his horse into a side street, struck her, and knocked her down. She had run almost blindly against the horse's shoulder.

It shied now and looked askance at her, lying there on the wet road, her hat off, her basket rolled into the ditch.

"Oh, my dishes, my dear dishes!" she wailed. "They'll be broken all to tiny bits." She hid her face in the crook of her arm and broke into sobs.

The man jumped out of his cart and came toward her.

"Are you much hurt?" he asked.

"Oh, I'm not hurt at all! It's my tea set. My Granny's tea set that I've never been parted from yet all this long way."

"Why, it's Delight," said the man. "The girl from The Duke. Whatever are you doing here at this hour of the morning? Whoa, Bessie, whoa, girl. I'll tie her to this post and help you onto your pins."

It was Fergussen, the fishmonger. Delight had talked to him often when he brought fish to the hotel. His broad face looked friendly but she wished he had not seen her. He would tell them all of her mishap and they would think it served her right. He might even tell them that she had run out of the tailor's door.

Fergussen got her to her feet and picked up the basket of dishes. He lifted the canvas that covered them and said cheerfully:

"Nary a crack. They've just rattled about a bit. They're like yourself, they're made of the best material. Now, what I want to know is where you're running to. Are you in some nasty fix?"

"I'm turned off. I'm taking the train to the city."

"Well, you'll never get her, for there she goes now. You'll have to wait for the next."

The train hissed. The bell tolled, changed, and then the locomotive came into view on the level crossing at the end of the street.

"Yes, you've missed her. The next train's at nine o'clock. Four hours to wait, my good girl."

"Oh, whatever shall I do? I can't go back to the hotel, and I don't want to sit waiting at the station with everyone staring at me and all."

"Now, look here, why do you want to go to the city? Cities is no good. They're bad for your 'ealth and bad for your moralities. You're too good-looking, that's the trouble. Now the country's the place for 'andsome girls all over the world, and I've seen 'em all over the world." He struck a heroic attitude in the middle of the road. "I've seen 'em in the Andes with black hair to their knees that a man might choke himself in. I've seen 'em in China with their lovely little eyes like two hot coals. I've seen 'em in Australiar with sunburnt cheeks you'd like to take a bite out of; and let me tell you it's always in the country that you sees 'em at their best."

"I'm going home to England, if ever I can get there."

"Well, old England's not so bad. Never shall I forget the first time I sailed into Plymouth early one Sunday morning. An old tar with me grabbed me by the arm and says— 'There's a pictur' for you, lad,' and a pictur' it was to make you sing with joy."

"But whatever shall I do? I've missed my train, and there's the sun coming up. It's day."

"Now, I'll tell you what. You get into my cart with me and I'll take you somewheres where you can get work. I've a load of fish here I must deliver in Northwood by eight. That's back through the quarry road, past Stebbing where they raise brook trout. Old man Heaslip lives out that way, a well-off old cadger but a little close. He has a farm and a good bit of fruit but the drought made his Indian pickers leave him, and now this grand rainfall will make the thimbleberries fit to burst with juice, and nobody to pick 'em."

"Me to pick fruit? I don't know how."

"Not know how to pick a berry? Come, now, that's too thin! Just hop into the cart with me and I'll set you down at Heaslips'. They'll be kind to you, too, and no one here will know that you're about, if that's what you want. What did you get fired for?"

"Mrs Jessop turned against me. There's my trunk, too."

"Where?" He looked up and down the street.

"Henry was taking it to the station on the wheelbarrow."

"That's easy. We'll pass that way and get it. Hop in now, there's a good girl. You're just the girl for Heaslips." He led the horse about, with the step of the cart invitingly before her.

Delight looked up and down the street. Factory folk were beginning to stir. Windows flamed in the upward slanting sunlight.

"I'll do it," she said. "Anything but sit in that station for hours and hours."

They found the trunk on the end of the platform. Boy and wheelbarrow had disappeared. Fergussen put the trunk before him in the cart and had to sit with his feet dangling. Delight nursed the basket in her lap. And then they jogged out of Brancepeth, the horse's feet splashing into sunlit puddles, the wind blowing Delight's hair all about her face, and throwing down green branches before her on the road. It was a wild, free morning and, as they left the town behind, Delight began to feel happier in spite of herself and to ask the fishmonger questions about himself and his travels. She did not want to be questioned about her present misfortunes or her past life. If she were to speak of the little lodge in the great park in England where she had lived with Gran, she'd break down, she couldn't bear it.

They jogged on through a hilly, stony country of small farms, and old quarries, and bits of cedar wood. White and blue and purple Michaelmas daisies and flaming goldenrod bloomed gladly on the roadside. Shining shocks of grain dotted the stubble fields and, here and there, in vivid green lay a field of young fall wheat.

At seven Fergussen drew up his horse beside a coffee-coloured stream that crossed beneath the road. He said:

"Look here, I think you'd better get out here and wash your face. You got more than a bit of mud on it that time you fell. I've got some sandwiches, too, in the cart and I'll give you one. You don't want to arrive at Heaslip's dirty and hungry, do you? Besides, both my legs is sound asleep along o' this bally box of yours."

They got out. Fergussen loosed the horse's headpiece and she began to crop the wet grass. He opened the canvas curtain of the cart and Delight looked in to see the glittering mass of salmon trout, whitefish, and lake herring lying on broken ice. There were his scales, his knives, his chopping board. There was a basket packed with slabs of finnan haddie. He took out his packet of lunch and a bottle of cold tea.

Delight was ravenous. She had eaten only a few mouthfuls of bread at breakfast and the long drive in the pure morning air had put her healthy body in a glow.

"I'd better wash my face first," she said.

"Well, p'raps you had. You'd be prettier company. There's a log we can sit on across the ditch. This here stream was all but dry when I passed it last, and now look at it, fairly boiling over."

Delight scrubbed her face with her wetted handkerchief till it shone like a schoolboy's and then came and sat down on the log beside the fish-dealer. He put a thick sandwich of bread and cheese into her hand and set the bottle of tea on the grass between them.

"You won't tell a soul you saw me?" urged Delight.

"Never a word, except I seen the boy a-trundling the barrow with your box on it to the station and you after it with your basket."

"And you'll tell Mr Heaslip not to say I'm working for him?"

"Never fear him. He's the greatest man to hold his tongue you ever seen. Now, look you, Miss What's yer-name, this Canada's a great place for opportoonities. You might walk along a country road 'ere, alone in the world, and in the first house you'd stop at to ask for a drink, you'd meet someone who'd want you as a partner for life. You can pick up a mate in no time."

"But I don't want to get married."

He had a pull from the bottle of tea and then observed:

"Well, if you like the single life—same as I do—your own boss, your own bedfellow, and no one to dash cold water on your gladness, it's a great country for that, too, for you've any hamount of chance for adventure. I travels light. I've been livin' in a little shack outside Mistwell three years. Three winters in a little shack on four posts, covered with tar-paper. . . . I may want to move on tomorrow. Wot do I do? I gets a few dollars for my old shack, a few more for my old nag, and I 'eaves the old cart in the river. You won't catch me putting my neck in a yoke."

"Nor me, neither."

"Well, you stick to Heaslips. They have no daughter and they might take a fancy to you and adopt you as their own if you're a good, willing girl, and fall in with their plans. . . . Now we'd better be movin' on. I'd like to spend a silly hour with you on the bank of this stream but I can't afford to do it 'cause my fish'ud go bad on me, so come along, my girl."

IV

Heaslips' farm lay in a fold of two hills, a hot, sandy, secret place where grain headed sparsely yet weeds grew shoulder high, finding fit nourishment in the light soil. The farmland was laid out with no regularity; patches of fruit, of vegetables, or irregular fields of corn were divided by thickets of stunted cedars. All the land was tunnelled by the burrows of rabbits and ground hogs, and the bank of the sluggish stream that moved unheard through a strip of undergrowth and wild shrubs showed strange foot and claw marks.

If this were safety and a harbour, it was mournful safety, thought Delight when Fergussen had driven off and left her with the Heaslips. She had not felt this till his hearty, wholesome presence was removed and she was face to face with her new life.

The house was small and grey, built of thick stone. It looked as though it had sprung from the hillside on which it stood, scarcely emerging, and ready at any time to retreat into the darkness again. Mr and Mrs Heaslip were small and grey like the house. He had little grey side whiskers and round pale eyes. She had a narrow henlike face and a tufted mole on each cheek to match his scant whiskers. They were past seventy and seemed in perfect accord, scarcely needing the aid of speech to communicate with one another. Indeed, they spoke but little, giving each other, instead, understanding looks, composed and secretive. Delight felt that they knew all about her without asking a question. They asked very few, seeming to be intent on settling the question of work and payment and, when that was settled, to desire nothing but to retire into some inner chamber of thought. They moved about noiselessly, speaking in half-whispers. Nothing they did disarranged the order and shining cleanliness of the dim rooms. There were no pets about the house and the barn was too far away for the sounds from there to pierce its stillness. If only poor little Queenie were there, Delight thought, to stamp up and down singing her marching song, and now and then wanting to be hugged! If only Charley were there to trip over his own toes and make one laugh. Delight supposed she would get used to the order and quiet, but after the disorder and cheerful bustle of The Duke of York this was like being suddenly entombed.

It had been arranged that she was to pick thimbleberries, and later on plums at so much a basket and out of her earnings she was to pay for her board. When the fruit was done, if she were satisfactory, she would be paid regular wages as a domestic, that Mrs Heaslip might not have the work of the farmhouse to do in the wintertime. The berries had been so soaked by the rain that it would take a morning's sunshine to dry them sufficiently for picking. In the meantime there was nothing to do but sit in the kitchen and watch those two grey shadows, one reading, one knitting.

She discovered that it was the Bible Mr Heaslip read, and it was a disconcerting discovery. No one she had ever known had read the Bible. Gran had liked to read an almanac or a good tale if she could get one, or even a tract for the sake of the story. Not that she hadn't believed in God! But— "His ways is mysterious, dear child," she had said, "and we'd best not look into them too partic'lar." Yet here was a farmer reading the Bible of a morning and now and again smiling in a triumphant way, as though he and God had a secret between them.

It was ten o'clock. Would it never be noon? Delight longed to go out and wander about but the place held her in a spell. She could not make up her mind to ask Mrs Heaslip if she might.

It was eleven. The clock did not strike. It wheezed a little at the hour but it did not speak. No one spoke. At last Delight whispered:

"Have you any children, ma'am?"

Mr Heaslip looked up from his Bible. His wife looked at him and they smiled their secret smile. Then Mrs Heaslip answered:

"One son. He is married. He lives in that cottage across the line. Maybe you saw it as you came in?"

"Yes, I saw a little cottage. Has he any children?"

Mr Heaslip answered this time:

"He has a son, a year old. We have never seen it."

Delight's cheeks became hotly red. She had unwittingly exposed their secret trouble. Their son, whose child, a dear little baby boy, they'd never seen. Oh, what a troubled world it was! Full of trouble. But, oh, how empty her stomach was! Like a live thing drawing itself into a knot between her ribs. She saw no sign of dinner. Visions of the dinner prepared at The Duke of York rose before her—the great roast of juicy beef, the pork and apple sauce, yes, and it was the day for the Queen of puddings. She could smell the hot jam and see the white drift of meringue. Oh, she was so hungry! She pressed her broad palm against the pit of her stomach. She thought of creamed butter beans; she thought of potatoes and brown gravy; she thought of barley broth, and drowsed, sitting in her chair.

The clock wheezed. It was twelve. Mrs Heaslip was standing by the stove over a frying-pan. The table had been laid for four so noiselessly that Delight had heard nothing. She noticed now that the fourth person had come into the room. He had been washing his hands in the summer kitchen and was pulling down the sleeves of his shirt. He was looking at her out of the sides of his eyes, a thin, sallow boy of eighteen with a shock of stiff mouse-coloured hair.

"Set the chairs up, Perkin," said Mrs Heaslip, and the youth glided to do her bidding with the same secretive quietness of movement as the old people.

"May I help?" inquired Delight, coming forward timidly.

"You can set those on the table." She handed a dish of fried potatoes to Delight who all but dropped them when she saw how few there were. She could easily have eaten them all herself.

"Now we'll sit down if you are ready, Pa," said Mrs Heaslip.

Her husband marked the place in his Bible, laid it down, and came to his place at the head of the table, smiling at her. He said mildly to Delight:

"This young man is Perkin Heaslip, our adopted son. I hope you and him will get on."

The boy smiled sheepishly at his plate.

Mrs Heaslip said:

"Young folks always get on together. In a lonesome place like this you could hardly help it, could you?"

Delight scarcely heard what was being said. Like a greedy child she watched Mr Heaslip lay a bit of cold meat and a small spoonful of potatoes on her plate. She ate them quickly and then noticed with dismay that the others had not much more than begun their helping. Covered with confusion she sat with eyes downcast, her long lashes shadowing the velvet bloom of her cheeks. The three Heaslips observed her beauty with furtive glances, and seemed silently to discuss her points among themselves, as they partook of the light meal.

Small dishes of preserved pears were passed around, also pallid tartlets, containing some custard mixture. Delight was given a cup of hot water coloured with skimmed milk.

"We do not drink tea here," said Mrs Heaslip. "It is bad for the nerves. Perkin does not know the taste of tea. Do you, Perkin?"

"No, Ma," replied Perkin, in a thin, high-pitched voice.

Mr Heaslip said:

"I suppose you saw lots of strong drink at The Duke of York. Mr Fergussen told me you have been working there. If I had my way I'd pour the stuff into the gutters. I never spend a cent in a hotel. I put my horse in the stable of The British American when I go into Brancepeth and I eat my lunch which my wife prepares for me in their parlour but I never spend a cent in the evil place."

"Had you ever heard tell of me in Brancepeth?" inquired Delight anxiously.

"Never a word till the fisherman set you down here this

morning. I had told him to be on the lookout for a likely young girl. I asked no questions except as to your character and he said that was good. . . . Well, Ma, I guess I'll go back to my work. Perkin can show her all about the berries."

He returned to his Bible with a smile at his wife.

V

It was glorious to be out of doors walking beside Perkin toward the barn to get baskets, to feel the soft breeze and smell the delicious country smells after the stuffiness of that dim house, the stagnation of that whispering atmosphere. After the full-blooded people of the hotel these seemed but a company of ghosts. Even the boy looked old and sad, and no wonder he did, poor lad!

"Don't you never go into the town?" she asked.

He shook his head.

"Don't you never have any young company?"

"No."

"Look here," she exclaimed generously. "We'll try to have a little fun while I'm here. I'll liven things up for you. Not in the house, of course, but out among the fruit or in the fields."

He gave her a curious sidelong look, but said nothing.

"My goodness!" she cried, "why don't you speak? Has the pussy got your tongue? Oh, I wish that May were here!"

"Who is May?"

"May's my pal. She's gone home now. She's a regular dear, May is. . . . O-o, what's that writing on the side of the barn? What's it mean?"

In white letters four feet tall on the weather-stained surface were the words—

IF THINE EYE OFFEND THEE
PLUCK IT OUT

The noontide glare struck the words into dazzling brightness. The girl was filled with sudden apprehension. She shrank from entering the barn.

"My goodness," she said, shivering, "what's it for?"

Perkin's look was one of quiet amusement now. "Oh, that's for Joel to see. He's Pa's real son. I'm adopted. Pa and him are enemies, so Pa paints a message up there for him every month. Last month it was somethin' about the serpent's tooth, and we've had lots of 'cursed be he's'—oh, the old man's done some great ones! That's what he reads his Bible for—gettin' new hate-texts dug up to scare Joel."

They stood beneath the letters now that seemed to radiate a fierce heat and energy in the noontide glare impossible to associate with that mild little man in the house.

"And do they scare him?" asked Delight, shivering in spite of the heat.

"I guess they do. He can't take his eyes off that wall as far as he can see it. I often watch him comin' down the road glarin' at it, and when Pa paints up a new one Joel'll sometimes take to his bed for a whole day, he's that upset."

"Pore lad! And his mother—is she against him, too?"

"Against him? Why, she's the fiercest of the two. But she hates his wife far worse than him. That was the trouble. Joel, he married Steven Thurtell's daughter, Mary, and Steven and Pa has been enemies all their lives. Pa would rather an earthquake'd swallow the farm up than to have a grandson of old Thurtell's own it. The day that baby was born all our blinds were pulled down as if we was in mourning, and a new text was painted about the sins of the father being visited on the son. You know the one. Pa did it wonderful. It just glowered at you. The midwife told us that when Mary sat up in bed and saw it she went right into a screamin' spell, and Joel was runnin' round pullin' his hair and cryin' and cursin' like a crazy man."

Perkin's sallow face was alight now with malicious mirth.

"You've found your tongue, haven't you?" Delight said drily. "You can talk fast enough to tell of cruel doings like those. You'd ought to be ashamed. Why it's no better than a bullfight, the way they do in Spain. My Granny had a picture of it. There was the poor bull on his knees and there was three men sticking little knives into him. Oh, it was a sorry sight!"

Perkin was convulsed with laughter, queer, giggling laughter that disgusted Delight.

"A bull," he stammered, "a bull! You'd ought to see Joel. If he was a bull no butcher livin' would give fifty cents for his hide. He's over forty and hump-backed and all broken down with work."

"Working for his father, I suppose, when he was too young, before his bones were set. Where does he work now?"

"He don't get much to do. Folks are afraid to give him work because they're scared of Pa. Now and then we give him a day, so's he won't starve. And he can have all his wood and turnips and potatoes off the place."

"If I was his wife I'd starve before I'd let him take a day's work from that old man."

"Not if you was nursin' a baby, would you?"

"Oh, my goodness," cried Delight, "this is the most unnatural place I've ever struck! Let's go get the baskets so I can begin my work. They're inside, aren't they?"

They went into the barn where sweet-smelling hay, spilled from the lofts, clung to the rafters, strewed the floor. In one corner crates and baskets were piled in disorder, many of them broken or scattered among straw and discarded harness.

Perkin began languidly to delve among them and extricated some of the least battered for Delight's use.

"The Indians have left these in a nice mess," he explained.

Delight watched his movements with interest.

"Who does the work on this comical farm, anyway?" she asked.

"Well, an old feller named Peake and his grandson mostly, this summer. He comes from Mistwell but he's stayin' with his daughter up this way for a while. The Indians do the pickin'. We get Joel in to plant the new beds and hoe the old ones. Pa does the prunin' and I milk the two cows and cultivate when I feel able. I've always been kind of sickly." He straightened himself with a sudden look of pride, and added: "We don't care whether we work or not here. Pa's got lots of money in the bank, and everything's to be mine when he dies. I've seen the will. Don't get it into your head we're poor farmers. I bet you we could buy your old Duke of York twice over, if we wanted. Pa's too busy with his Bible an' everything to care about farm work much. But I'll give you one piece of advice. Don't you try to get seein' Joel and Mary, because you'll lose your place if you do. Pa won't stand for any mixin' between the goats and the ewes. Come on, now, and get at your pickin'. You got to fill your boxes good and full, and don't you go puttin' leaves and stems in the bottom to make them look full, neither."

Delight could scarcely believe her ears. This sickly boy to dare to suggest that she'd do such a thing! In a sudden rage she caught him in her arms and dragged him toward an opening in the floor through which hay was put into the stable below.

"Here, what are you doin'?" he spluttered, clutching her.

"I'm going to throw you down this hole."

"If you do I'll take you with me. Let go! I didn't mean nothin'. I just wanted to see you mad. Let go! Delight! Say, if I had a name like that I'd go an' drown myself. I would truly."

He was laughing now. She laughed, too, and released him.

"You're as strong as a horse," he commented, looking her up and down.

"Well, take care you don't anger me, then, Mister Perkin. If I had a name like Perkin, I'd hang myself to that old rafter."

They picked up the crates and set out for the thimbleberry canes. Perkin was giggling as he walked ahead of her along the hot, sandy path that ran beside a heavily laden orchard.

"What is the joke?" asked Delight, staring at his narrow back and sloping shoulders.

"You thinking you're stronger than me. I could put you down and hold you if I had a mind to, you'd soon find out."

"I advise you not to try any tricks with me."

He looked over his shoulder at her with his malicious smile.

"Wait and see," he said.

The thimbleberries stretched before them now, a myriad of graceful, bending canes, swarthy berries clustered among the thorns. Here and there a bright spear of goldenrod shot upward, or a milkweed pod had burst and scattered its drift of silver down upon the russet-coloured leaves. A partridge had brought her young out from the woods to feed upon the fallen berries that lay thickly on the hot ground; but she called them and they sailed away with a loud drumming as the two approached.

"That's the way when you haven't got your gun," mourned Perkin.

"Ah, the dear little things," said Delight.

She was glad when he had gone and she was left alone among the canes. It was a pretty spot, she thought, and though the brilliant sky, the vivid colours, and sharp lights and shadows gave a foreign look, still there was something homely here, something very sweet.

She began to pick berries, dropping them swiftly into the box which was set inside another, conveniently tied against her stomach with a piece of binder twine so that both hands might be free. Perkin had tied it on for her and so equipped she felt at once competent and business-like. It was to be the emblem of her craft, as the tray had been in the dining-room of the hotel.

When the box was half full she thought she would taste the fruit. She popped a berry into her mouth, glancing hastily about beforehand to see that none of the Heaslips were in sight. It lay on her tongue large, warm, and soft as velvet.

She pressed it against the roof of her mouth, and the juice spurted from it and trickled down her throat like honey. She had to smile, it was so delicious. Her body contracted in a little shiver of delight. She began to eat the berries even faster than she had picked them for her box. She did not stay in one spot but darted here and there like a great golden butterfly after the biggest and ripest. Her arm struck the box she had half filled and upset it, scattering the berries over the ground. She did not mind. Deeper and deeper into the forest of canes she went, deeper and safer and farther away from the troubling world. Her heart danced out to meet the solitude and peace. Her hungry lips advanced, pouting, toward each approaching berry.

She thought she would sit down, here in the middle of the canes, and rest a bit. She was not really tired but a little sleepy after being awake all but one hour of the night and so harried by Mrs Jessop. She found a little sandy knoll overgrown with coarse grass, just big enough to sit on. Here she dropped with the canes arching over her head. A light breeze stirred them and the reddish leaves whispered together. A tiny goldfinch sprang on to a spray beside her and burst into the sweet medley of his autumn song. The spray swayed beneath him but he clutched it, all on a slant, and still sang on. A bit of milkweed fluff sailed shining between the canes. It caught in her hair and clung. This country scene seemed to enfold her, to make her one with it. Oh, if Jimmy were only here! If he only loved her as he had! She would be willing to marry him and settle down to be a quiet, good wife in a spot like this. Her head drooped to her updrawn knees. Soon, she was fast asleep.

Something in the springlike sweetness of the air made the goldfinch think that, after all, it might be as well to reline the old nest, just in case—well, his mate (he thought she was the one who had been his mate but, at any rate, another just as good) had cocked her head in a funny way at him only that morning. He espied the bit of fluff in Delight's hair. He darted downward, caught it in his beak along with one of Delight's curly hairs, tweaked angrily to get it free, gave up in despair, abandoning all hope of a new brood, and broke into a fresh ripple of song.

Fast asleep Perkin found her when the afternoon was waning, her boxes empty, her mouth berry-stained, her eyes, when she raised them to him, hazy with dreams of Somerset and Gran.

She was conscience-smitten at what she had done, deeply grateful to Perkin when he promised not to let the elders know of her delinquency. A new pride straightened the youth's shoulders as he found this lovely big creature suddenly timid and submissive to him. He would help her fill her boxes but she must work hard, too, or nothing worth while could be accomplished. He kept her beside him, ordering her brusquely about, sending her down the long rows for the crates, showing her how to pack the boxes in them with the fillers between.

Two crates were filled by six o'clock. Fifty-four boxes, at a cent and a half a box, meant eighty-one cents for Delight. Perkin paid her (though he had picked the greater part) in little red tickets to be redeemed at the end of the week.

VI

She was in her little room under the eaves, getting ready for bed at last. Mr and Mrs Heaslip had their bedroom downstairs. She and Perkin had climbed the short steep stair and entered the two doors opposite each other in the boxlike passage that smelled of old clothes, old boots, old cooking, and candle grease. But in her room there was a rather nice smell of fruit. She could not locate it at first. Then, putting the candle on the floor, she looked under the bed and discovered a basket filled with yellow-and-red striped Duchess apples. Gently she took one from the top and rose to her feet, candle in hand. She gave a guilty look about the room before she set her teeth in it. Was she never to be anything but hungry on this unnatural farm? But what healthy girl wouldn't be hungry after a tea of one thin slice of bread, a saucer of sweet preserves, and a scrap of stale cake? No wonder the boy looked half-starved, no wonder the son, Joel, was broken down at forty. Probably Perkin kept this basket hidden here for his own private eating. Well, he would scarcely grudge her one.

As she stood, pensively eating the apple, with the candlelight touching the red of her lips, the tawny tints of her skin and hair, she was like some simple Eve, tasting the fruit of life, unheedful of what lurked in the shadows about her.

Her room at The Duke of York seemed spacious in comparison with this closet that was overcrowded by the cot-bed, a battered chest of drawers, a broken spinning-wheel, and her tin box. The house was terribly quiet, though it was only nine o'clock. Between tea and bedtime the hours had seemed endless, helping Mrs Heaslip with the dishes, holding yarn for her, looking at a catalogue of one of the great city stores and, at last, nodding while Mr Heaslip read a chapter from the Old Testament and prayed in a low conversational tone to God. It was so intimate. It had made Him seem terribly near. Mr Heaslip had spoken about the text on the barn in his prayer, and she thought of God as leaning down from a low purple thundercloud to examine it. She wished some one would make a noise in the house. The preparations for bed of these people were made in stealthy quiet. She, too, laid her shoes carefully under the bed and her garments one by one on the trunk. She put on her coarse nightgown, buttoned close to the neck, and braided her cloud of strong wheat-coloured hair.

She knelt to say her prayer—a stalwart young figure, her face buried in her arms. She said slowly, in a husky whisper, "Now I lay me," as Gran had taught her. She had never in her life made a personal appeal to the Deity, but the intimacy of the old man downstairs gave her assurance. Surely if He would listen to a cruel old man with whiskers. He would lend an ear to a nice-tempered, decent young girl like her. Of course she knew He was partial to men, and to whiskers, too. She had always known that. But still, she was an honest girl, if not very religious, and would become, as she grew older, even better and more religious, especially if He granted this prayer.

She bent her head lower, and breathed:

"Oh, God, please let Granny's tea set not be broken. I fell on the road in Brancepeth with it this morning and I've been afraid to look at it all day. Please, God, it rattled terrible, but even if it was broken, I know Thou canst mend it in a twinkling if only Thou willst. I know it's only a tea set but Gran set great store by it, and it's all I have of her, and please, God, it's apple-green and it's in the covered basket behind the door—please don't leave it broke. Amen."

She was breathless. She did not rise from her knees at once. She would give God time.

When, at last, she took the basket up and set it on the trunk she could hardly find courage to open it. Cautiously she removed the canvas cover, and examined the cups, each wrapped separately, one by one. Green and smooth, and glowing like jewels, she set them out. Twelve of them without a chip, except, of course, the old, old chips that scarcely showed and did not count at all. The sugar bowl, fat and round, like a crinolined old lady with her hands on her hips. The milk jug with its generous curling lip. But dare she look at the teapot, most precious of all? She had seen Granny drain the last drop from its curly spout, her head in its frilled cap thrown back, both hands clasping the pot. Cautiously she undid it from its wrapper. *Not a chip!*

Safe. Darling old teapot. Darling teapot. Darling, darling God.

Oh, but she was grateful to Him! Her whole body quivered with love and gratitude. She could not bear to part with the pot tonight. She would lay it on the other pillow, next the wall where it could not roll off. It would be company, a bedfellow, almost. She placed it snugly on the pillow, smiled at it tenderly, blew out the light, and got in beside it.

It really was company in this lonely place. She laid one warm hand on its shiny fluted belly. Its spout curved toward her parted lips.

She thought:

"I am so happy I cannot sleep."

And, in a moment, she slept.

CHAPTER VIII

SEPTEMBER KISSES

DELIGHT had finished her day's picking. She and Perkin had filled baskets with Damsons and Golden Drops and Green Gages from six that morning. It had been beautiful among the plum trees in the hazy sunlight, with the piles of gold and purple fruit getting higher and higher as more baskets were added. Perkin and she were good friends now. A change had come over him in the last month. He was as silent, as mysterious in the house as ever but, out of doors, at their work he had become companionable. They were always together now, and the old people did not seem to mind. In fact they looked pleased when the two came in together. Joel was given more and more work to do on the farm, ploughing, cultivating, pruning and, when he was there, Perkin never left her side. She never had a chance to speak with Joel, though she would have liked to, till Perkin told her that Joel and his wife hated the very sight of her, and after that she turned her head the other way.

Perkin was almost always kind to her though occasionally sombre fits would overtake him when he would not speak to her for hours or, if he did speak, it was to find fault with the way she filled her baskets or missed branches that bore fruit. Sometimes he would jostle her out of his way, shoving his thin body against hers, with a strange, sullen gleam in his eyes. She was almost afraid of him.

She had earned enough at the fruit picking to pay for her board. Not a cent had been saved, though, and such board! Black, leathery meat, sodden pastry, half-sour bread, and not enough of anything. She had not minded much because she almost lived on fruit, but what would one do when the fruit was over? They had said nothing yet about her staying on, though she knew from remarks Perkin had made that it was intended that she should. Mrs Heaslip had once said something about teaching her to knit later on.

The truth was that she was afraid to leave. If she did, she must drive to Brancepeth to take the train, and whom might she not meet in Brancepeth? The last night there seemed a nightmare. Her life there was but a dream. Now this life, as another dream, enfolded her. She rarely thought and, when she did, it was in a puzzled, groping way. She hated to think. She lived from dawn to dark among the fruit, and at night slept dreamlessly beneath the eaves. There she was, strong, vital, rosy among these sallow, silent Heaslips, a creature of instincts, emotions, not much more developed intellectually than the soft-eyed Jersey in the byre, nor the wood pigeon that called among the cedars. Like the birds she felt a stir within her that urged her to fly before the winter, but she knew not where to fly, nor had she the money to take her farther than Brancepeth.

The past month had made a change in her. She was thinner, and her face, neck, and arms were tanned a deep golden brown. Her hair, from going hatless in the sun, had been bleached almost to straw colour. Her eyes looked larger, deep, and ambient, beneath the thick lashes. Her hands and arms were covered with innumerable tiny scratches from thorns of the thimbleberry canes, and the skin on them was dry from constant burning of the sun....

She was going to the stream to gather watercress for her tea. A fresh new growth had appeared and, though the Heaslips looked askance at her plate heaped with it, she still brought it to the table, for her stomach was stubborn and the hunger refused to be appeased by bread and jam and tarts. She pictured herself in the winter going to the roothouse to gnaw the turnips and mangolds. Why had God made her so hungry and then set her down here where there was so little food? Still she must not think hardly of Him, for there was her tea set all safe and sound. . . .

The sky was like the inside of a shell this evening, all blending shades of pink and mauve and blue. Little gold-edged clouds as light as thistledown swam slowly in the silken air. No birds sang; but the stream gave forth a dreamy, sensuous song of its own as it pushed its sluggish way through reeds and grass. Down here she was so alone. It was her own safe place where no one came. She knelt on the narrow bridge of moss-grown boards and plunged her hands into the water among the cress. It was icy cold, delicious on her hot arms. She bent lower and pressed her palms on the cold sandy bottom of the stream among the roots of watercress. The old growth was covered with pretty white flowers, like candytuft, and its leaves were bronze, but the new was short and green and tender. She began to pluck it carefully and lay it on the boards beside her. When she had a fair bunch she still lingered, pressing her cold, wet palms to her cheeks, her finger ends against her temples. It was inside there her brain was, the part one thought with, was cautious with, religious with. But the heart, right beneath the left breast, was the part one loved with, suffered with, sinned with. Gran had told her all this, and she was very glad she knew such things, for some poor girls were desperate ignorant of their insides and they got into trouble like as not.

She gazed dreamily at the tangle of lush growth around her, the tall Michaelmas daisies, the dogwood with its red stem and lead-coloured berries, the elderberry's richly purple cluster, the flaming spear of the butterfly weed, a patch of fringed gentian, like a bit of the sky fallen. No bluer, though, than the blue heron that started suddenly from among the cattails and flapped his great wings upward into the blue above. What had startled him? Someone moving there in the shadow of that black cedar.

It was Perkin. He came toward her slowly, his feet sinking in the moist velvet of the stream's brink, his large grey eyes fixed on her with an odd look.

"Why, Perkin, is that you?" And she explained: "I'm gathering watercress for my tea."

He came out on the board and knelt down beside her.

"Getting watercress, eh? You've struck a quiet place all right. It's as quiet as the bottom of the sea, ain't it?"

"There's a fresh growth come up. It's as tender as can be. Don't you like watercress?"

He shook his head. "I don't like any green stuff."

"Not when it's young and tender?" She did not like him so close beside her in that lonely spot. She did not like the way his breath came, so quickly and yet so heavily. Trying to be unembarrassed, a little playful, she held the fresh wet bunch of watercress against his mouth.

"Buy my watercress," she intoned, imitating an Old Country vender. "Fresh and tender. Fresh and tender."

In a sudden anger he tore it from her hand and flung it back into the stream. Then with a boy's sudden brutality he caught her to him and pressed his face cruelly against hers, twining his arms about her, struggling to join his lips to hers.

"You're fresh and tender," he gasped. "I want you. Now . . . now. . . ." He kept on repeating—"Now—" as they struggled. He seemed beside himself with passion. Could this be the sickly boy Perkin? Why, his arms were like steel. His head like a darting snake's.

Delight was filled with terror, as a doe that, having come to drink at a peaceful stream, finds herself attacked by some fierce creature of the forest.

"Let me go! Let me go! I'll scream."

Perkin laughed, his lips hot against hers. "Scream then. Go ahead, scream."

He said no more and she ceased to struggle, lying quietly in his arms, her eyes half-closed. She felt faint under the fury that blazed in his. She was conscious that his cheek and chin were beardless as a girl's, that he smelled of straw, of fruit, of hot human flesh. She lay so quietly that the boy laughed again in triumph.

"I said you'd find out some day which of us is the strongest. Now you know, eh?" He drew his head backward, with that snakelike gesture. He wanted to look into her face just a few inches below his, lying there, flushed, terrified, weak.

"Now you know, eh? Say, I've been dreaming of when I'd do this for a month. From the first minute I set eyes on you. As soon as I knowed you was to be my wife."

Her eyes were wide-open now, tragic; her clenched hands against his breast.

"Your wife, Perkin!"

"Well, that's what Fergussen brung you here for, isn't it? Aw, don't pretend you didn't know!"

"Fergussen. But why—why? He brought me here 'cause I ran away from the hotel. I didn't know where to go and he brought me here."

Perkin giggled. "Say, you are a little goose. Do you s'pose you've been any use here, to speak of? I mean the thimble-berries. Why it'd have taken ten like you to have picked enough to be worth while. It made me laugh to hitch up the wagon to take them to the station. We'd decided to let the crop go. The price wasn't worth pickin' them for anyway. We just put you at 'em to give you something to do, see?"

She was utterly bewildered. "But what did you want me for, then?"

"For this." He kissed her again. Then—"To marry me. To be my wife. Mrs Perkin Heaslip. Fergussen knowed. Pa told him to fetch us a likely girl from town, so's I could marry her and make things sure. And make Joel sicker than ever . . . and he fetched you. . . . And Pa's got texts picked out to paint on the barn to celebrate the marriage and when you get a baby, and all. . . ."

He kissed her again in ecstasy, rocked her in his arms. . . . A shadow fell, a chill rose from the stream. Something crept out of the water onto the brink and, with a squeak of anger and fear, leaped back again, making a tiny splash.

Delight shivered. Perkin's wife . . . forever shut in that secret farm . . . all that hate . . . those terrible texts on the wall . . . Perkin's arms about her, his blazing grey eyes. . . .

Suddenly Jimmy's eyes were looking into hers, pleading, blue as a little child's; and his mouth, tender, a little sulky, but a dear mouth, after all. Oh, she loved Jimmy; she would not give in to Perkin. Stronger than she? Ah, but not more knowing. Her fingers twined themselves in the breast of his shirt. Her muscles stiffened. Her legs gripped the planks. Another effort, and she had thrown him from her into the water. Down among the watercress—into the soft, cold bed of the stream. He cried out as he struck the water. It splashed all over her, yet through the flying drops she saw his face upturned, terrified, contorted with rage.

She was flying from the place. She kept out of sight of

the house, dodging behind bushes till she reached an old broken wall, alongside which she ran in a crouching posture till she gained the barnyard. A flock of geese waddled toward her, squawking with wings upraised, their roguish little eyes twinkling up at her, Delight, the poor farm girl, dripping wet, exhausted, her pulses throbbing like so many separate hearts. She could not hear the noises of the barn for their din. She pressed herself into the strawstack and listened. By degrees the geese settled down again to their supper, still scolding about her in an undertone, still casting jeering looks and rocking on their short legs when they noticed her. The sound of milk hissing against a tin pail came out to her. Old Peake was milking, then. She might safely reach the loft.

She crept around the corner toward the door that led to the loft. Mr Heaslip had been working on a new text that day Now, in the reddish light, the letters blazed out at her:

VENGEANCE IS MINE

She fled with terror into the barn. Up the ladder she scrambled, thinking:

"Oh, let me once get up into the hay, and I'll hide there until morning. Then, in the early morning, I'll run away. Anywhere away from this frightening place."

She buried herself in the clean, prickly hay, drawing it over her in great sheafs, burrowing into it till she was out of sight.

Long fingers of sunlight quivered between the cracks. She could smell the fresh paint of the text outside the wall. . . . After a time Peake came up the steps to put down hay for the horses. They knew it, for they were stamping and uttering little impatient whinnies. Old Major was kicking his drinking pail about, as he always did when he heard the swish of the falling hay. What if Peake should stick his fork into her, kill her dead? They would find her body and perhaps they would be sorry. Tears of pity for that poor pierced body filled her eyes.

At last there was silence, save for the happy munching below and, now and again, the rattle of a chain or a sleepy low from the byre, or the anguished cry of a fowl on the perch. Darkness fell.

The blackness of night closed over her like a great wing. She stared, open-eyed, into the dark. She thought:

"Ah, if I only had the tiniest bit of company! If only Lizzie, the cat, knew I was here she'd come and snuggle in beside me, I know. It's an awful thing to be in a big barn alone at night, with a comical text like yonder one on the wall."

As she stared, a firefly darted out from a crack somewhere and began to flit here and there before her eyes. Fiery little dashes it made, like bright stitches on the dark skirt of night. A sense of comfort warmed her. She thought:

"There, now. I hardly wish a thing till I get it. I always was a lucky one. If he will only stop about till I can get to sleep. . . ."

Even when she slept he did not leave her but flew about the loft with his little lamp all night.

CHAPTER IX

BEEMER'S

I

SHE awoke in the silver dawn, her limbs cramped by a curled-up position, the rough hay scratching her tender neck, the chill of an autumn morning sending shivers to her very marrow. Her dress had not yet dried from the splash caused by Perkin's fall into the stream and clung damply to her bosom. She crept to a crack, and through it looked at the farmhouse. It squatted, low and grey, on the hillside, a scarf of mist rising toward it from the stream. A dead house sheltering ghosts it seemed. Sinister ghosts who were angry because she would not stay and be another ghost. Not that Perkin had not life in him. But it was a cruel flame that frightened her. She must run from all this. She did not know where except that it must be the opposite direction from Brancepeth, somewhere past the quarries and Stebbing where they bred brook trout, to some place where no one had ever heard of her.

She descended the ladder and went to the byre. The Jersey cow was lying down, her black face resting against her bony cream-coloured flank, her liquid eyes gazing dreamily before her.

"Get up, Jersey," said Delight, slapping her.

The cow could not understand such an unusual proceeding, and closed her eyes as though to shut out the apparition.

But when she was slapped again she rose and swished her plumed tail about her legs and put her nose in her drinking pail.

Delight found an empty tin and washed it at the well in the corner, by the pulping machine. She brought a stool then, sat down by the Jersey, and milked the tin full. The cat came bounding and rubbed herself against Delight's skirt, rolling her beseeching topaz eyes at her. Delight sent a stream of milk toward her, and Lizzie, her tigerish jaws distended, received every drop into her greedy throat.

"You don't deserve it, you naughty little cat," said Delight, "for you wouldn't come and sleep with me last night."

She raised the tin to her own mouth then and drank the foamy, warm contents. She was alone in the world, as poor as a girl could well be, stealing a breakfast of milk in a byre, yet she was happy; a sense of freedom, of early morning adventure, made her pulses thrill. Through an open window a fresh breeze came but a few drops of rain came with it, and a shadow fell, making the byre dimmer than before. Perhaps it was not so early as she had thought. She had better hurry away before old Peake appeared. It might, after all, be nearer seven than she imagined.

Even as the doubt crossed her mind she heard a heavy step outside. Then the door of the stable was swung open and the horses broke into eager whinnyings.

"Morning to you, old Major," she heard Peake's thin voice saying.

She dropped the tin and flew to the ladder. She clambered up breathlessly, and then stood listening. He passed below, pitchfork in hand.

"Morning to you, Jersey," he greeted. "Morning, cows."

She was trapped up there in the mow.

What a pity she had run away! Better have stood her ground and brazened it out before old Peake. He could not have stopped her running away. Even now it would be better to descend the ladder and face him alone than to be caught up there by Perkin or Mr Heaslip who would soon be at work on the new text. She went down slowly and met the old man carrying a pail of water. His look of vacant busyness changed to the one of dazed admiration with which he always regarded her. He set down his pail.

"Morning, girl," he said, showing his gums beneath his ragged moustache.

"Morning, Mr Peake. I'm going away."

"Going away! Well, now. What'd that be for? Ain't they givin' ye enough to eat? I know their ways. I've worked for 'em, livin' in, and I know their table with no more grub than'd fatten a chipmunk. I bring my own dinner-pail with meat sandwiches and a bottle of tea or I wouldn't have the stren'th to hoe their old weeds that grows like all possessed on this pesky farm."

"It's not the food. It's Perkin. I'm expected to marry him and I don't want to."

"Marry Perkin! No, no, you're too fine a big lass. Oh, no, no, no. I wouldn't have you marry Perkin. He's only a Home boy. Still—they say he's goin' to inherit all the money."

"I don't care. I threw him in the stream yesterday."

"Threw Perkin in the stream! Well, I never. My, but you're strong! A fine strong young girl. Now, tell us what he did to make you give him a duckin'. Don't be afraid. Every word, now." He laid his horny hand on her shoulder and stroked it.

But she was not listening to him. She was listening to a rattle of wheels, to the sharp sound of a horse's hoofs outside.

"Hallo, in there!" a voice called.

Peake hurried forth.

"Where's Mr Heaslip?" went on the voice. "Is he about yet?"

Delight began to creep toward the door at the far end of the byre. She would escape while the stranger engaged Peake's attention. Then something in the stranger's voice caught her ear, held her motionless. He was saying:

"I want to complain of the milk he's sending in to me. It's no' up to the standard. He says he keeps a Jairsey and a half-Jairsey. Weel, the unnamed half must give water, I suspect."

It was the voice of Kirke.

"I wouldn't put it past him," the old man answered.

Delight threw open the door and ran to the nigh wheel of the cart in which Kirke, in a raincoat and bowler hat, with a long whip in his hand, was perched. His lean, highly coloured face was fresh with the moisture of the morning. His gimlet eyes were sternly fixed on the labourer.

"Oh, Mr Kirke," cried Delight. "Will you give me just a little lift away from here? I'm that upset. I've thrown Perkin in the stream and I won't marry him and, dear me, I'd all but gone and left my china—" She burst into tears.

"So this," said Kirke, "is where you're hanging out."

"The poor girl is all upset," explained Peake. "By the look of her I believe she's spent the night in the mow."

Kirke bent over her as she clung, sobbing, to the wheel. "What have they been doing to ye, lass?"

"Oh, my poor china," she wailed, "how can I ever get it out of that house, after me throwing Perkin in the stream and all?"

"It's terrible," said Peake. "They want to marry her to their boy, and she handled him rough, and she's hid all night in the mow, and they're holdin' her belongings, and won't pay her her wages, and she's half-starved."

"Weel," bit off Kirke, cracking his whip, "you have got yourself in a fine pickle."

Delight clung to the wheel and raised her eyes piteously to his. "Mr Kirke, if you will only go to the house and get me the china tea set that I brought across the ocean and have never been parted from since I lost my Granny, I'll bless you the rest of my days. I don't mind about my clothes. I'll leave them gladly if only I can get my—"

"Hop into the cairt," interrupted Kirke. "I'll see what can be done."

She climbed to the seat beside him and, wheeling rapidly about, he drove to the side door of the farmhouse. He jumped out and knocked with the butt of his whip. To Delight he seemed nothing less than a god come to deliver her, a god in a raincoat and a jaunty bowler hat, but a god, nevertheless. Oh, but she was afraid! Even sitting up there in the high cart, with Kirke between her and the door, she was afraid of the Heaslips. Her eyes, wild and mournful, were fixed on the panels. A dragging sound came from within. Then the door opened softly and Mr Heaslip appeared on the threshold, the basket containing the tea set in his hand. With lowered eyes he set it outside on the stone step, then turned back again. Mrs Heaslip now appeared holding one end of the little tin trunk. Her husband took up the other end and together they set it out beside the basket.

"Now about that milk," began Kirke, in a high, complaining voice.

The door was shut in his face. The lock clicked. The red in Kirke's cheeks became scarlet. He turned angrily to the window where Mr Heaslip was now visible, seating himself with a benign expression, his Bible before him.

"You've used this poor geerl very badly!" shouted Kirke.

A hand—Mrs Heaslip's—appeared inside the pane. The blind was drawn.

"Weel—I'm domned!" said Kirke.

II

They were bowling along swiftly toward Brancepeth now. Delight was nursing her basket, scarcely able to believe that she was delivered safely from the Heaslips, that her tea set was safe on her lap. Kirke had even arranged with Peake to take her trunk to his daughter's house on his wheelbarrow, and to have his daughter's husband deliver it at Kirke's shop the next day, when he was driving in with a load of turnips. Delight had, by his order, lifted the lid and found her clothes neatly packed within. She had taken out her brown cloth jacket and rather crushed velvet tam with a quill in it, and a clean print dress. She had put on the jacket and tam, and laid the print dress on the top of the basket, blindly obeying Kirke.

She did not speak till they were long out of sight of the farm, then she asked in a trembling voice:

"Where are you going to take me, Mr Kirke? I hope you don't think as I could ever go to work in Brancepeth again, for I couldn't. Besides no one there would ever give me work after the tales Mrs Jessop would tell of me, and all. Perhaps you'd know of some village where I could get work in a factory."

"We'll talk of that later," replied Kirke. "What I want to know first is how you came to get into Heaslip's hands. By the way, is that the basket I carried up the stairs for you the nicht you first arrived?"

"Yes. I've never been parted from it since my Granny died. It's all I have in the world that belonged to her."

Kirke looked down at her inquisitively.

"It's always—'Granny—Granny' with you. Had ye no mother, then? I've often wondered about you, and I think, considering everything, it's only fitting you should tell me the truth about yourself. You've got some blood in you that's not a common sort, I'll be bound. . . . Is your mother dead?"

"Yes. She died when I was born. I only knew Gran. She kept the lodge on a gentleman's estate, and after she died I went up to London with another maid and got work in a public house."

"I see. Now what about your mother? Where did she get you? You needn't be afraid to tell me. I can keep a secret if ever a man can. . . . Was it the gentleman whose lodge your grandmother kept? Or did she go up to London, too?"

The horse's hoofs made a pleasant clatter, the wheels a humming sound. A shaggy hill, with the first frost-touched maple crowning it, stood out against the rainy sky.

Kirke peered into her face.

"She was a beauty, eh?"

"Yes, Mr Kirke, and she did go to London, sorely against my Granny's will."

"To work in a pub?"

"Oh, no." She was indignant. "She was stage-struck. And she learned how to dance with a lot of other girls. She was that beautiful that everybody noticed her. But not the same as me—finer like. All pink and white, and eyes as blue as harebells."

"And then she met your father, eh?"

"You'll never tell a soul one word of this? I've never told anyone here but May and Jimmy. Oh, please tell me about Jimmy. Is he well? And has he taken out another girl yet?"

Kirke replied curtly: "We'll talk of Jimmy later. . . . So your mother lairned to dance, and a handsome young man—or oldish, maybe—noticed her? Is that so, Delight?"

"He came with some Russian dancers, and he had grand dark eyes, and he could dance—dear me! Mother told Gran he could leap his own height in the air, and stamp and twirl and bound till he took your breath away. All London came to see him. And his muscles was like iron and his hair like beautiful black fur. Mother told Gran about him just once, after she'd come home, and then she never spoke of him again. I reckon her heart was broken. And Granny hated the very thought of him, but she told me 'cause she thought I'd a right to know."

"Weel, weel," said Kirke, staring meditatively between the horse's ears, "it's an interesting tale, and it's safe with me, you may depend." He was gratified by this revelation of the girl's origin. It pleased him to think of that bounding, leaping Russian giving his grand dark eyes to this sweet Delight by his side. No wonder dancing came naturally to her! No wonder she had a strange, exotic charm! Somerset and Moscow! A strange mixture.

"And who gave ye the name?" he asked.

"Delight? Mother named me that before I was born, because he used to call her his delight in his queer English—not much better than baby-talk, and she told Gran that if the child was a girl, it was to be Delight, and if it was a boy it must be Ivan, after him. And Gran held to it though she thought it an unchristian sort of name but she used to say afterward that it just suited me."

"It does. Now, then, tell me how you got to Heaslips'."

She poured out the story of her quarrel with Jimmy, of Bastien's asking her inside his room a moment to see some trinkets he had brought from Africa, of Mrs Jessop's finding them. (Here Kirke smiled grimly, remembering his own part in the discovery.) She told of the terrible night she had spent with the storm raging outside and Mrs Jessop watching her door the long hours through, of her departure, of her meeting with the fishmonger, of her life at the Heaslips'.

"Weel," commented Kirke, "you've managed to pack an extraordinary lot of experience into a brief while. We haven't been exactly dull in Brancepeth, either."

"Please, tell me about Jimmy?"

"Jimmy!" answered Kirke laconically, flicking the mare's shoulder neatly with the whip, so that she plunged forward. "Ah, he's gone. Went the day after you did."

"Gone!" She was aghast. She clutched her basket, fearing she would let it fall in her agitation. "Gone! But where? Why?"

Kirke grinned at her with amusement.

"Why, to sairch for you, to be sure. When Mrs Jessop told in the morning that she'd sent you packing, Jim had already gone to his work, but as soon as he came in for his dinner he haird the news and he raised a fine to-do. He told the old geerl she was no better than a murderess to send a lass like you into a city all alone. Bastien ordered him to leave the house. Bastien and I had words, for he'd got it into his silly head that I had set Mrs Jessop after you. Annie and Pearl were crying. The cook burned the joint to a cinder. But it was good for business, for you couldn't have packed another man into the bar that night. Then Fergussen appeared and said he'd seen you going to the station before sunrise, and that you came out of Mayberry the tailor's shop. Jim had been drinking a good deal in the afternoon, and he hit Fergussen fair on the mouth. Fergussen knocked him down. Then Bastien and Charley Bye put him out. Jimmy—"

"Oh, my own pore Jimmy!" broke in Delight, rocking her basket. "Pore lad!"

"Jimmy went straight to Mayberry's and asked him if it was true and the poor little man took his oath he'd never laid eyes on you. That didn't help him much, for Jimmy lifted him off his bench and gave him the finest beating he'd ever had. That done he took the train for the city and hasn't been haird of since. He told the station-master he'd walk the streets till he found you. But he'd soon change his mind when he sobered up, and by now he's happy with another lass you can be cairtain."

"But I'll never forget him, and mebbe when he doesn't find me in the city he'll come back to Brancepeth to look for me. Don't you think he might, Mr Kirke?"

"Weel," agreed the Scot, "I should think he micht. His box with his clothes in it is still in his room. The room's vacant yet. Things aren't prosperous at The Duke of York. Lovering and I have left. We're stopping at The British American now."

"Oh," said Delight, trying to be agreeable, "and do you like it there?"

"It micht be better and it micht be worse. The house is dingy and dark, but the board is fair. I'm out to help Beemer improve it. You know, I have a nice dairy business stairted, and I've a produce shop now in connection with it. I supply Beemer with fresh eggs, milk, cheese, butter and poultry from the country. . . . Now my plan is to supply him with another product of the country—a nice, fresh dining-room geerl—"

"No, no, no, I wouldn't go to Beemer's to work—right next door and all—I couldn't do that."

Kirke turned his head sharply toward her.

"Don't be a fool, my geerl. It's your one chance of meeting your lad again, to stop here in Brancepeth, where he's bound to turn up sometime to fetch his box. Now I'll tell you what I'll do. I'll get his box for you, and you can keep it in your room at Beemer's, so he can never get away with it without your knowledge. And another thing, I'll see to it that Beemer gives you five dollars a month more than you got from Mrs Jessop. Now be a sensible lass and be guided by a man who knows the wairld a little better than you do. And I'm fond of you, too, though I may not be willing to be your slave as these other silly blighters are. Now, will you do what I tell you?"

"Y-yes, I'll do it," she answered sadly. "Though I'll never put my nose outside the door where I might meet Mrs Jessop, or any of the other folk from The Duke."

"Nobody wants you to put your nose outside the door. All you have to do is to wait at table and look pleasant. Now I'm going to take ye to my shop and you'll sit there while I telephone to Beemer. It may be that he won't want ye at all, but I think I can manage him."

III

Delight was sitting in the whitewashed room behind Kirke's shop, waiting with much trepidation while he rang up the proprietor of The British American. The little room was beautifully clean. Through the polished windows the yellow September sunlight, suddenly flaring along the slanting rain, fell on rows of mellow cheeses ranged on shelves against the wall. In a cupboard with glass doors, she could see pound prints of butter and sections of honey in the comb. On a table stood a deep basket filled with clean brown eggs. She wished that she owned a shop like this. She pictured herself behind the counter in the shop selling this tempting produce to dear old ladies with little round baskets, and to young wives carrying red-cheeked babies in their arms. She would give a little taste of honey to the babies, just to see them smack their funny little lips.

She could hear Kirke's voice talking on and on in the next room. His words did not come to her, but he broke now and again into a cackling laugh. The truth was that Kirke's body was tingling with triumph. Ever since his quarrel with Bastien and his departure from the house, he had been filled with vindictive energy against The Duke of York and its two managers. He was trying to persuade the Byes to leave, and start a small boarding-house of their own. He knew of several of the third-floor boarders who would be willing to go with them. He sneered at the pair for being slaves to Bastien and Mrs Jessop. . . .

She sat quietly, her hands in her lap, while Kirke's voice hummed on and on; like a great bee she thought. She wondered why she felt so light-headed; the cheeses seemed to be dancing up and down. Then she remembered that she had had nothing to eat since her dinner the day before save some plums and the drink of milk from the Jersey. Oh, she was so hungry! If only she had a little bit of cheese! Or a mouthful of honey! A knife lay on the table. One of the largest of the cheeses was already cut. Desperately she snatched up the knife and cut herself a large thin slice. She sat down again and began to eat it, her eyes fixed anxiously on the door through which Kirke would enter. There was no sound in the other room. Kirke must be listening to Mr Beemer for a change.

It was nearly noon and she was so hungry. She finished the cheese. Then she went to the cupboard and opened the door upon the squares of honey. A fat bumble-bee that had been knocking his head clumsily against the glass, flew in before she could stop him. A puddle of honey lay on the wooden frame of one of the squares. She put her finger, first in it then in her mouth. Strange how many lovely, sweet things there were in the world—and so much trouble.

"Ha!" said Kirke's voice behind her. "Into the honey, eh?"

She was dreadfully ashamed.

"Oh, Mr Kirke, I didn't hear you coming," she stammered.

"Weel, never mind. We're friends." He came and put his hand under her chin and kissed her in an offhand, arrogant fashion. "We're friends, aren't we? We micht be very good friends." (Another kiss.) "Sweeter than honey, eh?" (Another.) "Ah, Delight, Delight, you're going to fall on this town like another blight. It's terrible. It's fair rideeculous."

She pulled herself away from him, and snatched up her hat.

"Is Beemer goin' to take me on or isn't he?" she demanded, colour flooding her face.

"He is, thanks to me."

"No thanks to you, Mr Kirke, for treating me like this. It's an outrageful thing, I say. I threw Perkin Heaslip in the stream for no more."

Kirke's face was transfigured by a delighted grin to see her in a rage. He advanced a step toward her, but she snatched up the long black-handled knife with which she had cut the cheese. Her eyes were two shining dark slits. She said:

"If I ran this into you, they'd hang me, wouldn't they? And then it 'ud be all over."

"Come now, come now," said Kirke soothingly. "You're not in airnest, and I was only in fun. . . . We must make haste along to Beemer's now, for it's almost dinnertime. Put down that knife, my lass."

She laid it down, but looked at him threateningly still, out of the sides of her eyes.

"Dear, oh dear," commented Kirke jauntily. "I never thought to stage a melodrama behind the wee shop." He took off his bowler hat and made her a little stiff bow. "The carriage is waiting, your ladyship, daughter of Ivan, the acrobat."

IV

The British American Hotel, commonly called Beemer's, was a low-roofed, dark, musty place, a weather-beaten frame building, with a leaky roof, a sagging verandah, and small-paned windows. But there was something homelike about it, after all. There were men—the saddler, the auctioneer, and a down-at-heel lawyer—who had lived there for years. Once one got used to the smells and the disorder and the children that sprawled over the verandah in summer and the halls in winter, one found that the cooking was good; the beds, though never properly made, were fairly comfortable; and the whiskey, Canadian brands, cheaper than at The Duke.

Mrs Beemer, a black-browed, light-eyed heavy woman, did the cooking, except for one week in the year, when she had her annual baby. During that week the maids managed as well as they could, but she usually found things in a sorry tangle when she got about again, and she had violent outbursts of temper as she put them to rights. For years she had had her babies in November and December, very suitable months, since they were among the quietest in the year, but the last two years, through rather unseemly haste, she had decreased the period between the births till she had twice taken to her bed, not only in October but in Fair Week, the busiest week of the year. Beemer liked plenty of children. He saw in them future waitresses, kitchen girls, barkeepers and hostlers, hard-working on small pay. Children were easily fed in a place like this. But he did resent the lack of consideration shown by his lady in laying off, and lying in, just when he most needed her.

Now, as Fair time was approaching and her figure showed that her retirement was imminent, she knew herself to be in black disgrace and it did not improve her temper. From under her heavy brows she shot resentful looks at Delight as she stood in her fresh print dress in a corner of the kitchen, keeping out of the way of the bustle. Mrs Beemer had told her to keep out of her way until clearing-up time. She did not want to be bothered with a new girl while she was serving the dinner. She did not like the idea of engaging Delight at all. She had never had a handsome girl in the hotel before and the sight of her standing there, her wild, bright eyes flying from face to face, put her in a smouldering rage. She thrust out her under lip and scowled as she cut thick slabs from the roast of pork. She rapped her ten-year-old boy sharply on the knuckles as he reached for a crisp bit of rind. . . . Kathleen and Nellie, two sisters who had been at Beemer's for years, going there straight from a rigid Catholic home, did not enjoy the sight of her any more than their mistress did. They had their boys, quiet-living, faithful boys, but how long would they remain faithful with Delight Mainprize in the house?

Delight looked longingly at these three women. No sensitive intuition told her of their unfriendliness. Folk were often stand-offish with a newcomer. She liked the little round heads and freckled faces of the sisters and their brisk movements. They worked together like two good stocky ponies. As for Mrs Beemer . . . after Mrs Bye's long-legged leaps across the kitchen, she seemed like an elephant ponderously going through the motions to which it had been trained. But presently she saw that Mrs Beemer accomplished more than Mrs Bye, for all her frenzy, and that, with the utmost economy of movement, she kept the machine of the kitchen running in deadly earnest.

After the big airy kitchen at The Duke and the animation of the occupants, this low-ceilinged room, these silent women were rather depressing. Even the children were odd, not a bit like Queenie Bye. They were fat, whey-faced urchins with clumpy boots and drab, tousled heads. They were eating their dinner at a table in a corner, and every now and again one would slide from his chair, come to the stove with an empty plate, and reload it from the various platters and vegetable dishes. As they passed Delight they looked askance at her, resenting, like their mother, this new presence. One little fellow, bolder than the others, ran to her, and shutting his chubby fist, struck her on the side, then scuttled away to safety under the table.

"Here, Johnny, quit that!" said his mother, but a grim smile played about her lips.

Delight's face grew red from the heat of the stove, all her blood seemed to be singing in her head. It was queer to think that she was here at Beemer's, and just across the way was The Duke of York, and Charley and Mrs Bye, and Annie and Pearl. What would they think when they heard she was here? Was there a chance of her ever meeting Jimmy Sykes again?

She saw the women moving about her in a haze. Very lonely she felt. . . . It was two o'clock when Mrs Beemer said:

"I guess we can have our dinner now," and wiped her

forehead with the back of her hand which still held the carving knife.

Delight got a chair and joined the others at the grease-spotted, untidy table. But she leant her head on her hand. There was a lump in her throat. For the first time in her life she was not hungry at mealtime.

CHAPTER X

THE RISING TIDE

I

THE news that Delight Mainprize was at Beemer's spread like wildfire through the town. Women who had never seen her, who never expected to see her, felt disturbed at the thought that the strangely beautiful girl was again in their midst. Kirke had refused to disclose the place where she had been hiding for the past months. He told mysteriously how he had discovered her on a lonely farm, kept a prisoner by the farmer who had found her wandering about the country with her basket of dishes after she had been turned out by Mrs Jessop, and who had become crazed by desire for her. Kirke said that she had been sleeping in a stable among the cattle when he had found her. Straws had been sticking in her beautiful hair. She had had a fey look. She had told him the whole story of her life and origin, and he was willing to say that it was not surprising she could dance like a sprite, in fact, there was nothing she could do that would surprise him after what he had heard. He almost wondered at Beemer's temerity in taking that remarkable woman into his house.

On market day, he sauntered stiffly from stall to stall, and from one stand heaped with produce to another, dropping strange hints about her, not only because of her great power over men, but also because of natural beauty and some potent —well—he might almost call it—poison, that emanated from her and drowned the senses. But, ha! ha! she was a fine geerl, after all. She meant no hairm; and she was worth seeing. They'd better get their dinner at Beemer's if only to see her, and a good dinner they'd get. He had left The Duke of York to go to Beemer's. He'd had enough of their overcharging and tough pastry. Bastien was a blow-hard, and the absent owner a fool.

Wherever Kirke went longing looks were cast after his tall rain-coated figure. If only he could be made to tell all that he knew!

That day the dining-room at Beemer's would not seat all the guests. The tables had to be laid a second time, an unprecedented thing except at Fair time. Beemer, a fat little man with bottle shoulders and oily hands, wished to Heaven that he had a Chinese gong such as was sounded at The Duke of York, but he placed the copper dinner bell in Delight's hand, as though it were the hunting horn of Diana, and bade her ring long and loudly.

It was a dark hall at Beemer's, and to overcome this he had had a bracket lamp with a reflector behind it set at right angles to the door of the dining-room. She stood before this, the black, closed door behind her, clad in her narrow black dress, her beautiful face illuminated, her eyes sombre and full of an unnamed longing, her lips parted as though she panted to be free. . . . As her right hand moved up and down, and the bell rent the air with its clamour, her left was laid against her breast as though to still the throbbing of her heart. She saw nothing, being bewildered by the glare in her eyes, the clanging of the bell, after the country quiet to which she had become accustomed. Men crowded about her, staring into her face, their breath, hot with spirits, stifling her, while Beemer, dizzy with elation, sidled to and fro across the hall, rubbing his oily hands, and repeating in a voice thickened by adenoids:

"I'm afraid there's no room in the dining-room for all you fellahs. Say, this is awful, ain'd it? My missus is half-crazy id the kitchen."

Kirke scarcely passed a pound of butter or a wedge of cheese across his counter that day without dropping a word or two to the customer about the return of Delight. His words were seed that sprang up and bore fruit with tropic swiftness. That evening he strolled across to The Duke and, after being served with a glass of Scotch by Charley Bye, draped himself in his old posture against the newel post. Regardless of Bastien's glowering looks, he hung there, tantalizing, shrewd, dropping the right word into the ear of each man who hesitated near him, now and then giving vent to his staccato laugh.

By half-past nine the bar of The Duke was almost empty and Beemer's was full to overflowing. There was excitement in the air of Beemer's, exhilaration. By comparison The Duke of York seemed lifeless, dull, an empty cocoon, from which the butterfly had flown.

II

The kitchen at The Duke of York was much perturbed by Delight's return to Brancepeth. The fact that she had come to Beemer's made social intercourse with her impossible, for it was an unwritten law that no calls should be made between the two houses. Mrs Bye and Annie hoped to meet her on the street, but their strolls to and fro past The British American brought no sign from her, and old Davy learned from Beemer's hostler that she never had set foot on the pavement since her arrival. Mrs Bye sent Queenie with a message to her, but it was never delivered for, after she had lingered timidly at the kitchen door for nearly half an hour, two of the Beemer boys caught her, pinched her, pulled her hair, and sent her home weeping.

A feeling of unrest possessed them. Bastien became exacting, ill-tempered. Everyone knew that things were not going well with the house and, as in all business concerns, the employees grew slack and indifferent as they felt prosperity departing.

Charley Bye was all for taking Kirke's advice and starting a boarding-house of their own. He was sick and tired of being ordered about by Bastien, of eternally tripping over his own toes as he carried endless trays of drinks to disrespectful customers. Now he pictured himself as head of a crowded boarding-house with nothing much to do but carve the roast and give a hand with the coals and slops.

"I were a-dreamin' last night of my old buck rabbit," he said. "That's the third night in succession I've dreamed on him and it always means a change. One ear for'ard he had, p'intin' towards The Duke, and one ear back'ard, p'intin' towards Beemer's, and he was a-wigglin' of his nose in a sneerin' way he had. By gum, I was all of a sweat when I woke, and I says to myself —'Charley, old boy, it's toime for a move.' "

Mrs Bye regarded him with a strange mixture of contempt and awe. Charley's dreams were a puzzle to her; yet it was never safe wholly to ignore them, for she could remember more than one occasion when disaster had followed the disregarding of their warnings. Dreams of the dead rabbit were especially significant.

nd of rite to her. . . . Again she examined it. Its
eyes stared up at her. Taking a crochet hook from
ble, she pressed its point against them till, with a
they fell back into the head.
threw herself on her bed and lay half-dreaming until

IV

le of October brought the Fair. It was held in the park
goon. Pens were cleaned out, booths set up, and the
ilding prepared for exhibitions of fruit, vegetables,
akes, pickles, fancywork, and even oil paintings. During
e days of the Fair, football matches, running races, and
ces were in almost constant progress before the grand-
nd at night crowds from the various factories and shops
e side shows, and thronged the swings and the merry-
d. They were great days for Brancepeth, and all the
yside looked forward to it throughout the year.

Delight had not intended to go to the Fair. She had kept
w to remain indoors while she worked at Beemer's. Now
lt that she would suffocate for lack of air and outdoor
ment. She was tired to death with serving the crowds that
ged the dining-room, so, when she met Kirke in the hall-
and he urged her to go with him on the last night of the
suddenly she could not resist. . . . To be out of doors, under
big bright moon, in a crowd of people, with soft grass be-
h her feet instead of boards, the temptation was too great.
would go for an hour.

When she and Kirke entered the Fair grounds, the air
s vibrant with the crash of the town band, the jigging melody
the merry-go-round, and the cries of hawkers. Inside the
ming circle of lights, laughing or stupid faces flashed out and
sappeared in an ever changing pattern. Bright hats with ribbon
ows, red and green balloons, bloomed like exotic flowers. Some
oys had made a jack-o'-lantern from a prize pumpkin. Their
udden sallies into the crowd with it brought shrieks and scurry-
ng from the girls. A man, with a fire blazing in an iron cauldron,
made waffles before an admiring circle. He looked like a sor-
cerer with the ruddy light on his swarthy face and bare arms,
dipping his irons in the pot of batter, then in the pot of sizzling
fat, then rolling the smoking dainty in powdered sugar. Kirke

It was through Pearl that they at last got intimate news of Delight. Pearl no longer worked at The Duke, so she was free to call on a friend at Beemer's, though she did so with a good deal of trepidation, for she was now somewhat of a personage herself, and a naturally shy girl.

Her romance with Edwin Silk had ended, less than a fortnight after Delight's departure, dramatically and with tragic splendour. Silk had died and left her all his fortune. He had driven to the village of Stead one Sunday with three other men, among them Bastien. They had played poker most of the night. In the morning, one of the men who had slept with Silk found him dead in bed by his side. There was no inquest. Silk had always been a weakling, and the strain of losing three hundred dollars that night had been the last straw to a heart already degenerated.

Edwin Silk's last gesture was theatric. He had left what remained of his fortune to a kitchen girl. There were about two thousand pounds and an old cottage in Surrey, with an acre of land. . . . The shock of this legacy, coming after the shock of her lover's death, had been almost too much for Pearl. His attentions had kept her in a sort of daze; this sudden wealth almost bereft her of the power of thought. She knew that she was now a fine lady, but she had no friends other than the servants at The Duke, and no life outside her work and her sweethearting. This last was denied her, for she was now afraid of all men—Mrs Bye had warned her that they would be hot-foot after her dollars—regarding them with fear and suspicion. She had no relations, so she took a room in a boarding-house that advertised itself as "refined," and sat there by the hour in her black velvet dress fingering her jet bracelet, and thinking of Edwin. She could not wish him back because latterly he had frightened her, but she had loved him, and the thought of his narrow head lying against her plump shoulder always brought the slow tears to her eyes.

She came to the kitchen one sultry afternoon toward Fair time to tell Mrs Bye and Annie that she had been to see Delight. She had gone up to her room and sat with her there, and Delight had kissed her and stroked her hand, and stared at her so hard with those wild, bright eyes that she had made her feel queer. She had Jim Sykes's trunk in her room and she had taken out a jersey of his and shown Pearl how it still held the shape of his body, just as though he were dead like Edwin. Not that she could do such a thing with Edwin's clothes—

"I'll bet you couldn't," interrupted Charley, "hisn 'ud lie flat enough, I'll be bound, fur he'd neither breast nor vitals to hold 'em out."

Pearl looked hurt, and Mrs Bye said sharply—

"Nonsense, Charley. He was a gentleman, and he didn't have any need of such things."

"I reckon," persisted Charley, "that I'd leave a impress on my shirt that a year couldn't flatten."

"I reckon Bill will flatten you, if you don't get a move on with that ice," put in Annie.

Charley picked up the pail of broken ice and moved heavily to the door, muttering:

"Well, he won't have me to bully much longer. Three nights hand runnin' I've dreamed on my buck rabbit and it never fails to bring a change."

"Just the same, it is very queer about Delight Mainprize," said Pearl, when he had gone: "Everybody's talking about her. Folks you'd never expect would have heard of her. I wouldn't dare tell my landlady, Miss Sniffin, that I've been to see her. Only this morning she said that a girl like that ought to be run out of the town. And then she asked me what she looked like. She couldn't hear enough about her looks and her dancing and everything. And then she said she was going to ask the minister of her church to preach against her."

Mrs Jessop's voice fell unexpectedly on their ears. She had come in softly, in felt slippers. She grinned broadly.

"What's that?" she asked. "More about that street girl I threw out?"

"Nothing," answered Pearl, "only folks don't seem able to talk of anything else but her. She's like a magnet at Beemer's. I saw her today and she gets lovelier all the time."

"She'll come to a bad end," said Mrs Jessop, her grin changing to her scowl. "You'll see."

"There's no harm in her," blazed Mrs Bye.

The two women faced each other for a brief space, their eyes like swords, then Mrs Jessop turned away and shuffled out of the room.

"I say there's no harm in her," repeated Mrs Bye sturdily.

"Still, you can't help wondering," said Annie.

Mrs Jessop was a much strang
ever guessed. Hers was a domin
grey hair, glistening grey eyes, a
appearance of great energy, whil
scowl made her moods felt in a
her passing moods lay her real se
except Bastien whom she loved, a
fierce caresses, violent fits of wee
She looked sometimes as though sh
knife into a man.

Mrs Jessop had independent
position of housekeeper because her
not be dammed into the sluggish p
needed other women to domineer over
for favours; men, with whom to be
sullen.

It was known that she was the w
keeper. No one knew that he had marr
vagrant, half-gypsy horse-dealer who, b
for a long term for stealing and assault,
man to marry his only daughter, threate
dealings they had had together. Mrs Jessop
deed. She remembered hearing as a child wil
of her father's father, whose last necktie had
hempen one. Dark, murderous blood was Mr

When she left the kitchen she went st
room. From a drawer she took out a small f
She had dressed it in a neat black dress with a l
with shoulder-straps. This doll she had bought
day after she had found Delight Mainprize in
To her it was the symbol of Delight, and on it sh
she could contain it no longer, her spleen towar
pinched it. She struck it on the face. She pulled its
by one till now it had a bald spot on the back of
stuck pins in it, making, as they entered its body, lit
noises to represent its pain.

Now, holding the toy in her hand, she looked
a ferocious, yet baffled, expression. After all the in
had suffered, it still retained its sweet smirk, its pink
. . . Slowly, meticulously, she did the things to it w

become a k
brown glass
her workta
tiny clatter
She
teatime.

The midd
by the la
main bu
pastry, c
the thre
horse ra
stand, a
filled t
go-roun
countr

her vo
she fe
move
thron
way
Fair,
the
neat
She

wa
of
fla
di
b
b
s
i

bought half a dozen, and he and Delight strolled along, eating them from a paper bag.

"Would you sooner have had hot popcorn?" he asked.

"No. I like these. We can have the popcorn after a bit."

"True. Would you like to dance?"

"No." She shrank from the thought of mingling with the dancers. She had seen some of the boarders from The Duke on the floor.

"There's a fortune-telling booth. Like your fortune told?"

"Yes, I'd like that."

But when they got inside the door, she saw the gypsy from whom she had bought the green earrings, and fled, leaving Kirke to follow.

"Weel," he observed, "you seem to be in skittish mood tonight."

She did not answer but pushed out her under lip like a stubborn child. He stalked beside her, frowning and yet amused. She fascinated him, more and more. He did not half like it and yet took a certain grim pleasure in observing the effect she had on him, as a cool and somewhat cynical outsider might. The more he felt her power, the more arrogant he became with her.

"We'll go on the roundabout," he said, and held her arm while he bought two tickets.

She pushed the last of her waffle into her mouth, gently submissive.

"What beast do you fancy?" he inquired.

"I dunno."

"The lions look comfortable."

"No. I don't like the lions."

"The war horse, then! Try a war horse."

"No. What's that animal with the horn?"

"A unicorn. We must mount something, quick, geerl. The platform's trembling."

The music burst forth in a peal. The roundabout commenced to revolve. They were side by side on two rearing, wild-eyed unicorns. The brazen vibrations rocked their bodies, the music drugged their senses. Faster and faster they sped. They had taken off their hats and the night wind blew between their parted lips, whistled in their teeth, filled their lungs. All outside their whirling circle became a shining blur of lights and faces. To be flying like this with her beside him on a unicorn fired Kirke's spirit into a wild joy. They two! They two! They were worth more than all this throng of clods that peopled the Fair grounds together. Delight and Duncan. Duncan and Delight. Ha! What a ride together!

His hand that held the dagger seemed inspired. Time after time he thrust it through the golden ring. Ride after triumphant ride they had for nothing. The crowd gathered not only to see the girl but to watch his prowess. . . . When at last they descended, she was so dizzy she could hardly stand. She stood leaning against the support of a tent while he went to fetch her a glass of lemonade. She clutched a tent rope as the dark earth seemed to rock beneath her.

The jigging music drummed in her ears. She was afraid of the obscure forms that moved about her, their faces distorted into strange grimaces by the flickering lights. She almost cried out as a hand was laid on her arm by someone who had come up behind her.

"It's me—Bill," said Bastien's voice in her ear. "What are you jumping for? I'm not going to hurt you." He gave a short, excited laugh and looked over her shoulder into her face, his white teeth gleaming in his dark face. "I've been watching you spinning round on that darned whirligig with Kirke. Are you gone on him, Delight? I tell you, he'll never marry you, if that's what you're looking for. All he cares for you is to use you as a tool to spite me. I care more for your little finger than he does for your whole body. Look here, I could have shot old Jessop when she fired you. I'll get even with her for it, too."

"Here comes Mr Kirke with the lemonade," breathed Delight. She feared trouble between the two men. The air seemed charged with danger, full of sinister tension.

Bastien pressed her arm. "All right. I'll get out. But I've got to have a talk with you. I want us to work together instead of against each other, see? I've got a plan. I'll tell you this much. I've been to the city to see Mr Hodgins—the owner, you know—and he's firing Mrs Jessop next week, see?"

Kirke stood before them, a bottle of lemonade in his hand.

"Is this young woman here with you or with me?" he bit off, an angry gleam in his eyes.

"Keep your hair on, Scotchie," laughed Bastien. He pressed closer to Delight and whispered in her ear: "I'll slip out tomorrow night at ten. Meet me just outside the gates here and we'll talk things over." He moved away, and melted into the crowd. Kirke remarked, looking after him fiercely:

"I'd a mind to break this bottle over his head."

The lemonade was gratefully cool. . . . Delight, her head thrown back, was draining the last drop when she saw Mrs Jessop emerge from the tent beside which they were standing. It was the gypsy's tent and the housekeeper had evidently been having her fortune told. She walked rigidly with a stony face, a strong, squat figure that gave way to no one. Delight breathed a sigh of relief because she had not seen her.

V

The next day everything was slack at Beemer's. The crowds were gone, everyone was dog-tired, and no one was doing his or her own work because they were plunged into their annual muddle on account of the arrival of a new Beemer baby. Mrs Beemer had behaved better than Beemer had hoped for. She had been about the three days of the Fair. She had even cooked the supper on the last night, though she put so much pepper in the fried potatoes that the whole dining-room was in a state of panting, and had to have gallons of tea to ease their burnt throats.

It was her last fierce gesture before taking to her bed. She threw the empty pepper-pot on to a shelf, kicked the cupboard door to, and rolled out of the kitchen and into her bed.

Neither the maids nor Beemer, himself, had had much sleep that night. It was white dawn before the little new Beemer arrived. It was too late to go to bed, so Delight and Kathleen set to work and scrubbed the dining-room and kitchen floors, while Nellie began to cook the early breakfast.

Delight was drowsy, and as she described soapy arcs with the scrubbing brush, her mind revolved, without arriving at any answer about one question. Should she or should she not meet Bastien that night? If Mrs Jessop were discharged, how homey it would be to go back to The Duke with Mrs Bye, and Queenie, and Charley, and Annie, and old Davy, like dear friends around her! She knew they were friendly toward her, for Pearl had told her so. Here none of the women were friendly. There was only Kirke, who would be in a fine rage if she left Beemer's. She didn't care. Let him rage. Old "Fine Nicht."

When she went to her room to put on her black dress for dinner she found an envelope lying on the floor inside. It had been pushed under the door. It was addressed to—

Miss D. Mainprize,
British American Hotel,
Brancepeth.

She could scarcely believe her eyes. Who would be writing to her? It was not Jimmy's neat, firm script but a large scrawl, half printing. She turned it over and over in her large gentle hand, still moist and red from scrubbing, before she opened it with a hairpin. The sheet inside was heavy, with a narrow gilt band. She read:

My dear Miss Mainprize—

Having had dinner at The British American in Fair time and seeing you then and also later on the grounds, i beg to tell you i am desperately in love, i am a wealthy cattle breeder and can give you the best of everything, fine house and clothes and everything. i think it a shame for a girl with your grand looks to be working in a hotel. i make you this formal offer of marriage hereby. Now Miss Mainprize this is what i want you to do. i want you to meet me on the other side of the lagoon tonight at sundown. Cross the Park to where the lagoon is narrowest, and you will find a green rowboat tied among the willows. Get in and row yourself to the far side. i will be there. You better bring your basket of dishes with you as i will have my motorcar waiting and if we come to a proper understanding there won't be no need for you to go back to Beemer's at all. We can be married at once by special licence. Now my dear Miss Mainprize don't fail me for my heart is set on making a lady of you as you deserve. Meet me at Sundown sure don't be afraid.

Your sincere admirer and lover,

J. Adams,
Manor Farm.

Red and white. Hot and cold. Still and trembling. Delight was shaken by a flood of emotion. A proposal on beautiful gilt-edged paper pushed under her door! A terrifying, delicious, arrogant proposal. A gentleman farmer! A breeder of prize cattle! There had been several to dinner, she knew. If she had only known which was he, so she might know what he looked like! Just when she had been worrying about whether she should meet Bill. Now this stupendous thing, blotting out all else. A lady! She looked about the stuffy room, a mere closet, lighted by a skylight. She looked at her red hands, her feet in down-at-heel slippers, wet from the wet floor. She looked at her tin trunk, at Jimmy's trunk—Jimmy's trunk. Oh, if Jimmy hadn't run away from Brancepeth! She would never see Jimmy again. Except, perhaps, as she rolled along in her motorcar—and he trudging in his workingman's clothes. Poor Jimmy. If only he hadn't been so hasty with her! And she a lady in a motorcar, wearing a pink plumed hat with lace falling from the brim.

Pearl called on her that afternoon. Pearl in a new fall suit lined with satin, long kid gloves with innumerable buttons, and shoes with wide silk ties. A black velvet toque, too, with white roses. Pearl was greatly wrought up over the letter shown her on a pledge of secrecy. Delight must do it, must go to meet this wonderful man, this prize-cattle breeder.

"Do you suppose he really is rich?" asked Delight. "It would seem too good to be true. Like a dream, Pearl."

"I know. But look at Edwin. Folks said no good would come of me trustin' him. And look at me now."

Delight looked at her, deeply admiring.

"Think of havin' your own motorcar."

"I'm afraid of them. I've only seen a few."

"Pshaw. There's nothing to be afraid of. Every well-off man'll own one before long."

"Pearl, think of me with no work to do. Not at anybody's beck and call."

"Like me. I tell you it's grand to lie in bed as late as you like and never have your ankles swelled up with being on your feet all day."

"It must be grand, Pearl."

But her face had become thoughtful.

"There's Jimmy, Pearl. He might come back."

Pearl was a soft, gentle girl but, like many gentle women, quietly ruthless. She was fond of Delight. She thought that if Delight could marry a gentleman (though, of course, he would not be a *real* gentleman like Edwin), they might become companions, fast friends. In Delight's marriage she would find some sort of anchorage for herself, whereas now she was drifting among those who were not of her social standing. Her unexpected fortune had made everything seem possible. There was an unreality in everything she saw. She scarcely believed in herself.

Now, bending her soft gaze on Delight, she said:

"My landlady" (she could not quite bring herself to say—"I, myself") "My landlady was in the city three weeks ago and she saw Jimmy Sykes at a show with another girl—a little bit of a plump girl with straight black hair. They was both laughing fit to kill."

Fit to kill. . . . The stab that went through Delight's breast was fit to kill. When Pearl had gone, she went to Jimmy's little trunk. She took out the jersey that still was curved to the form of his compact body. With her scissors she snapped a strand of yarn. She began to unravel. . . . Larger and large grew the mass of crinkled yarn. Small and smaller, the shape of Jimmy, clinging desperately to her hand. At last she stood motionless gazing down at the last strand in her fingers with the fateful look of an Atropos.

CHAPTER XI

THE LAGOON

SUNDOWN, red, and blurred with golden haze, ended the day of Indian summer. It was a languid, whispering day, hazy with the smoke from northern forest fires. A sweet, yet acrid, scent hung in the quiet air. Slender leaves like little golden fish fell from the bending willows into the lagoon, sinking slowly, mirrored for one lovely moment in the still water.

Mirrored, too, was the green boat, and Delight, fearfully dipping the oars. . . . There seemed to be two boats, two Delights, crossing the deep lagoon.

The sun, like a great red rose, lay at the water's edge, its rich light streaming like a banner from shore to shore. A little flock of gulls floating with folded wings watched the passing of the boat, with turnings and archings of their downy necks.

The basket, in which lay the apple-green tea set, gently rose and sank with the motion of the boat.

CHAPTER XII

THE TRIAL BY WATER

I

SHE made the boat fast to the twisted root of a tree, where it would be hidden among the bushes. Her feet sank into the moist earth from which water oozing into her footprints formed tiny glistening pools. She hid the basket among the elder bushes on the shore, and there, shading her eyes with her hand, scanned the fields for the figure of her unknown lover. Evening mists were gathering in the hollows; the hillsides were velvet brown. Would he be coming down a hillside maybe? Or at the far end of that narrow ribbon of a path that disappeared into the pine wood? When she saw him she must have courage, walk up to him and say—"Are you Mr J. Adams? Please, I'm Delight Mainprize. . . ." But, of course, she wouldn't need to say who she was. He'd know the minute he saw her. Still it would be more polite to say—"I am Miss Mainprize, please. I have received your kind letter."

She had on her best dress, wine colour, with elbow sleeves and a little black bow at the neck, and her black velvet tam with the quill. In the rich light her tawny yellow hair and the tawny and red tints in her cheeks glowed like bright wine, alive, changeful. She turned this way and that, but there was no sign of any human being; just the rolling, velvet fields, the rose-tinted lagoon, the deep pine wood, and a silence that was not a silence, for it was full of whisperings that seemed no more than the breathing of the grass, or the sighing of the earth as it turned toward sleep.

Then from out a little copse of dense cedars a low whistle came, deep and flutelike, repeated thrice. It startled, almost frightened her. She stood like a deer, head up, listening, her great eyes fixed on the copse. He was there. She was to meet him there. It was only a very small copse, but a shelter, if he were a shy man. If she did not like him, if he were too forward, or a wretch, well, there was the lagoon. She would throw him in there as she had thrown Perkin into the stream. Full of curiosity now she hurried toward the copse. It was darker in there than she had expected, but in one place there was an opening where the light shone redly, and from just beyond it the whistle sounded, softer and yet more urgent.

She went into the open space and stood there smiling expectantly.

There was a crackling of twigs as someone emerged from the shadows. She drew a step nearer and saw, not a man but a woman, a thickset woman, bareheaded, with untidy grey hair.

It was Mrs Jessop.

The meeting, the letter, was a hoax. Mrs Jessop had played her this trick. Her pulses began to beat quickly. Rage flamed in her heart.

"How did you dare?" she said. "You ought to be ashamed. You'd better get out of here before I hurt you. I'll do it and no mistake. I'll give you a proper beating, I will."

Mrs Jessop stood stock-still now. When she had entered the clearing she had been wearing her broadest grin. Now it changed to her black scowl.

"Now, you slut," she said, "I've got you."

"Got me! It's me that's got you. I'll throw you into the lagoon as quick as look at you."

"We'll see whether you're going to come back to this town and ruin our business after I've put you out."

"I'll come any place I like—"

"And ruin our men, too."

Delight thought: "If I can get hold of her wrists, I'll put her down on her knees and make her say she's sorry. She might get drowned if I threw her in the water." She moved toward Mrs Jessop, holding her eyes with hers.

The housekeeper glared at her and again uttered that strange deep whistle which came from her coarse lips like a spring of sweet water from rough clay. . . . At the note every tree and shrub and clump of spiny undergrowth seemed to come alive. In every place that a woman could hide, there was a woman hidden. Like birds of prey, with skirts that flapped like flapping wings, uttering cries of rage and exultation, they swooped forth.

The sun had set. The bright space where the two stood became dusk as the other women gathered about them. For one instant Delight had seen their faces, transfigured by the last fiery glow into strange burning masks, more like metal than flesh, with jewels for eyes. Now, as the shadows fell, she only saw them surging about her, blurred, menacing, darker shadows from the shadow.

She struck out at them, as they surrounded her.

"Don't dare touch me!" she shrieked. "Keep your hands off me!"

She grasped the one nearest her and threw her to the ground. She caught the next one by the throat and threw her into a bush. One from behind tore off her velvet tam. Another pulled down her hair. She turned and faced them like a wild thing at bay. A short girl with a broad flat face spat on her. She struck the flat face with her fist. There was a scream.

"Ow, she's broke my nose! It's streamin' blood."

They were a wave now that submerged her. They struggled with each other that they might get near her to deliver a blow for some harm they fancied she had done them, or just because she was so strangely beautiful, and they had her at their mercy, and Mrs Jessop had aroused the savage in them.

Mrs Jessop had taken no hand in the attack as yet. She stood apart, her arms folded, her head on her strong neck thrust forward. Mrs Jessop, respectable for all these years, obeying only the incalculable promptings of her fierce heart. Once more the grin was enthroned on her face, such a grin as might have stretched the lips of one of her cutthroat ancestors. Her blood danced singing through her veins. She felt and looked twenty years younger.

But she did not want her girls to go too far. She did not want her victim to be seriously hurt or rendered unconscious. She raised her voice and shouted to the little mob that moved here and there in the dusk of the copse like a strange animal in pain:

"Easy there, girls! No more now—take her into the open —down to the lagoon. I'm going to duck her!"

They did not seem to hear but they must have heard, for very soon the animal that had seemed to be in pain in the copse writhed out into the field, and down to the water's edge, as though it would end its suffering there.

II

Lovering was leaning against the bar, sipping a glass of whiskey and water, with a feeling of deep content. He had got a raise, and at last he had been able to send for his wife and two little girls. A telegram had come that day from Quebec to say that they were arrived. He was thoroughly tired of hotel life. It was all very well in its way but, after all, there was nothing like a home of his own for a man. He had had enough of rooming with Kirke. Duncan was getting more overbearing all the time, especially since he was going with the mayor's daughter.

He came in now, and said to Lovering:

"It's a fine nicht."

"Ay. But sultry."

"Nothing of the sort. It's balmy. You couldn't ask for a finer nicht." He ordered his beer and then continued—"The Byes have given notice today. Going to start on their own. Five of the third-floor boarders are leaving with them. Charley told me just now that Mrs Jessop had a letter from Mr Hodgins this morning giving her a month's warning, too. Mark my words, Jack, Bastien himself will be out of a job before spring."

"He can marry Mrs Jessop, then."

Kirke's light eyes moved sharply over the room.

"Who's that just come in? Why, it's Mayberry! He's in a fine stew about something. He's gibbering like an idiot. Let's see what's up, Jack."

He hurried over to the tailor, and Lovering, sucking his "clay," lazily followed him.

Mr Mayberry was in a pitiable state. He, who rarely moved faster than a snail's gallop, had run wildly through the street from his shop to Beemer's, forcing his weak limbs and sluggish heart to such violent action that he stood now, open-mouthed, gasping like a fish, clinging to the bar for support, while he tried with all his might to tell the men who were excitedly crowding around him what was wrong.

"Gi'e him a drop of liquor," suggested Kirke.

"I'm afraid he couldn't swallow it the state he's in," said Eddie, the barman.

"I'll see that he swallows it," said Kirke.

He approached Mr Mayberry with a commanding look, but the tailor put up his hand to keep him off, looked imploringly at the others, and then got out the words:

"De-light—"

There was a sudden and spontaneous roar of laughter. So this was what all the anguish was about! Delight! Poor old Mayberry.

Mr Mayberry glared at them. He was recovering himself. By the time the laughter had subsided he could speak coherently.

"Delight Mainprize. Some of the womenfolk—factory girls—Mrs Jessop—ill-treating her in the field across the lagoon

—my niece told me—she got scared and ran home. Men! They're ducking her—drowning her perhaps. I came here to see if she'd got back. Oh—what can I do?"

"Godamoighty!" shouted Lovering, "coom along, Duncan! Everybody! Lead the way, tailor, if you know where they've got the lass; coom on, boys." He stuffed his pipe into his pocket.

The tailor, suddenly galvanized into new life, sprang forward, tottering in a kind of anguished speed, like an autumn leaf in the gale. He was first into the hall, first out of the front door, first to round the corner by The Duke of York. The men nearest the window of that bar saw him pass, his thin hair flying, his spiderish legs almost doubling under him. And in his train stout Lovering, rushing like a curly-polled bull; Kirke, in angular leaps, like a deer; fat Beemer, waddling at the tail of a score of others.

Forgetting his feud with Beemer, Bastien strode to the door.

"Hi, Beemer!" he called. "What's the matter?"

"Batter enough," choked Beemer. "The womenfolks is gone clean crazy and they're killin' my girl—you know, the Prize girl—I mean the Mainprize girl—Delight. Oh, don't keep me, Mr Bastien!" He ran on, vainly trying to overtake the others.

Delight! The syllables clutched at the men's hearts like fingers of fire. They burst into incoherent babbling all at once and rushed for the doors. Some of them ran with glasses in their hands, hesitated in the street to drain them; then dashed them into the road as they sped on.

Charley Bye was among the leaders when they started. His noble head thrown back, his chest inflated, he looked, in truth, like some classic runner. But his erratic legs played him false, he tripped over his own toes, fell to the road and lay there groaning while Kirke leaped over him, Bastien gave him a kick and, at last, fat Beemer trotted round him. When he gathered himself up, the others had turned in at the park gates. He sighed, brushed the dust from his legs and, remembering that the bar was deserted, ambled back there and had a glass of gin and water in peace.

Meanwhile men from doorways of cottages joined the others. Men, chopping wood for their wives, dropped their axes and made the streaming tail of the rescue party longer. One man, leaning on a gate, nursing his baby, ran for a space after the others with it in his arms, till his wife overtook him and brought him back, shamefaced, but muttering the name that thrilled them all.

As the first of the men reached the park gates, strange muffled cries came to them from across the lagoon. They had half believed that they were on a wild-goose chase, but those unearthly cries brought the sweat to their foreheads and deadly certainty of danger to their hearts. They could see nothing beyond the race course but the topaz glint of the water between the willows that fringed the lagoon.

All other noises were now drowned by a wild clamour among the crows. They rose out of the pine wood and swept like a tumultuous cloud above the lagoon. Flying close together, fanning each other with their heavy wings, uttering cries of fear and rage, they cast their black shadow on the limpid mirror below.

Delight saw them as, bruised and drenched, not certain whether it were not all a horrible nightmare, she raised her terrified eyes to the sky. Above the drumming in her ears, she heard their cries. Jimmy's crows were calling, rowdy, noisy, faithful crows:

"Caw! Caw! They've got her—Jimmy's girl—Jimmy's pretty girl—Jim's Delight. Delight! Delight! 'Light! Give us 'Light! Give us 'Light!"

Mayberry, almost fainting, cursed the birds for their noise. If it were not for them he might know just which opening to head for. As it was they bewildered him till he felt that when his feet were once on the racecourse he might have no more wit left than to run there in a half-mile circle till he dropped. . . .

Kirke was the first to crash through the undergrowth to the water's edge. His small eyes screwed into two points of light, he peered across. He saw the crowd of women on the opposite shore, Mrs Jessop in the foreground. She stood up to her waist in water, clutching in her hands something—someone that hung limply like a doll.

Kirke gave forth a great yell:

"Mrs Jessop! Woman alive! Are ye gone mad? Ye've killed the lass. Are ye all out of your senses?"

A scream of defiance rose from the women. One shouted: "Never fear. She ain't dead—yet!"

The other men now thronged to Kirke's side. As the women had screamed defiance at them, they shouted impotent rage at the women. They shook their fists to heaven. Macy, the constable, took out his handcuffs, and waved them in the air, threatening to clap them all in gaol. . . . But Kirke, more practical, was pulling off his coat.

"I'll swim across," he snarled.

Other men began to follow his example, though the water was icy cold. Seeing what they were about to do Mrs Jessop turned and spoke to her girls, with a jerk of the head toward a pile of broken bricks, ruin of an old smokehouse. They fell on the pile with screams of triumph and half-hysterical laughter. They were more like malicious children now than furies. With Mrs Jessop as captain, they would hold the fort. Pelt any man who ventured near their side till he would be glad to turn back. They filled their skirts with the fragments and some began to throw pieces into the water, and to invite the men sarcastically to join them. When Mr Mayberry saw that Kirke was preparing to enter the water, a heroic flame transfigured his sallow face.

"I go first, Mr Kirke," he said, and without waiting to remove his coat, he leaped into the lagoon, his long coattails flying like the tail of some grotesque water fly. His body smote the water flatly with a loud splash and he struck out with short, pawing strokes, coughing and groaning. A cheer went up from the opposite shore and a shower of missiles splashed into the water.

Kirke was after the tailor. In three clean strokes he had passed him. His gimlet eyes were fixed on the figures of the two women in the water. With every nerve in his hard muscular body he strained toward them. He could see Delight's face now, white and still. But she must have seen him coming, for a piercing scream came from her cold lips:

"Help!"

That scream and the shock of the cold water were more than Mr Mayberry could bear. He flung up his arms and in a weak voice echoed the cry—

"Help! I'm sinking."

Kirke turned on his side and threw an angry glance back at the tailor. He had a mind to let him sink. Still, the old cadger was better plucked than the string of goggle-eyed men that fringed the shore. Not one of them—yes, one—Bastien! Now, another—Fergussen!

"Help!" came weakly from Mr Mayberry, and he sank out of sight.

Could these devils of girls on the shore see that a man

was drowning? Or did they think it fun for men to be stoned in the water like stray cats? A piece of brick struck him on the head, inflicting a sharp pain.

"Hello, Kirke! Hello, Scotchie! What are you turning back for?" came with jeers and laughter, and a fresh volley of broken bricks.

Bastien and Fergussen had got the tailor between them.

"Come back, men!" shouted Lovering. "They vixens'll stone your heads in. Mrs Jessop's trying to say something. Let's hear what she has to say."

The four men, perishing of cold, climbed onto the reedy shore. The constable and another began to apply first aid to Mayberry. Kirke turned on Lovering.

"You blasted coward, Jack! Why did ye no stand by me?"

"I knew it would do no good. Tha'rt as wet as a rat and I'm dry. That's the only difference. Listen what tha auld girl has to say."

Mrs Jessop had a magnificent voice. It came to them now, clear and vibrant, across the lagoon.

"You're a fine lot, aren't you? And we've a fine reception waiting for the next that ventures over here. You've had it all your way for the last few months. Now, we've got it all ours."

"You'll spend the night in gaol," cried Macy.

"Just wait a minute and listen. I sent this girl out of the town two months ago because she was making fools of all you men. But she wouldn't stay away. You wouldn't let her stay away. We know who brought her back. And we've reached the end of our patience. Haven't we, girls?"

"Ah-h!" groaned the girls.

"Now we're giving this Jezebel a fair trial by water. I've ducked her twice, and after each ducking she says she's innocent. Now—I'm a-going to duck her a third time and I may bring her up—or I may not—"

"Shame! Shame! For God's sake, no!"

The men, goaded into recklessness, prepared as one to rush into the water, while the women opposite, reinforced by fresh arrivals, frantically tore at the ruin for more ammunition.

"Wait!" thundered Mrs Jessop, and held up her hand.

The pine wood stood black against the red curtain of the afterglow. The hunter's moon had risen and the reflection of her lovely shape lay on the ambient oval of the lagoon. Far away the crows could be heard, a distant black-winged band, mournfully crying.

"Now, listen." Mrs Jessop's voice was compelling. "You men love this girl. Have any of you got the spunk to marry her and take the responsibility of her? Have you? Because if you have—and she'll agree—I'll pronounce her innocent this minute, and she can set on the bank while you fools make it up between you which it's to be. Will anybody marry this Delight Mainprize?" Her big voice shook with sardonic laughter. "A handsome filly—sound in wind and limb—will not shy at anything—guaranteed to be fond of gentlemen."

A shrill chorus of laughter rose from the other women, exhilarated beyond measure by all the unloosed passions of the senses.

"Tak' that lass out of the water," yelled Kirke, mopping his bleeding forehead, "or I'll have you hanged."

"Hanging's nothing new in our family. My grandfather was hanged." Mrs Jessop cast all those cherished years of respectability from her now, as a snake casts its skin. In new, fierce colours she reared her flat head and sparkling eyes among them.

"Will *you* marry her?" she demanded.

"I will," shouted Kirke.

He had forgotten his fine ambitions. He had forgotten the mayor's daughter. He was only Duncan Kirke, who had been a wild barelegged boy among the heather. He wanted, more than anything on earth, to marry the half-drowned servant, Delight.

Mrs Jessop, now that her lust for revenge was satisfied, now that she had crushed the girl, became almost tender with her. With a fawning gesture, she bent over her and whispered, and hung waiting for an answer. When she had got it, her voice came with a cooing note across the lagoon.

"She says she'll marry anyone."

"Take her out of the water," shouted the men.

Mrs Jessop helped Delight to the bank. She herself was soaked to the thighs, but she felt neither chilled nor stiff. Delight was drenched, through and through. Her heavy hair, in long wet strands, half hid her marble face as she sank to the ground, her head resting on her hand—her strong right hand that now felt so weak. . . .

The tailor, now resuscitated, had heard Mrs Jessop's

question and Kirke's answer. Scrambling to his shaking legs, he ran to the Scotchman and grasped him by the arm.

"No, no," he entreated. "Don't take her from me. It was me that saved her. She ought to be mine, I tell you. I want to marry her! She's mine by right."

"Rot!" said Kirke, shaking him off. "Do you suppose she wants to tie up with a skinny old gaffer like you?"

But what was this? Bastien at the water's rim. He curved his hand at his mouth and shouted:

"Mrs Jessop! Ask her if she'll have me? I'll take her fast enough."

"Oh, is that you, Billy, my beauty? Yes, I'll ask her if she'll have you. . . . She says she doesn't care. She loves you all so well, she'll marry any, or all of you. Settle it among yourselves, gentlemen."

Burly Fergussen pushed his way to the front.

"Marryin' hasn't been my long suit," he said. "I'm all for travellin' light. But, blast my eyes, if I aren't ready to marry this poor girl."

"You," said a sneering voice beside him. "Do you think she'd marry a coarse brute like you? Smelling of fish and dirty with tobacco juice? Have a heart."

It was the slender, dark-haired schoolmaster who spoke. He had been in the park before it all began, so absorbed in his own dreams that he had heard nothing of what went on beyond the lagoon till the other men came running in.

"Fish, hell! Tobacco juice, hell! I'm a man, you silly blighter, and it's a man she needs, not a chalky-faced—what the hell's your business, anyhow?"

"Teaching school."

"Teaching school, eh? Is that a man's job? You'd be no more to her than a toe-rag. Ho, you fellers, here's a white-livered schoolmaster wants to marry my gal!"

"Your geerl," snarled Kirke, digging his bony elbow into the fisherman's stomach. "You must think she's badly off."

"Friends—friends. Don't let us quarrel at such a moment," beseeched Mr Mayberry. "Let us pick out the most suitable man—regardless of age—and send him over to the maid. See, two of the women are starting across in a boat to fetch him. At least, it appears that way to me. Now, let us choose the best—"

"I'll put a head on him—" growled Fergussen.

"Do you mean me?" asked Kirke.

"Yes, I mean you."

"Ah, I'd like to see you."

But their voices were drowned in a cheer, half-welcoming, half-threatening, as the faces of the two young women who rowed the boat now became recognizable. Mrs Jessop had picked out these two to approach the men for good reasons. Nannie Wilcox, the stouter and older, was the daughter of Tom Wilcox the baker, a jolly girl and a favourite with all the men whom she had served in the little ice-cream parlour behind the shop. Always good-humoured and ready to chaff a customer, it was hard for the men to believe that she had taken part in such a cruel persecution as they had just witnessed, without deep provocation. The truth was that Nannie had held no personal spite toward Delight but she was tired of hearing her praises sung by the infatuated men. Mrs Jessop had, for years, been her father's best customer. Beemer had bought nothing. Now Beemer (through Delight) was ruining The Duke of York. A little rough-house, Nannie thought, would clear the air, and it was a grand outlet for high spirits.

The other girl, Gertie Reed, was a sharp-featured factory girl. Mrs Jessop had chosen her because she was afraid of no one.

"Nannie, Nannie, I never thought to see you mixed up in a mess like this," cried fat Tom Wilcox.

"Oh, Father, we didn't hurt her. It was only what she deserved, anyway."

Kirke shook his fist at her.

"The buckle end of a strap is what you desairve. And you'd get it if I had the handling of ye!"

"You let Nannie alone," said Wilcox. "She's no worse than the others."

"Jump into the boat, Mr Kirke," invited Gertie Reed, "and we'll row you across to your ladylove. This here is the river Jordan and she's waiting in heaven on the other side." She leaned on her oars, raising her vixenish face to the fringe of men on the shore.

"I'll come fast enough. You'll be made to suffer for this, I warn you."

Mr Mayberry struggled to the front and raised a trembling hand. "I beg you, don't let this man in the boat. He's not fit. He's a loose liver. I tell you I'm going to marry that poor, dear girl. I will marry her! I will—I will—I will—" He would have hurled himself into the boat but Fergussen pushed him ruthlessly aside and himself charged toward the prow that now nosed seductively against the shore.

The two girls in the boat gazed up, with envious interest at the men struggling on the shore. Each wished that she were waiting across the lagoon while angry men fought to reach her.

Now the schoolmaster was talking and flourishing his hand but no one would listen to him. Now a shadow fell like the wing of a crow. The afterglow changed from petunia to orange. The hunter's moon sailed upward in the melting twilight of the sky.

Another figure had entered the far end of the park. A man, alone, running like the wind, all the muscles in his strong, compact body moving in sweet accord. Along the racecourse he ran like a race horse. Now he left it and sped toward the lagoon. . . . Above him in a dark column flew the crows. All those that lived in the pine wood were there, winging along the evening sky with great, strong strokes. Soon they would be going South —tomorrow perhaps—the urge was in their blood. But now there was this wild flying together.

To Jimmy Sykes they were friends. He stretched his legs the faster when he heard their cries of encouragement:

"Here's Jimmy! Young Jim's here! Come to fetch his gal. His pretty gal—pretty gal! Help them, lads—hurt those that hurt them—peck their eyes out—tear their hearts out—Delight's foes—Delight—'Light—'Light—" A mad uproar of caws.

Jimmy was shoving his way among the men now, his face flaming, his sandy hair erect. He made as though to leap into the boat but some of the men caught him by the arms and held him, struggling. Only a moment they restrained him, for Kirke was at his side.

"Fine nicht, Jim," he bit off. "You're the mon. I'll uphaud ye."

Guarded by Kirke's steel arms, heaved by Kirke into the boat, Jimmy, the bridegroom, was on his way across the lagoon. It was now the dusky red of ashes of roses, reflecting a cloud that had caught the last of the afterglow. A sudden breeze stirred and all the reeds along the shore were whispering.

Timidly Delight crept to the shore to see whom they were bringing to her in the boat. She was afraid, ashamed, to look in his face, with her hair all streaming loose and wet, and her bare shoulders and breast showing through her torn gown, but when she saw that square honest face, those faithful eyes under the broad white brow, she was no longer ashamed. She ran to the water's edge. He sprang from the boat.

"Jimmy!"

"Delight!"

Each sobbed the other's name, and they fell, half-dead, into each other's arms.

III

Some of the girls, not the ringleaders, but those who had taken part on the outskirts of the attack, were sorry and ashamed. They brought Delight her coat which she had laid on her basket of dishes among the elder bushes, and they found the velvet tam and would have helped her to fasten up her hair under it, but Jimmy would not let them touch her.

Neither he nor Delight would enter Brancepeth again. He had a cousin who was a blacksmith in the hamlet of Mertonbrook, three miles along the road to Mistwell, and his plan was to walk through the pine wood, strike the road on the other side, and reach his cousin's that night. He had given Delight a mouthful of brandy from a pocket flask and it had brought the colour to her cheeks and lips and set her blood into motion.

But more effective than the brandy, had been the coming of Jimmy at the moment when her heart cried out for him. Now, simple and trusting, she put the terrible events of the evening behind her, behind her with all frightening remembrances—Perkin—the Heaslips—other things that she did not distinctly recall. With all dark shadows of the past she cast Mrs Jessop and her followers, and threw herself upon Jimmy's love. Her stalwart young body rebounded quickly as a boy's from the effects of the buffeting and ducking. . . . To be sure, she was a little dizzy, there was a humming in her ears, she had to cling tightly to Jimmy's arm as they walked. Jimmy, too, was feeling a little shaky, after all his excitement and violent exertion.

"O-o, Jimmy, it's good to be together again, isn't it?"

"My own darling girl! I'll never let you out of my sight again, I swear that."

"Don't swear anything, Jimmy. Let's just be good as good, all the rest of our lives, never say one cross word to one another, and never do a single bad thing."

"All right," agreed Jimmy. "I'll try. But you know I've got a quick temper."

"I know you have. You see it was that temper you got

into that sent me downstairs crying, and made Mrs Jessop turn me out and all."

"Yes, I know, darling. But she said she found you in Bastien's room. That was a lie, wasn't it?"

"Well, I was just inside the door. He'd been so sorry to see me crying, he was showing me some little trinkets he'd brought from South Africa to take my mind off my troubles."

"Huh!"

"Really people are kind, though. Why those men tonight, they were fighting cruel to see which one would come over to marry me. Just think of it, Jimmy."

"Well, I showed them which was *your* man. And Kirke, he helped me, Delight. He's a good head. A regular brick is Kirke."

"Good old Fine Nicht! He wanted to marry me, too. He was asking me two months ago in his wee dairy to be his wife."

"He was? Oh, I like his cheek! When he knew you was promised to me."

"But he knew you'd broke it off, Jimmy." Jimmy groaned and held her closer.

"Well, I'll never let you out of my sight again till we're safely tied up. It's an awful thing to love a girl like you, Delight, that other men can't look at without something inside them just turning over."

"Yes, isn't it, Jimmy? Even the schoolmaster and all. . . . But I'll be true to you and never give you any cause for worry. Have you got my tea set safe?"

"Yes, dear. Are you all right? It's not hurting you to walk? I do feel anxious about you in all those wet clothes."

"But my coat is so warm and dry on top. I'm as snug as can be. . . O-o, Jimmy, see the moon!"

"Yes, and hear the crows! *My* crows. Dear old fellows, they were almost wild at the way those women were treating you. Listen to 'em now. Cozy, I call it."

Truly, the crows were going to bed, folding their long black wings, pouting their breasts, snuggling their sharp black beaks against the down. Now they uttered only sleepy little croaks as they settled on the resinous pine boughs.

"Jimmy's safe," they seemed to croak. "Jimmy's safe. He's got his gal. His gal, Delight."

Dim as a cathedral aisle the path lay through the wood, and in the tallest pine, like a garland, hung the moon.

IV

The walls of evening closed about them, but the moon lighted their path, smooth and sweet-smelling with pine needles. With arms clasping each other they told of all that had happened while they were separated. Delight, of her sojourn at the Heaslips', of Perkin's passion for her, of Kirke's coming, just at the moment when she was desperate. Jimmy, of his weary search through the city, inquiries at agencies, false clues, of his return to Brancepeth, almost in despair, and of Charley Bye's meeting him with the awful news of her persecution in the park.

As for going out with another girl, as Pearl had said, he had never spoken to another girl except to inquire for Delight since he had last seen her.

"And, oh, Jimmy," she said, "I was that vexed, I unravelled your poor jersey every bit, and there it lies in your tin trunk in my room at Beemer's! Oh, whatever shall I do?"

"My trunk in your room at Beemer's? How did it come there? I left it at The Duke."

"Fine Nicht had it sent to me so you'd never get it away without me knowing it."

"He did?" shouted Jimmy. "He's a good head, that's what he is! I wish I'd shaken his hand before I jumped into the boat. But I'll search him out when I go back for our trunks."

"We'll have him come to visit us when we're married, won't we?" she cooed. "And I'll tell you what I'll do. I'll get a pair of knitting needles and knit your jersey all up again, as good as new."

"What a darling you are," said Jimmy.

At last they were before the blacksmith's door. The forge was open. A sharp, musical tapping came from within and a ruddy glow lighted the arms and leather apron of the smith. In his cottage next door the windows were alight and they could see a supper table set with a cold joint and a loaf and a huge pot of tea.

"The kindest people in the world," said Jimmy. "They'll do everything for you, sweetheart. . . . Now Tom sees us. He's taking off his apron."

Delight's deep gay eyes were shining. She was so happy, and so very, very hungry. If only Gran could see her! Lucky girl that she was. She knew God saw her. . . . He had saved

Gran's tea set and now He had saved her. Darling Gran! Darling Jimmy! Dear, dear God!

V

While Delight and Jimmy were being reunited, Macy, the constable, and his assistant were hastening in a jog trot around the end of the lagoon, with the object of heading off Mrs Jessop. Macy was burning to arrest the woman who had defied him, and thoroughly to frighten the other women who had been led by her into such an outrage. But, while the two men were panting on their way, the women, yearning toward the lads in the park, and being tired already of this antagonism of sex, were crossing the lagoon in relays by the little green boat.

Mrs Jessop was the last to leave, sitting in the stern with Nannie and Gertie to row her. They were midway on the moonlit water when Macy arrived with his handcuffs. Brandishing them aloft, he shouted:

"Don't think you can escape me, Mrs Jessop! You shall spend tonight in gaol."

"Gaol!" Mrs Jessop's resonant voice threw back the word in scorn. "Gaol! As though I was afraid of your little one-horse county gaol! Now, I'll tell you, I was born in a prison—a real penitentiary—a lot I care for your little tuppenny-hapenny gaol!"

After that terrible speech the two girls were glad to put her ashore and turn in the opposite direction. She was a bad woman and they wanted nothing more to do with her. . . . That night she disappeared and was not seen again in Brancepeth.

The older men, and the sadder, had drifted away, but the young, light-hearted ones hung about while succeeding boatloads of girls landed and imperceptibly group melted into group. What was the use of holding spite? And on a night like this, warm with the last kiss of summer?

They merged together. Soon a game of hide and seek was in progress. Dark forms holding hands darted among the willows. Faint cries were uttered.

The great red moon, shining on the racecourse, transformed the white dust to gold, so that it resembled a huge wedding ring couched on the velvet of the turf.

THE NEW CANADIAN LIBRARY

n 1. OVER PRAIRIE TRAILS / Frederick Philip Grove
n 2. SUCH IS MY BELOVED / Morley Callaghan
n 3. LITERARY LAPSES / Stephen Leacock
n 4. AS FOR ME AND MY HOUSE / Sinclair Ross
n 5. THE TIN FLUTE / Gabrielle Roy
n 6. THE CLOCKMAKER / Thomas Chandler Haliburton
n 7. THE LAST BARRIER AND OTHER STORIES / Charles G. D. Roberts
n 8. BAROMETER RISING / Hugh MacLennan
n 9. AT THE TIDE'S TURN AND OTHER STORIES / Thomas H. Raddall
n 10. ARCADIAN ADVENTURES WITH THE IDLE RICH / Stephen Leacock
n 11. HABITANT POEMS / William Henry Drummond
n 12. THIRTY ACRES / Ringuet
n 13. EARTH AND HIGH HEAVEN / Gwethalyn Graham
n 14. THE MAN FROM GLENGARRY / Ralph Connor
n 15. SUNSHINE SKETCHES OF A LITTLE TOWN / Stephen Leacock
n 16. THE STEPSURE LETTERS / Thomas McCulloch
n 17. MORE JOY IN HEAVEN / Morley Callaghan
n 18. WILD GEESE / Martha Ostenso
n 19. THE MASTER OF THE MILL / Frederick Philip Grove
n 20. THE IMPERIALIST / Sara Jeannette Duncan
n 21. DELIGHT / Mazo de la Roche
n 22. THE SECOND SCROLL / A. M. Klein
n 23. THE MOUNTAIN AND THE VALLEY / Ernest Buckler
n 24. THE RICH MAN / Henry Kreisel
n 25. WHERE NESTS THE WATER HEN / Gabrielle Roy
n 26. THE TOWN BELOW / Roger Lemelin
n 27. THE HISTORY OF EMILY MONTAGUE / Frances Brooke
n 28. MY DISCOVERY OF ENGLAND / Stephen Leacock
n 29. SWAMP ANGEL / Ethel Wilson
n 30. EACH MAN'S SON / Hugh MacLennan
n 31. ROUGHING IT IN THE BUSH / Susanna Moodie
n 32. WHITE NARCISSUS / Raymond Knister
n 33. THEY SHALL INHERIT THE EARTH / Morley Callaghan
n 34. TURVEY / Earle Birney
n 35. NONSENSE NOVELS / Stephen Leacock
n 36. GRAIN / R. J. C. Stead
n 37. LAST OF THE CURLEWS / Fred Bodsworth
n 38. THE NYMPH AND THE LAMP / Thomas H. Raddall
n 39. JUDITH HEARNE / Brian Moore
n 40. THE CASHIER / Gabrielle Roy
n 41. UNDER THE RIBS OF DEATH / John Marlyn
n 42. WOODSMEN OF THE WEST / M. Allerdale Grainger
n 43. MOONBEAMS FROM THE LARGER LUNACY / Stephen Leacock
n 44. SARAH BINKS / Paul Hiebert
n 45. SON OF A SMALLER HERO / Mordecai Richler
n 46. WINTER STUDIES AND SUMMER RAMBLES / Anna Jameson
n 47. REMEMBER ME / Edward Meade
n 48. FRENZIED FICTION / Stephen Leacock
n 49. FRUITS OF THE EARTH / Frederick Philip Grove
n 50. SETTLERS OF THE MARSH / Frederick Philip Grove
n 51. THE BACKWOODS OF CANADA / Catharine Parr Traill

n 52. MUSIC AT THE CLOSE / Edward McCourt
n 53. MY REMARKABLE UNCLE / Stephen Leacock
n 54. THE DOUBLE HOOK / Sheila Watson
n 55. TIGER DUNLOP'S UPPER CANADA / William Dunlop
n 56. STREET OF RICHES / Gabrielle Roy
n 57. SHORT CIRCUITS / Stephen Leacock
n 58. WACOUSTA / John Richardson
n 59. THE STONE ANGEL / Margaret Laurence
n 60. FURTHER FOOLISHNESS / Stephen Leacock
n 61. MARCHBANKS' ALMANACK / Robertson Davies
n 62. THE LAMP AT NOON AND OTHER STORIES / Sinclair Ross
n 63. THE HARBOUR MASTER / Theodore Goodridge Roberts
n 64. THE CANADIAN SETTLER'S GUIDE / Catharine Parr Traill
n 65. THE GOLDEN DOG / William Kirby
n 66. THE APPRENTICESHIP OF DUDDY KRAVITZ / Mordecai Richler
n 67. BEHIND THE BEYOND / Stephen Leacock
n 68. A STRANGE MANUSCRIPT FOUND IN A COPPER CYLINDER / James De Mille
n 69. LAST LEAVES / Stephen Leacock
n 70. THE TOMORROW-TAMER / Margaret Laurence
n 71. ODYSSEUS EVER RETURNING / George Woodcock
n 72. THE CURÉ OF ST. PHILIPPE / Francis William Grey
n 73. THE FAVOURITE GAME / Leonard Cohen
n 74. WINNOWED WISDOM / Stephen Leacock
n 75. THE SEATS OF THE MIGHTY / Gilbert Parker
n 76. A SEARCH FOR AMERICA / Frederick Philip Grove
n 77. THE BETRAYAL / Henry Kreisel
n 78. MAD SHADOWS / Marie-Claire Blais
n 79. THE INCOMPARABLE ATUK / Mordecai Richler

o 2. MASKS OF FICTION: CANADIAN CRITICS ON CANADIAN PROSE / edited by A. J. M. Smith
o 3. MASKS OF POETRY: CANADIAN CRITICS ON CANADIAN VERSE / edited by A. J. M. Smith

POETS OF CANADA:

o 1. vol. I: POETS OF THE CONFEDERATION / edited by Malcolm Ross
o 4. vol. III: POETRY OF MIDCENTURY / edited by Milton Wilson
o 5. vol. II: POETS BETWEEN THE WARS / edited by Milton Wilson
o 6. THE POEMS OF EARLE BIRNEY

CANADIAN WRITERS

w 1. MARSHALL MCLUHAN / Dennis Duffy
w 2. E. J. PRATT / Milton Wilson
w 3. MARGARET LAURENCE / Clara Thomas
w 4. FREDERICK PHILIP GROVE / Ronald Sutherland
w 5. LEONARD COHEN / Michael Ondaatje
w 6. MORDECAI RICHLER / George Woodcock
w 7. STEPHEN LEACOCK / Robertson Davies
w 8. HUGH MACLENNAN / Alec Lucas
w 9. EARLE BIRNEY / Richard Robillard
w 10. NORTHROP FRYE / Ronald Bates
w 11. MALCOLM LOWRY / William H. New
w 12. JAMES REANEY / Ross G. Woodman